Depravity

A story about the darkness of the human soul

Geoff A. Wilson

kindle direct publishing

kindle direct publishing

First published 2020
Kindle Direct Publishing (UK Office)
44 Ashbourne Drive
Coxhoe
DH6 4SW

About the author

Born in London to a British father and a French mother, ***Geoff A. Wilson*** grew up in southern Germany where he went to primary and secondary school. He is trilingual in German, French and English. He studied for his Masters degree in Geography, Cultural Anthropology and Archaeology at the University of Freiburg (southern Germany), before completing his PhD in Geography at the University of Otago in Dunedin, New Zealand. From 1992-2003 he worked as a Geography Lecturer/Senior lecturer at King's College London, and from 2004-2019 as Professor of Geography (Emeritus Professor since 2019) at the University of Plymouth (south-west UK). Geoff became a world-renowned academic expert on questions about the resilience of human communities, more specifically about how rural communities cope with, and adapt to, change, disturbances and disasters. He has published over 100 academic articles on the subject and has written several books including *Environmental management: new directions for the 21st century* (with Raymond L. Bryant; UCL Press, 1997), *Multifunctional agriculture: a transition theory perspective* (CABI International, 2007) and *Community resilience and environmental transitions* (Routledge, 2012). Married and with

one son, he lives in a small village on the south coast of Devon, UK. Geoff retired in 2019 to become a full-time writer, specialising in young adult fantasy and dystopian novels/psychological thrillers, including the best-selling *Lllobillo* fantasy series (Austin Macauley). *Depravity* is his 4th novel.

Books by Geoff A. Wilson:

Children's fantasy:

Lllobillo: the secret portal (Austin Macauley, 2017)

Lllobillo 2: the Viking curse (Austin Macauley, 2020)

Dystopian fiction:

Pandemic: A dystopian story about what might have been ... and about what could still happen in future (KDP Publishing, 2020)

Foreword

Psycho-therapist George Williamson struggles to help his patients and increasingly realises that he is himself embroiled in complex psychological problems as he attempts to interpret and deal with himself, his patients, and the world around him. It has often been said that three topics should stay off-limits in literature – politics, religion and sex – but this book tries to show that there are times for hard story-telling about touchy topics, and that too often the over-cautious language used to talk about sexual misdeeds, religious biases and political prejudices, in particular, risks back-firing even when intentions are good. This book openly and unashamedly addresses sexual misdeeds and misconduct, as well as thoughts about religion and politics, without hiding between an over-moralistic façade of artificial restraint. The result is a politically incorrect story that cynically and polemically broaches complicated and challenging topics such as sexism, religion, political bigotry, friendship, marriage and divorce, nihilism, Brexit, alcoholism, gambling and drug addiction, poverty, philosophy, thuggishness, misguided masculinity, complex gender issues, dysfunctional relationships … you name it. It is a novel of intolerance and compassion, resilience and vulnerability, love and loss, with at its centre a flawed but, at times, sympathetic character whose life is rocked by actions and emotions often beyond his control. It

panders to human's raw instincts and the fact that our brains get off on many of the things we are ashamed of. It is about power and relationships and hovers uncomfortably at the intersection between violence, desire and madness. Reader, be aware, there is no safety net in this story. Proceed at your own peril.

Part 1

Life ... itself

OMNES QUI CECIDERANT
OMNES ECCLESIAS DESTRUCTAS
PINNATIS
CAESIS OMNIBUS MARITIS
CONIUGES LIBEROSQUE
OMNES CIVITATES DESTRUXISTI
CIVILISQUE
IMPOTENTIA HOMINIS OSTENDE
VIVERE IN PACE
ET PER MAXIME BASIC PRAECEPTA
ETIAM PUDOR COERCET
ET PRAVITAS HUMANI GENERIS NON
EST NUMERUS

All the fallen men
All the destroyed churches and spires
All the slaughtered husbands, wives and children
All the destroyed cities and civilisations
Show man's inability to live in peace
And in accordance with even the most basic rules of decency
The depravity of the human race knows no bounds

(Verucca of Rotterdam, in 'The Book of the Fallen', written AD1645 towards the end of the disastrous European 30-year religious wars that left millions of dead)

George Williamson adjusted his office chair yet again. Somehow, he could never find the right position for the backrest, and every time he sat down again his body required a different posture, a new back support, and a different angle and head position for viewing his computer screen. After fiddling angrily with the backrest lever, and twisting his back into the most comfortable position, George turned his attention back to his computer. “Bloody crap!”, he hissed, hoping that Daniela, his receptionist, had not heard him through the half-open door to the waiting room where Daniela’s desk was situated. *I can’t believe it, but I have yet again forgotten which sequence of keys to press to get into this new idiotic software for logging receipts!*, George thought utterly disappointed in himself. He scratched his stubbly chin, closed his eyes, and tried to remember what Daniela had told him only yesterday. OK, first press the ‘claims’ icon … He pressed the icon and the message ‘invalid entry’ appeared. “Fuck!”, George shouted out, cursing the not-user-friendly, anti-intuitive and opaque setup of these stupid computer programmes. Why could they not invent software that was truly user-friendly and sympathetic to the needs of a 52-year old like him who had not been brought up in the digital age as a kid and who, as a result, had found it difficult to understand the apparent ‘logic’ behind the workings of software programmes and electronic devices. George grudgingly admitted that he even found his iPhone difficult

to use, a problem that elicited wry smiles and incomprehension from people younger than him.

"Are you ok in there?", came the worried voice of Daniela from her receptionist's desk. Daniela was a 50-year old with dark curly hair, short, and relatively fit looking woman with a permanent tan. George had 'inherited' Daniela from his predecessor who had run this psycho-therapist practice in the heart of Devonmouth, a middle-sized city located on the south coast of Devon. George was very glad that Daniela had agreed to stay on as his receptionist, as he liked her as a person and particularly valued her experience with helping to run a practice with over fifty regular patients with complex psychological problems and needs. George was still not sure why his predecessor, Paul Sutherland, had suddenly quit, seemingly abandoning his practice with all its patients from one day to another. Indeed, nobody seemed to know anything about Paul's whereabouts and George and Daniela still had to tie up a lot of loose ends left by Paul's sudden disappearance. But it had been a great opportunity for George who just happened to be looking for an individual practice of this size in this part of England, and he had immediately jumped at the opportunity when it had come up about a month ago.

"I am ok, Daniela!", George shouted back, not wanting to admit that he was not ok at all. "Just trying to remember how to open a new file for this claim I am putting in for our tax return.

There is a message that says ‘invalid entry’.” George heard the rustling of a chair on the wooden laminated floor of the waiting room, and Daniela came into his office with a smile on her face. “George, remember, you need to press ‘data entry’ first, before pressing ‘claims’”, she said patiently, leaning over his shoulder and pressing the ‘enter’ key. George could smell Daniela’s subtle perfume wafting towards him, a not unpleasant fragrance with a hint of roses, lemon and lavender. He looked sideways at Daniela’s wrinkled and tanned neck as she pressed one icon and then another. “There!”, she said, “now you are in and ready to enter the amount from your receipt. Remember to press ‘next’ to access the second page and to save it before you exit, otherwise you will lose the information again”. This was a subtle reminder that, after entering a hole list of items the day before, he had forgotten to press ‘save’ at the end and had lost all the data.

“Thank you so much once again”, George said smiling at Daniela, “I don’t know how I would cope without you!”

“I know, George, I know”, Daniela said and patted him in a motherly way on the shoulder. “Paul, your predecessor, had exactly the same problems”.

George briefly hesitated and wondered whether he should use the opportunity to enquire further about why Paul had so suddenly abandoned his practice, but the stern expression on Daniela’s face made it clear that she was not

yet ready to talk about it. Maybe she did not know much about the reason why his predecessor had left anyway? Daniela walked back to her cubicle and closed the door behind her, subtly suggesting that she did not want to be disturbed again with an IT-related question, at least for a little while.

George leaned against his still badly adjusted backrest, his arms folded behind his head, and looked around him. He had not changed much in the room since moving in four weeks ago. He was using Paul's desk, his office chair, his office furniture and, most importantly, Paul's psycho-therapist's couch, the first thing that comes to mind when people think about psychiatry. Still leaning back in his chair, George's gaze drifted towards the couch located in the far corner of the room. It was about two metres long with an elevated pillow-sized headrest and covered with a dark blue sheet. George thought about the many patients he had already seen in the four weeks since he had taken up Paul's practice and the fact that most of the time Paul's psychiatric couch was not used at all but that, instead, most discussions took place with his patients sitting in the comfortable chair opposite him. Only in a few instances did modern psycho-therapists use what many referred to as the 'Freudian couch', named after the father of modern psychology, Sigmund Freud, who started using it regularly after 1909 since when the term 'on the couch' became accepted as a symbol representing what psycho-therapists do. From his training as a

psychology student a long time ago, and his long career as a psycho-therapist working in London, George knew that there were subtle but important differences in patients' reactions, openness and candour, depending on whether they were just sitting in the chair opposite him or lying down on the couch. As psycho-therapy mainly involved treating emotional problems and mental health conditions, the 'talking cure' was still a crucial aspect of any treatment, allowing George to look deeply into his patients' problems, worries and traumas. A congenial atmosphere, helped by appropriate ambiance, lighting and furniture, was, therefore, crucial to put patients at ease and allowed them to 'open up' to a stranger with their deepest secrets and worries. Compared to a chair where a patient would sit upright and look George in the eye while talking, the couch, by forcing a patient to lie down without direct eye contact to George who sat near the couch but behind the patient, helped create an environment that was practical yet intimate and allowed a patient's ideas and thoughts to flow more freely through so-called 'free association'. George almost always found that patients on the couch where less inhibited to say whatever readily came to mind without him intervening, allowing a patient to freely explore ideas that could build a picture for George to work with. Key was to build a trusting, working relationship with the patient, and George used his experience and subtle interpretations of the

patient's behaviour to assess whether a patient was 'ready' for the couch.

George scanned the room again. He knew that it was not perfectly laid out, the lighting was a bit too harsh, Paul's furniture and the couch looked at bit worn and tired, and he was still unsure about whether the few pictures on the walls – the ubiquitous assortment of cheaply framed van Gogh reproductions and idyllic landscape and seaside scenes – helped or hindered his patients opening up. But George had already overspent by taking on this practice and the rent was high in this central city location, which meant that, currently, there was little spare cash to kit out this room and the adjacent waiting room with new and more fancy furniture.

A knock on the door roused George from his thoughts. "Mr Miller is here and ready for you", Daniela said while opening the door. George glanced at the old-fashioned ring-bound paper diary lying next to his keyboard. Ralph Miller was the first of three patients this morning, each of whom had been long-standing patients of his predecessor Paul, and each with complex histories of neuroses, psychoses, and childhood-related traumas. "Let him in", George said to Daniela while putting on his reading glasses and taking out the notes on Ralph Miller from the top right-hand drawer of his desk.

*

Daniela let in a gaunt-looking man in his later forties with a haunted looked on his face. George pointed at the chair in front of his desk and motioned to Ralph Miller to sit down. Ralph had not yet looked once into George's eyes and, after sitting down, kept looking at a spot on the floor in front of him. George ruffled through Paul's typed notes and his own hand-scribbled notes. George briefly hesitated at one of Paul's pages which showed the message 'handle with extreme care: high risk of suicide!' which had been circled three times with a red felt pen. George was well aware of recent statistics in the UK that highlighted that one of the most important cause of death for men was suicide. "I last saw you two weeks ago, Mr Miller, how have you been?", George probed looking at the hunched man sitting in front of him. Ralph sat uncomfortably in his chair, rocking his upper body slightly in a regular motion which suggested extreme unease.

"Alright", Ralph replied, still not looking up towards George.

Although George remembered Ralph's case well as he had seen this patient twice since he started this practice in April, George glanced again at the complex notes in front of him. Paul had seen this patient off-and-on for years and had clearly struggled to help. Ralph's life story had an all too familiar ring to it. He had once been a successful businessman, but then his life had begun to fall apart linked to a gambling addiction

with online poker, rapidly rising debts, and the resulting loss of his house, wife and children. Like many poker players, Ralph had thought that he was good at poker and bluffing, not realising that, other than most gambling games, poker was actually about mathematics and quickness of mind to assess the likelihood of winning with a specific combination of cards. As a result, poker addicts like Ralph, who were not that bright, quickly lost money, but never fully understood why, always hopeful that the elusive 'big win' was just around the corner.

After losing a fortune, Ralph had been homeless for a while, mainly roaming the streets of Devonmouth and begging passers-by for coins to feed his worsening alcohol and substance abuse problem. Social services had eventually picked up Ralph's case, and he was currently living in sheltered accommodation with the cost at least partly covered by Devonmouth Social Services. While looking at Ralph's files, George forced himself not to fall into his usual rant about how social services in the UK had declined over the years and how the so-called 'care-in-the-community' scheme instigated by misguided Tory governments in the 1990s was just a cost-saving exercise that had led people like Ralph fall through the cracks of an increasingly leaking and cash-strapped social safety net, making it virtually impossible to get desperate cases back again onto their feet. Things were even worse in other countries. George had read recently that in the USA, for example, in as many as one in four

of all fatal police shootings the victim suffered from severe psychological problems, suggesting a complete breakdown in outpatient psychiatric care.

George tried again to make eye contact with Ralph but his patient continued to stubbornly look down onto the floor. "How is your new medication working?", George asked hesitantly. "Have you managed to take it regularly as we discussed last time?" George continued to be frustrated at the fact that, as a psycho-therapist, he was not allowed to prescribe medication to his patients himself, but that, instead, he was dependent on what GPs and hospital doctors had prescribed his patients. Occasionally, but in George's view not often enough, GPs and hospital-based psychiatrists sought his advice about patient medication, but George felt that communication between them was often poor.

Ralph shuffled his feet and after a while mumbled "… gives me headaches".

"Does this mean that you have stopped taking the pills?", George enquired more insistently.

For the first time, Ralph looked up. George could see the haggard, gaunt, red-veined and heavily wrinkled face of a man who was younger than him but had a face that bore the marks of alcoholism, drug addiction and personal neglect. *He probably was an attractive man a few decades ago*, George thought with a great sense of pity for Ralph and a feeling of heartfelt sorrow for the life pathways some people embarked on,

whether out of choice or not, and for how difficult it was to help patients like Ralph.

"I still take them", Ralph replied and patted the pocket on his battered shirt, suggesting that he had tucked the packet of pills away in easy reach, "but I have felt very down again lately."

"Are they treating you well at your new accommodation?", George asked with a worried look on his face.

Ralph looked down again onto the floor. "It's been alright … There was a nice girl in there last week who helped me a lot … some kind of volunteer helper linked to a charity … but she left. Couldn't stand the constant groping from the other blokes. Shame, really, as she was nice."

George assumed that Ralph himself had not tried to grope the girl and that there was probably still a sense of decency, and even gentlemanliness, hidden behind Ralph's uncouth, dishevelled and disintegrating exterior.

"That's a shame", George replied with sincere candour, "but I am glad to hear that you are gradually getting used to your new accommodation."

"Better than sleeping on the street!", Ralph replied, and for the first time a smile punctuated his ravaged face.

"Indeed", said George, "indeed". Ruffling the papers in front of him, George held up a sheet towards George. "I have good news Ralph, and the main point I wanted to discuss with you today is that, after I sent my latest psychological evaluation of your case to both your GP and

hospital doctor, our application for you to attend one of Devonmouth's citizen rehabilitation groups has been accepted". He passed the official-looking sheet with lots of stamps and signatures to George. "As of next week, you can attend this group here", and he pointed towards a specific paragraph on the sheet. "I have heard many good things about this group, and the lady who runs it is very passionate about helping patients like yourself. Indeed, she mentioned that they have had good success in reintegrating people who have gone through challenging life-changing circumstances like yourself back into the community, especially by providing them with access to jobs". At this point George felt more like a social care worker than a psycho-therapist, recognising again how the boundaries between these different professions had become increasingly blurred.

Ralph's mood clearly improved after receiving this news and his face lit up with a smile. "As we discussed last week", George continued, "psychologically this could be very important for you and may just be the boost you need to get back on your feet. I suggest that we set our next meeting for after you've had your first meeting with the group and then talk about how it went. In the meantime, please continue to take your pills regularly."

Ralph seemed happy with this suggestion. He got up, looked George firmly in the eyes and shook his hand. "Many thanks, Dr Williamson, you have been a great help so far."

George shook Ralph's limp and sweaty hand, smiled, and felt reasonably reassured that Ralph would be ok for the next few weeks. He was sincerely hoping that the new citizen rehabilitation group would be able to implement what they so optimistically promised in their promotional leaflets.

For years it had been George's practice to transcribe a session with a patient as soon as it was ended. George opened the file on his computer entitled 'Ralph Miller' and started typing everything he remembered of their discussion. He knew that the ability to accurately record what had been said was of paramount importance to a therapist, as much detail was quickly forgotten and, most importantly, the immediacy of the emotions lost – something a taped recording could not capture. Before seeing a regular patient, George would always spend a few minutes going over his previous notes, not only to remind him about what they had discussed but also of the patient's deepest emotions and feelings during the last meeting.

When he was ready, George buzzed Daniela and she let in the next patient. Fergus Rumpley was again one of Paul's previous long-term patients, and, ruffling through the next folder, George was reminded what a strange and unfortunate case this was. Fergus was a 30-year old man with pale skin and dark hair. He sat down in front of George and his demeanour was the exact opposite of the previous patient: Fergus looked very self-assured, almost cocky, and had

a warm inviting smile on his face. At their first encounter four weeks ago, George had immediately sensed that Fergus was the kind of character gullible people would immediately trust, and he rightly guessed that Fergus's job was associated with making money, not necessarily in the most moral or, indeed, legal way. Over the years, many of his patients had been like Fergus, suggesting that the boundary between being a potential financial whiz-kid and having deep-seated psychological problems was a fine one. Since his early 20s, Fergus had been a dealer in bitcoin, the crypto-currency introduced to the world after the financial crisis of 2008 as a blockchain-based techno-libertarian project aimed at bypassing dealing with hated 'conventional' banks. After meeting Fergus for the first time a few weeks ago, George had read up a bit about this crypto-currency and had learned that bitcoins are created, or 'mined', by having computers solve a maths problem where the first miner to find the answer is rewarded with bitcoins. Fergus had been involved for years with a British-based crypto-currency exchange that purchased and traded mined bitcoins and, having entered the game early, together with a friend he had amassed over a thousand bitcoins in 2009 when they were still nearly worthless. However, Fergus had told George at length at their first meeting that the relationship with his friend had turned sour and, as a consequence, his friend had changed the password for their encrypted laptop, just before dying in a

motorcycle accident. Fergus had initially not thought much about it, but shortly after his friend's death bitcoin's value soared, and a few years later their stash was theoretically worth millions of dollars. Despite repeated and diligent efforts Fergus could never find the password to access the encrypted files, and even consulting experts who could check bitcoin's public transaction register did not provide information on the inaccessible deposit. Unsurprisingly, in the aftermath of this catastrophe Fergus suffered a psychotic breakdown leading to episodes of violent outbursts which led to his incarceration in a psychiatric ward for several years. Upon his release Fergus had been assigned to regularly see a psycho-therapist which was how he ended up seeing Paul Sutherland, George's predecessor.

"How are you feeling today, Fergus?", George asked, still struggling to comprehend the intricacies of how Fergus had lost a potential fortune.

"I am feeling ok, thanks Dr Williamson", Fergus replied putting himself at ease in the chair. "As I told you before, it's great to have the opportunity to talk about my problems with someone like you".

"I am glad I can help", replied George, "and I hope I can do as good a job as my predecessor Paul".

"Yes, Paul was very good", Fergus acknowledged, "I think he may have dabbled a bit in bitcoin himself", he said with a wry smile.

“I was not aware of that”, George admitted. “Have you tried the little mental exercise we discussed last week?”

“Yes, I have. As you suggested, every time I think about the millions of dollars that lie inaccessible in this bl…” – Fergus hesitated a bit, still unsure whether he could swear in front of George – “in this bloody encrypted laptop, and every time I get angry about it, I force myself to think about food instead. Trust me, there has been a lot of thinking about food since!”, said Fergus laughing.

“That’s great”, replied George. “As I explained to you, this procedure which we term ‘parallel cognitive refraction’ can help shift negative thoughts towards those associated with pleasant things in life. Food, or sex, are often useful cognitive refractions.”

“Well, so far it seems to work”, Fergus said smiling at George. “I have the impression that guiding my thoughts away from this constant preoccupation with how much money I have lost has also affected this recurrent nightmare I had and has at least modified it. Now, instead of dreaming about standing in front of this gigantic unopenable vault behind which millions of shiny new dollar notes lie, my recent dreams have involved me standing in front of a fridge that I am unable to open!”

“Well, let’s hope that this will not affect your appetite!”, George replied, and they both laughed heartedly. George was pleased that, although it was still too early to say, parallel

cognitive refraction, as a relatively new therapy, appeared to have initially helped Fergus. Fergus talked a bit more about how his post-psychiatric-ward-life was gradually coming back together and that, based on his interest and experience in crypto-currency dealings, he had been offered a job by a relatively well-known accounting firm in Devonmouth.

"I am very pleased to hear that", George remarked sincerely and a little surprised, "although I would like to monitor how well you will cope with a job that is dealing with things close to what caused your initial psychotic shock. I think that sets a nice target for our next meeting which I suggest should be in a month's time."

Fergus agreed, and while making his way to the door promised to keep up with the cognitive refraction exercise, and said he would keep George informed over the next few weeks if there were any adverse changes to his condition.

George leaned back against his poorly adjusted backrest. He could feel his back with all this sitting, and was looking forward to a round of golf soon to stretch his back and legs. He took off his reading glasses and swiped his eyelids with his fingers. He was feeling a bit tired after what had been a busy week, and he was looking forward to a cappuccino at his newly-discovered café not far from his practice. He looked at his diary. His next patient was probably the most difficult one so far. Marlies was a sixteen-year old girl with a history of severe psychological

trauma. She had been another patient of Paul Sutherland, and this was the first time George was seeing her. He scanned through the files left behind by Paul but there was surprisingly little information about Marlies and her circumstances. Paul's notes, normally neatly typed and detailed, comprised in the case of Marlies only a few roughly hand-scribbled remarks. From what George could make out, Paul noted that Marlies was always accompanied by her mother, and in one hand-scribbled remark Paul had warned *'beware of the mum, she is enough to give an aspirin a headache!!!'* with three exclamation marks.

But George could not find any information about the detailed history of Marlies's problems, why the mother may pose a problem, nor any summary notes of her previous meetings with Paul. Instead it appeared that several pages had been ripped out of the folder. George had not realised this before, when he had cursorily scanned Paul's vast legacy of paperwork. He checked again whether there was a file on Marlies Brown in any of Paul's computer files, but there was no file under that name. George went over to the filing cabinet on the wall and checked whether some loose sheets may have fallen out, but again there was nothing. *How strange!*, George thought. While Paul's filing system had been relatively thorough and while he had left a reasonably informative paper trail on all his patients, Marlies Brown seemed to have been an exception even though Paul had

seen her for over 12 months since she was 15 years old. George looked at the old-fashioned wall clock, checked his diary to confirm the time for Marlies's appointment and pressed the buzzer that gave Daniela the signal that he was ready for the next patient.

*

Marlies Brown and her mother entered the room, led by Daniela. Daniela looked at George with a strange expression. *Is she trying to tell me something?*, George wondered, *or am I reading too much into the fact that files are missing on this patient?* Marlies was a very pretty, slim, and petite girl with short dark hair and pale skin, large brown eyes and small freckles around her nose. She wore a plain white t-shirt and tight-fitting black jeans that accentuated her boyish and still relatively undeveloped features. *She looks more like 12 than 16!*, was George's first thought, inadvertently glancing at Marlies's small breasts that only barely protruded through her t-shirt like a whisper of things to come and did not yet need a bra to hold them in place.

George motioned the two women to sit down. Marlies's mother was the complete opposite of her daughter, and, at first glance, George found it hard to believe that the two were related. Esther Brown was a plump unattractive brown-haired woman with pasty fatty skin of an unhealthy reddish colour criss-crossed by small

veins, a large reddish mole on the edge of her upper lip, and a porcine face with small eyes surrounded by fatty-greasy wrinkled skin. She wore what George thought was a dreadful greenish poorly cut dress and was holding a small mock-crocodile-skin handbag which was, in George's eyes, testimony to a woman with garish and vulgar taste. The outline of her large sagging breasts could be seen through the vulgar dress, withered breasts that hung like wet weighted socks, and which, George caught himself thinking, must have at one point suckled this beautiful daughter of hers. While Marlies looked at George with a mysterious almost dreamy expression on her face and with a hint of a smile, Esther looked grumpy and ill at ease as she adjusted her poorly fitting dress before she sat down. George thought that Esther did not want to be there at all. George could not interpret from Marlies's face whether she wanted to be here or not.

"I am very pleased to meet you", George said looking mainly at Marlies. Marlies got up from her chair and shook George's hand, and he was surprised at her firm and confident grip. Esther just grunted something incomprehensible.

"I see from my notes that you regularly saw Paul Sutherland before I took over his practice?", George enquired in order to break the ice.

Esther looked up as if reminded of an unpleasant dream. "Yes, indeed", she replied on behalf of her daughter. "We have tried to stop these ridiculous and unnecessary appointments,

but for some unfathomable reason both our GP and Dr Cranston at the hospital have insisted that Marlies continues with her treatment here!"

George briefly looked at his notes and tried to remember whether he had seen any reference to Marlies's GP or a Dr Cranston, but could not find anything. Maybe this was part of the notes Paul rad ripped out for unknown reasons?

"Remind me again why they have sent you here?", George tried to ask, sounding as nonchalant as possible to hide the fact that he had so little information on Marlies's case.

Esther looked askance at George, probably suspecting that something was not quite right. "Well, as your notes will say", she said pointing a fatty finger at George's pile of paper, "Marlies has been diagnosed with severe psychosis linked to the fact that …". Esther hesitated and looked at her daughter with a worried look on her face. Marlies continued to stare at George showing no reaction.

"You can tell me everything, Mrs Brown", George replied. "As Paul will have told you, everything we discuss here is treated in strictest confidentiality."

"Call me Miss Brown, please", Esther replied grumpily, "I am divorced now and both Marlies and I have taken my original surname."

Maybe there is another file with Marlies's father's surname?, George wondered, *and that's why I can't find any information?*

"As your notes will show", Esther interrupted George's thoughts, pointing her fat

fingers again at George's desk, "Marlies's father …", she hesitated again, "did things to her … which caused a traumatic psychotic reaction. Marlies became … what d'you call it …?"

"Catatonic, mum", Marlies replied, looking impatiently and embarrassed at her mum.

She has a nice, melodic voice like an eiderdown pillow, but also still a very child-like voice, that fits her boyish exterior, George thought.

"Catan … catatonic, yes", the mum continued. "And she also stopped talking for over two years …".

George looked at Marlies again. How often had he heard a story like this in his long career as a psycho-therapist: attractive young girl molested, possibly raped, by father, destroyed lives and shattered marriages, causing unfathomable pain, sorrow and mental problems. Although psycho-therapy was undoubtedly helpful in these cases, George knew that traumatic psychosis was among the most difficult mental problems to cure, and that in most cases only damage-limitation was possible. Often patients had to grapple with their problems for the rest of their lives, feeling depressed and often suicidal, and often unable to fully integrate into society. And yet, he did have cases in the past where patients with a story similar to Marlies had gone on to live relatively fulfilled and successful lives. He looked at Marlies again with an encouraging smile but also with an

immense sense of passion and understanding. He really wanted to help this girl!

Marlies saw this as an invitation to speak. “Yes, my dad did things to me which were horrible, but I think that I am beginning to get over it … gradually.”

This sounds too much like a rehearsed response by this child-like 16-year-old!, George thought with suspicion. “Can you tell me in your own words what happened?”, George asked cautiously.

Marlies continued to look straight at George and then, with an uncertain look, at her mother. Esther was twisting her ugly handbag in her hands, looking down on the floor. George wondered whether she was crying and did not want George to see. A deadly silence spread through the room, the ticking of the old-fashioned wall clock appeared to George to get louder and louder. Through the door Daniela could be heard typing on her keyboard.

“Mrs Brown, it may be better if I speak with your daughter alone, if you don’t mind?”, said George breaking the silence. “I am sure that Paul will have also seen Marlies individually in the past?”

Esther still looked down, but eventually looked up with a tearful face. “I don’t understand why we have to go over this over and over again!”, she replied with an angry voice. “All of this has been discussed! I am divorced now, Marlies’s father is in jail and will not be let out for a long time. We are trying to put all this

behind us, and yet the GP, Dr Cranston, Paul Sutherland and now you force us to have these … these … humiliating sessions that are just a waste of time!"

George was familiar with such a reaction and fully understood Esther's criticism. He certainly had to get in touch with Dr Cranston at the hospital to get more information on Marlies's case and to jointly discuss the best way forward. "I can assure you that I have the deepest sympathy for both your daughter and yourself, Mrs Brown … pardon me, Miss Brown … but you have to trust us experts and what psychotherapy can do to help your daughter. Please remember that your daughter has been subject to a prolonged trauma that, if left untreated, may affect her for the rest of her life. However, my past experience and the many studies that have been done on these issues suggest that we can help your daughter, but we need to stick to the roster of meetings initially established by Paul, and this will also include me talking to your daughter on her own, just like Paul did in the past."

George hoped that his assumption that Paul had seen Marlies on her own was correct, as he had no information about this from Paul's scarce notes. Esther had taken out a handkerchief from her bag and blew her nose loudly with a horrible trumpeting sound that sounded more like an elephant being strangled to death. Yellow snot could be seen oozing out of the sides of the handkerchief, dripping onto Esther's dress.

George thought that even the snot could not make Esther's dress look worse than it already did, but he also immediately chided himself for thinking such horrible thoughts about one of his patients' mother. *Stay professional here, George!*, he inwardly warned himself. Without looking at George, Esther got up, briefly looked at her daughter with a placid face, and made her way to the door, her fake-leather handbag dangling against her large unshapely hips. This suggested to George that it was probably not the first time that Esther had been asked to leave her daughter alone with her psycho-therapist.

The room was again deathly silent after Esther had closed the door behind her. George pressed the intercom button and asked Daniela to make a cup of tea for Mrs Brown … Miss Brown … and make sure she was ok. He then looked at Marlies who sat still and upright on her chair, looking at him with an inscrutable face.

"Is it ok for you just to talk to me on your own?", George asked her prudently.

"Yes, that is fine with me", came the immediate reply, suggesting to George that his assumption that Paul had probably used a similar strategy was correct.

"You may be more comfortable talking about this over on the couch?", George ventured cautiously.

Without hesitation, Marlies stood up and walked over to the couch, again suggesting that this was not the first time Marlies had used the couch. George was amazed again how her

narrow frame looked more like a boy than a girl from behind. "Dr Sutherland often used the couch in our discussions", Marlies confirmed as she lay down on her back with her head on the pillow-like headrest.

Although George rarely used the couch these days, in some cases he found it easier for both himself and the patient. He pushed a chair close to the couch and looked at Marlies who looked relaxed and comfortable, confirming her familiarity with the couch therapy.

"So, in your own, words, tell me what happened to you", George said encouragingly. Marlies closed her eyes and swallowed. Maybe she was fighting back tears, George wondered. "Take your time …", George said.

"My father raped me regularly when I was 12 and 13", came Marlies's sudden and firm reply. "I told him every time that I did not want him to do it but he would not listen. I tried to push him away but I was not strong enough!"

Marlies opened her eyes and looked at George. He felt immensely sorry for the girl, but knew how important in psycho-therapy it was for her to talk openly about what happened. *Why had this information been ripped out of Marlies's notes?*, he wondered.

"After a few times I realised that I could not do anything about it", Marlies continued, "so somehow I relaxed and it was as if my soul started floating outside my body. It was as if I was watching myself, and my father on top of

me, from just below the ceiling. That somehow made it easier for me …"

"As Paul will have explained to you, this is a typical outer-body experience as a response to intense shock, and a natural coping mechanism many develop in such situations", George explained. "What about your mother? Did she not realise what was happening?"

Marlies hesitated. "My mum knew nothing about this ... or at least she claims that she knew nothing. She said that she thought … like … my dad was reading me bed-time stories or stuff like that! Most of the time he did it to me when mum was out of the house … like, she often came home late from work. He made me swear to say nothing and threatened to leave us if I did say something to mum. I often wanted to talk to my mum about it … but … like … we never had that great a relationship."

At this point Marlies could no longer hold back the tears. She turned her head towards the wall and sobbed quietly. George took her hand and caressed it gently. "You are doing very well telling me all this", he said, not knowing how else to respond to Marlies's sudden showing of grief. "We can stop at any time …"

"No!", came Marlies's immediate reply, "I want to talk about this now. I need to! I was quiet about if for long enough and it really helped talking to Dr Sutherland about it … I did not speak for over two years … I could no longer go to school … I felt that nobody would be able to help me. As Dr Sutherland will have told you,

my mum eventually found out … It was inevitable, really. It was a wonder that my father had gotten away with it for so long … Anyway, one evening she came home early, like, came into my room and saw my father lying on top of me … inside me. She threw him out immediately, called the police, and he was arrested one day later at work. He denied everything … I was not allowed to go the court hearing … and he now is in prison. I hate him!"

Marlies suddenly sat up from the couch and, before George could do anything, she put her arms around George and her head on his chest. She was still sobbing. As part of his psychology studies and his training as a psycho-therapist, George had been trained to cope with situations like these. Psycho-therapist-patient relationships were among the most complicated, complex and, at times, problematic in the medical world, and in no other circumstances – not with GPs or hospital doctors – did patients open up to such an extent to another person about their innermost problems, worries and fears, as in a psycho-therapist's practice. George knew that it was imperative to be understanding, consoling and that, at times, physical contact with patients was unavoidable. He had had many situations in the past where patients – female and male – had needed hand-holding or a hug after delving deep into their inner self. Psychological training also warned that psycho-therapists could often become the object of intense infatuation, and that it required great skill and professionalism by the

psycho-therapist to draw clear boundaries. In cases where a psycho-therapist suspected that a patient was interested in a closer relationship that went beyond the doctor-patient contract, it was common to talk about it and then refer the patient to a colleague in the gentlest way and with the least harm to the patient. In his career, George had had a few female patients who seemed to develop a personal interest in him, and in all cases the situation was subtly defused by referring these patients to other psycho-therapists.

These thoughts immediately came to mind as Marlies was clinging on to George, although he also understood that Marlies's reaction was unplanned and done on the spur of the moment. He had hesitated initially but then decided to gently put his arms around her. He could feel her slim body and her ribs through her t-shirt. Embarrassingly, the close body contact meant that he got an erection. He did not want to push Marlies away, but he was hoping that she did not see the rising bulge in his tight-fitting trousers, especially considering the traumatic story she had just recounted. *She will think that all men are the same, even her psycho-therapist!*, he thought, disgusted at his own primitive bodily reaction. He looked down at her head propped against his chest. Her eyes were now open and as far as he could make out she was indeed looking directly at his erect penis.

George immediately pushed her away. "I am sorry", he stammered, not knowing what else to say.

Marlies was still half clinging onto him and looked him straight in the eyes.

"That's ok, Dr Williamson, I am sorry too", and she gently let go of him and lay back on the couch.

George was now feeling rather hot and began sweating profusely. He walked to the window and opened it, forgetting the traffic fumes and noise which usually impelled him to keep the window closed. He looked back at Marlies and saw that she was still lying on the couch, staring at the ceiling. He quickly readjusted his erect penis to the left through his trousers so that the bulge was less evident.

"I think we better end this session", George said with his back turned away from Marlies. "I will contact your mum about our next session", but he was not sure whether it would be advisable to see Marlies again. And yet he felt that he had behaved as professionally as he could, that he had done nothing wrong, but nonetheless he was angry at his body's reaction to this attractive, but immensely vulnerable, young girl.

Marlies still lay on the couch, suggesting that she was hoping that the session would continue, but she eventually got up and left the room without a further glance at George.

She is only a child!, George thought with bitterness. *What impression does she now have*

of you? Embittered he walked back to his uncomfortable office chair and ruffled through Paul's notes, but his mind was elsewhere.

*

Over lunch George was sitting in his favourite café in Breakwater Street, the pedestrianised part of Devonmouth town centre. He enjoyed his lunch time breaks there, and, on this spring day, it was warm enough to sit outside at his favourite table in the far corner of the café's elevated wooden decking. George adjusted his sunglasses to ward off the strong glare of the May sun, chewing on a limp panini and sipping a weak cappuccino. *Just relax!*, he thought, but he could not stop thinking about Marlies hugging him, her small boyish body in his arms, the smell of her hair, and how she obviously had seen his erection. *Damn it! Why does this kind of stuff always seem to happen to me?*, he thought, briefly envying the people around him who were completely oblivious to the turmoil he was going through. *I think I will have to refer Marlies to another psycho-therapist. I should also contact this Dr Cranston at the hospital, and maybe talk to him about Marlies's case. I wonder how Paul Sutherland coped with all this? Why did he not leave me more complete notes on Marlies's case?*

George tried to think about something else while sipping his coffee. As a psycho-therapist

one of his favourite pastimes was to watch people around him and let his mind wander, at this moment in time possibly the best way to forget about Marlies. But often George wondered whether it was possible for him not to see people through a psycho-therapist's lens? Would it be healthier for him not to constantly try and second-guess people's thoughts, intentions and deepest problems? It was hard to put into words, but he knew that over a career spanning decades a psycho-therapist would become well attuned to recognising mental distress in people just by sitting in a place such as a café and observing people, especially by observing physical behaviour, speech, a glint in the eye, often revealing something haunted, afraid, and even mad.

It was lunchtime and Devonmouth city centre was beginning to fill with people taking breaks, having a rest from shopping, or just enjoying sitting down in the sun. A group of French schoolchildren, fresh from the nearby ferry from Brittany, was streaming past the café, loud and boisterous. George glanced at them and estimated that they must be between ten and thirteen years old, possibly their first time in Britain. At that age the boys and girls still tended to cluster in gendered groups, with some of the girls taller and more developed than most of the pre-pubescent boys. Despite of the desperate attempts of their exhausted-looking teachers, they were shouting and showing-off in French, oblivious to their unfamiliar surroundings, the

boys trying to impress the girls with fake fights, scuffles and rowdy behaviour which annoyed some of the passers-by who looked at them with deep frowns and a shaking of the head. Many of the girls wore skirts that were too short, bangles and fake plastic jewellery that glistened in the midday sun, and t-shirts that showed off their budding breasts, not realising what effect they had on the sex-starved Devonmouthian men trying to squeeze through their group which was increasingly holding up pedestrian traffic in front of the café.

George watched the kids and could not help himself seeing them through his psycho-therapist's lens. There was the shy girl who tried to fit in with her boisterous girly peer-group, but who was clearly ill-at-ease and who kept looking self-consciously around her. There was the extrovert boy who was hugging all attention of the cluster of boys around him, showing off his new-fangled watch while all the while glancing at the group of girls standing next to them and checking whether any of them was looking at him. There was the class clown, a short skinny boy dressed in a flowery shirt that seemed out-of-place, who was generating loud cheers and laughter from his group while he precariously balanced on a handrail for the elderly in front of the main café entrance until he was told to jump off by one of the teachers to the loud boos of the surrounding kids. Watching the boy, George thought that it was often those who performed the role of class clown who developed

psychological problems in future, outwardly joyous, boisterous and self-assured, but inwardly insecure and full of anxieties hidden behind a veneer of clownish behaviour. There was also the misfit, a tall slightly obese and ugly girl with thick glasses, who stood slightly aside and did not seem to be part of any of the groups. George felt sorry for her as she looked pleadingly towards some of the other girls hoping they would realise that she was there, that she existed at all, that she wanted to be included in their peer-group, that she wanted to be accepted and take part in even the silliest of their antics. And there was the ubiquitous street-wise kid, a cute black-haired and rather French-looking boy with fine features and an aquiline nose, not necessarily intelligent but street-smart, highly adaptable, who seemed to read the vibes around him well and almost always knew what could sway the mood of his peer group. Although their school grades were not often the best, these street-wise urchins often developed into leaders, company CEOs, staff managers, or generally successful people who succeeded in life not because they were the best at one thing, but because they were good at many things, and had a real knack for understanding the complex and intricate interactions between people with different needs, wants, yearnings and aspirations. As the black-haired boy was explaining something George could not hear and pointing towards something beyond the café, the boy clearly had the attention of the five or six

boys standing around him, and even some girls standing nearby had interrupted their giggling to follow what the boy was saying. As George watched these intricate power games, complex social interactions, and complicated inter-personal relationships among this group of budding adults, the exhausted teachers finally managed to move the group of kids on and, to the relief of the increasingly impatient passers-by, to disentangle the bottleneck of people that had built up where the footpath narrowed between the café entrance and the outer decking.

Watching the last French boys and girls disappear to catch up with their group, George settled back into his chair. In front of him a tired mother with two toddlers was adjusting the straps for one of the kids sitting in a battered buggy. The table in front of her looked like a bomb site with left-over food spilling over plates and molten ice cream dripping from the table onto the chewing-gum-riddled and dirty wooden decking floor. One of the children started crying as the mum tried to wipe a mixture of ketchup and ice cream from her son's dribbling chin. At the next table two young men in hoodies and muscle shirts were hunched over their milkshakes, their bulging muscles testimony to regular workouts at the gym. *Were girls and other people really impressed by such muscly bodies?*, George had always wondered. Their arms were covered in tattoos showing dragons, bare-breasted mermaids and skulls in faint colours ranging from dark red to deep purple.

They were talking in hushed voices, frequently and self-consciously looking over their shoulders as if to make sure nobody was overhearing what they said. George looked away as their gaze briefly met his, and glanced at an elderly couple behind the two young men. The old couple were both eating fish and chips, blood-red ketchup dripping from their fries as they tried to juggle the soggy yellow-golden fries into their mouths with arthritic hands covered in paper-thin whitish skin through which blue worm-like veins protruded. The old man put his hand forward and his wife gently put her hand on his. They looked at each other with their deeply wrinkled faces that suggested a life of poverty and hardship. *But they clearly still love each other*, George thought, *despite all the trauma and problems they may have gone through in life*. George had a vision of the old couple in one of Devonmouth's many shabby estates, a grimy flat where a vicious landlord charged overpriced rent, with unkempt streets and overflowing wastepaper bins, and yet here they were, enjoying each other's company and basking in the lunchtime sun eating their greasy meal. In many ways the old couple epitomised the vicissitudes of living in a tough place like Devonmouth, life … itself.

George adjusted his sunglasses to make sure that his table neighbours did not see him watching them. He looked back at the two young men, but they were again engrossed in whatever they were discussing. A drug deal maybe? Or

how to get laid tonight? While sipping his cappuccino, which was too hot and not made to Italian standards, George thought that all these people were somehow typical of Devonmouth and, although he did not recognise anyone he may have seen before at this café, similar to the usual crowd one would expect around lunchtime. People from Devonmouth often looked poor and shabby, not able to afford the latest clothing brands sold in the newly built arcades on the high street. They were also often obese and short, with pale pasty skin suggesting poor diet and lack of exercise. George smiled as he remembered a friend from London referring to Devonmouthians as 'fat dwarves with bulgy eyes', although he had always thought that this was too harsh a description of his fellow citizens who, after all, were just trying to make a living and survive like everybody else under difficult conditions. A certain London arrogance had been evident when his friend had made this comment, and George had at the time refrained from further commenting, although deep inside he did agree.

George took a bite from his panini which, by now, was rather cold, and let the squishy mayonnaise-laden tomatoes and cucumbers slosh around his mouth for a few seconds. He took another sip of cappuccino to hide the after-taste of the mayonnaise. By now the cappuccino had cooled down a bit and had become more palatable. Ever since he had moved to Devonmouth, George had developed a love-hate relationship with the place. Like many, he had

mainly decided to set up his practice in the south-west for its idyllic rural beauty and tranquil life compared to many other places in the UK. But, as someone living in a village outside the city, he also felt aloof and arrogant towards the city of Devonmouth and its inhabitants. In some ways the poverty of the place made it attractive to many as it prevented over-development due to its unattractiveness to profit-hungry developers, was relatively cheap to live in, and created a relatively 'genuine' and 'honest', non-arrogant feel to the city – characteristics which were the curse of places like London or Paris. But, at the same time, it also constantly reminded him of how difficult it was for an economically struggling place to properly provide for its citizens. Indeed, levels of poverty, malnutrition, teenage pregnancy, and childhood obesity were very high in Devonmouth, and the city centre, badly rebuilt and planned after the ravages of the Second World War, repulsed him for its shabbiness, dreariness and architectural ugliness that oozed under-investment and lack of maintenance at every street corner. George glanced over his shoulder at boarded up shops and bargain outlets that sold rubbish and plastic shit that nobody needed, and that would soon clog up landfills or end up as plastic waste in the oceans. He thought of the large number of beggars and homeless people in Devonmouth who made George feel guilty that he had a well-paid occupation and a nice house well away from all this ugliness.

Since when have I become so arrogant?, George wondered. *I am getting into my 'negative Devonmouth attitude' again!*, George admitted with a smirk and thinking about how over the past few weeks his negative thoughts about Devonmouth had consolidated, while scanning the café decking for new arrivals. He was abruptly awoken from his thoughts by a dark-haired woman in her fifties who had suddenly appeared in front of him and asked whether the chair opposite him was already taken. "No please, help yourself", George replied, placing a hand in front of his eyes despite of his dark sunglasses to better see her face, as the woman was standing in front of him with the sun directly behind her. With her black shoulder-length hair, her slim frame, and the way she smiled at him, the woman reminded George of his first wife Martina, although Martina would have never worn the woman's bright lipstick and cheap bangles around her wrists. This was not a pleasant memory as Martina and George had been divorced under acrimonious circumstances, but George could not avoid occasionally seeing women in the streets who reminded him of her. George watched the woman take the chair and place it at a table nearby where two other women of roughly the same age were sitting, sipping frothy latte macchiatos.

George had met Martina while travelling in Germany when he was a psychology student and they had rapidly fallen in love. She was besotted by his middle-class and educated 'English'

upbringing, the fact that he was 'foreign' and spoke English, and the rather 'exotic' aura he seemed to exude. Martina had come from a small remote town somewhere in the wooded hill areas of south Germany and was eager to get out and explore the world beyond the narrow confines of her small-town upbringing. George had been attracted to Martina by her intelligence, wit and beauty, while he was also interested in Martina's different culture and the challenges that it would bring to a transnational relationship.

The first few years of their marriage, when they had moved to London where he completed his PhD in psychology, were very happy and they talked about having children. But what George had not realised initially was that Martina could not jump over her shadow, cast away the path dependencies associated with her upbringing, and think critically and reflexively about herself and her family. He knew from the start that Martina had been brought up in a staunchly protestant household as the daughter of a vicar in a backward and conservative small town. But he had been misled by thinking that Martina's urge to leave the narrow cultural and geographical confines of her home and explore the wider world would translate into a growing open-mindedness. While Martina loved the hustle and bustle of London and its seemingly endless offering of culture, art and avant-garde thinking, she also became quickly over-awed by the energy and internationalism of the place. While initially she went out a lot, with him or

with friends from the accounting firm where she worked as an intern, she increasingly withdrew from London life. Instead, and for reasons George could never fully work out, his wife rediscovered her staunchly protestant religious roots, initially in a relatively subdued form through more and more regular visits to the local church, but eventually through an all-pervasive invasion of religion into her personal life. This did not only involve a tangible change in her day-to-day routine through regular prayer, the establishment of a what Martina called her 'spiritual room' – a bedroom converted into a prayer chamber with a small shrine that included a bible and cross on the wall – and an asceticism that made George shudder, but also less tangible changes in their lives especially with regard to how Martina viewed the world, their relationship, their friends, and George himself.

What riled George in particular was that suddenly every action was interpreted with moralistic religious undertones which had not been apparent in the first few years of their marriage. The most obvious was when he had a beer in the evening after a hard day reading and writing for his PhD, with Martina commenting on the fact that drinking alcohol was 'un-Christian' and that God would look unkindly upon those who promoted and indulged in debauchery and drunken behaviour. George remembered that his reply was that having one beer after work could scarcely equate to 'debauchery' and 'drunken behaviour', and he

reminded Martina that he had not been drunk since they had last been drunk together at a friend's party not that long ago, where they had both over-indulged on tequila and vodka shots and that she had indeed seemed to greatly enjoy the occasion at the time. Martina's response had been to take the beer bottle from his hand and smash it furiously against the kitchen wall, leaving an ugly wet brown stain on the wallpaper and pieces of broken glass all over the floor.

Soon after, Martina resigned from her internship and a promising career as an accountant, claiming that a woman's role was in the house and rearing children, not working and earning money, comments which greatly annoyed George. The straw that broke the camel's back from George's perspective, however, was when Martina decided to only have sex with him when they were trying to conceive a child. Gone were the days of hand-jobs, cunnilingus and fellatio, of sexual teasing, foreplay and enjoyment just for the sake of it. Instead, Martina had begun a rigid 'sex-timetable' as she called it, which meant intercourse – now under the sheets and with the light switched off of course – only at times of assumed fertility. In hindsight, they were lucky that Martina's strategy had not been successful for her getting pregnant, possibly linked to the rather naïve and unscientific approach Martina had chosen to identify her 'fertile' days. While George saw himself as a relatively open-minded guy and willing – at the beginning of Martina's

religious phase at least – to see her growing religiosity as simply a phase a protestant country girl like her, cast into a global city environment, may have to go through, the fact that her whole life became increasingly dictated by her religious zeal, eventually led to the breakdown of their marriage. George had also increasingly wondered whether their inability to conceive a child, despite of Martina's seemingly instrumentalist approach to the matter, also contributed to the breakdown in their relationship. George thought back about a typical exchange they would have had towards the tail-end of their marriage:

"You don't love me anymore", Martina would suddenly claim while they were watching one of her favourite programmes on one of the religious TV channels offered through their Sky subscription.

"But of course I do, and you know that", George replied. "The fact that I put up with your increasing religiosity is testimony to the fact that I still love you".

"If you really loved me, you would try to better understand why I have rediscovered my Protestant faith".

"But I try to understand, darling. It's just that I can't understand why an intelligent woman like yourself needs to believe in a God-like creature and thinks that such a God influences what you do or think, whether Protestant, Catholic, or whatever…!".

"You know that God, with his endless love and wisdom, is all around us", she would say with a gleam in her eyes.

"But how can you, as a woman, for example unquestioningly accept that this God is an old male? How can you accept the persistent gender inequality, the outdated views on abortion and marriage, the lack of tolerance towards other faiths, or the lack of reflexivity of clerics whose thoughts have not progressed beyond the pitiful spiritual mumbo-jumbo with all its pathetic icons and outdated ceremonies promoted by your Christianity? How can you explain that billions of people believe as fervently as you in other non-Christian Gods? Probably couples in Saudi Arabia and Myanmar are having exactly the same discussion as we have right now when talking about Muhammad and Buddha?"

As his voice was rising, George was working himself up into his usual rant against any form of religion. At this point, Martina usually shut up, as she had no logical explanation for his questions, nor any inclination in taking up George's 'scientific' approach to understanding religion, spirituality, and religiosity.

"As usual, it is not worth debating this further", Martina would say angrily, moving away from him and huddling up in a ball at the edge of their sofa, hiding her tears by turning her face away from him. At times like these, George had increasingly realised that he was living with a stranger.

George looked up from his day-dreaming and gazed at the woman again who had reminded him of Martina. The woman was animatedly chatting away with her friends, sipping her coffee and occasionally flicking the ash of her cigarette onto the floor, blatantly disregarding the non-smoking sign fastened to the wooden railing. After all, this woman seemed so different to what Martina had become at the end of their marriage.

The divorce from Martina was quick and very unpleasant, but based on mutual consent. George remembered an angry letter written by Martina's mother, in German, that accused him of not having looked after his wife properly and insinuating that it had been entirely George's fault that his wife had slipped into an unhealthy and over-zealous religiosity. But George was so shattered by the whole experience that he never brought up the courage to write a reply. Having been brought up in a non-religious household where religion was the butt of jokes, George had always been cynical about any form of religion. But the experience with Martina had hardened his views. Not only did he see religion – any type of religion, be it Catholic, Protestant, Muslim or Buddhist or anything else – as something inherently negative and nasty, where innocent people were indoctrinated by self-centred and bigoted older men, but he had also never understood the need for religion and spirituality engrained in most of his fellow citizens.

While he had read a bit about, and to some extent understood, indigenous people and tribal societies and their need for interpretations of nature as imbued with spiritual meaning, he had particular problems with the larger-scale religious movements that often could not easily be separated from politics and, indeed, maximising profits for a ruling clerical class. While he knew that, at a time of global terrorism and jihadism, it was particularly politically incorrect to criticise Muslim religion, George found it especially hard to understand why Islam, in its current violent guise and interpretation, had so many new followers around the world. George saw modern Islam as intrinsically interwoven with politics and, worst of all, perpetuating an anti-modernisation discourse that had stifled the implementation of enlightenment in the past that had led to most Muslim-dominated countries being stuck in a vicious spiral of primitiveness, poverty, gender inequality and unscientific worldviews. With sadness George thought about how the 'fertile crescent' in the Middle East, now the heartland of many bigoted Muslim autocracies, was once the cradle of civilisation with regard to the invention of agriculture, urban life and a specialised non-agricultural workforce. Indeed, right up to the 12th century Muslims were at the forefront of science, medicine and literature – most of the stars in the sky, for example, had been first identified and named by Arabs – and Muslim rule had generally been pluralist and

inclusive of other religions and faiths. Medieval Islam hungered for learning – for example by translating many Greek philosophical texts and inventing algebra – was innovative, curious and tolerant, allowed the arts to flourish, inspired brilliant scholarship, and was much ahead of Europe in the 12th century in science, discovery and statecraft. Paper was widely used, bookshops thrived, and libraries graced the homes of the learned rich when most Europeans could barely read and write. However, this worldview was gradually abandoned and even stigmatised in subsequent centuries because of the increasingly stifling narrow-mindedness of Muslim interpretations of the Quran and the rest of the world. Recent terrorist attacks claimed by ISIS-sympathisers that had killed hundreds, the mindless destruction of cultural artefacts deemed 'blasphemous' by ISIS bigots, and sharia law where religious courts convicted the accused in accordance with archaic notions of criminality and meted out draconian and gender-repugnant penalties including floggings, stonings, and amputations reminiscent of the Middle Ages, had only hardened George's anti-Muslim stance. George particularly recalled a news item about the sentencing to death of people for 'blasphemy', with one Christian woman in Pakistan having been accused by Muslim neighbours of insulting the prophet Muhammad after they balked at sharing a jug of water with an 'infidel'.

Of course, George also realised that the over a billion of Muslims on the planet came in all different shapes and forms, from extreme radical to very open-minded and globalised, and he continued to have great admiration for Muslim-related art and architecture, recollecting visits to the Taj Mahal in India and the Alhambra in Grenada. Similarly, he was well aware that jihadists only made up a minuscule fringe of Muslims, that terrorist attacks had disproportionally and erroneously turned Islam into a looming threat in many people's minds, and, most importantly, that far-right and populist parties had fed on and fanned such irrational fears. Still, despite his rational self, anything Muslim currently left a sour taste in George's mouth.

George was distracted by a large bluebottle that had settled on his half-eaten panini, sucking avidly on the mayonnaise oozing out of the soggy mess. The tiny hair on the flies' bulbous body were gleaming with an iridescent blue in the bright sunlight. George pushed the plate away, feeling relatively full and simultaneously disgusted at the thought of sharing the rest of his meal with an insect that may have been sitting on a moist dog's turd only a few seconds ago.

Glancing back at the chatting women, George's thoughts returned to his rant about religion. Apart from his negative perceptions of Islam, at least in its current and more violent narrow-minded guise, he had equal qualms about the role of other faiths such as Christianity, not

least because his personal life linked to his marriage with Martina had been so affected by it. Having been brought up in an atheistic family where, unusual for her time, even his grandmother had reneged on her Christian upbringing, George could never understand people's naïve belief in a Christian God, especially not in the guise of an old bearded white male. When people he knew talked in awe about this 'God' he tended to joke by referring to 'Goddess' instead, often eliciting incomprehension and shaking of heads by females in his audience as to why this should be regarded as funny at all. And the belief in Jesus as the impersonation of God was even more ludicrous. *Yes, sure*, George thought, *it is likely that there was a bloke who may have even been called 'Jesus' and who may have even lived in the area of Nazareth and Jerusalem around the time, as it was likely that 'Muhammad' or the man who would eventually be referred to as the 'Buddha' may have been real people*. But how billions of people could be indoctrinated to believe in the elevation of these characters to god-like figures by a corrupt class of self-professed clergy over the centuries utterly puzzled him. In Jesus's case, how could an infantile story referring to the 'resurrection' of a dead person, whose cast and ludicrous script belonged rather to a B-rated zombie movie, be taken as the 'truth' by self-proclaimed Christians who, after all, included many well educated and 'scientific-oriented' people? How stupid did

people have to be to voluntarily flock with fervour to obviously fake iconic remains of faith leaders, such as Jesus's shroud, his crown of thorns and even one of his pubic hairs, let alone believe in childish idiocies such as miracle healings or the appearance of stigmatas on believers' hands? How could people not see the evil done to millions of victims of religious wars, where subtle differences in interpretations of one ludicrous religious interpretation over another – as in the case of Catholics versus Protestants or Shias versus Sunnis – led to massacres and atrocities in the name of their respective narrow-minded and infantile interpretations of faith? The area in southern Germany where his former wife Martina had grown up was a case in point, where during the 30-years religious war in the 17th century neighbouring towns and villages were at each other's throats because of subtle differences in interpretations of the bible between Catholics and Protestants. In some towns, half of the population, including innocent women and children, were slaughtered in the name of religion.

In George's critical and cynical view, the modern Christian world was also characterised by hypocrisy, financial gain and enrichment at the expense of the gullible masses, the Catholic priests' idiotic promotion of overpopulation by banning abortion and women's right to self-determination contributing substantially to the 70 million plus new people overcrowding the planet each year, and, most sadly of all, utter

abuse of power towards children as the weakest in society through paedophilia perpetrated by sad, sexually frustrated and pathetic Christian clerics. In his mind, all religions were, therefore, first and foremost about exploiting the stupidity of the masses, stifling innovative thought, and perpetuating gender imbalances by chauvinist males.

George realised that he had, not for the first time, worked himself into a frenzy and that he needed to calm down. These negative thoughts did not get him anywhere! He took another sip of his cappuccino, but by now his coffee had gone cold. But he could not help continue his thoughts. There was, he admitted, also the beauty of art and architecture that religion had encouraged, especially the world's magnificent cathedrals, mosques, temples, churches and chapels, and of religious music that had inspired the world's best composers such as Mozart or Bach to compose some of the most heart-warming and inspirational music ever conceived by humans. Or what about the feeling of like-minded community religion and spirituality seems to instil, or the often selfless helping of unknown others through religious aid programmes, food donations, or the looking after of the help- and homeless? What about some forms of religion that venerated what George thought were much more sensible forms of deities, such as the sun-cult of Ra in ancient Egypt and several Central and Southern America's cultures? *That is a form of religion I*

can almost accept, that somehow makes sense through its veneration of the only true life-giver of planet Earth, the sun, that allows life to exist in the first place by enabling complex processes such as photosynthesis and the transformation of matter into energy, George thought as he was feeling his tanned forearm being bathed in the strong May sunshine. *Am I, therefore, too critical of my fellow human beings, especially considering how unique humans are and how unlikely it is, at the scale of our universe, that intelligent beings like humans evolve in the first place?*, George wondered once more, pushing his fly-infested plate further away. *Should I give my fellow human beings – however stupid and primitive they may appear to me – more latitude, more benefit-of-the-doubt, more acknowledgement that even the most idiotic and dumb human has nonetheless to be considered a miracle of evolution, with incredibly complex thinking processes occurring that eclipse even the wildest imagination? Am I again arrogantly elevating myself above others, thinking that my anti-religious view of the world is the only 'correct' worldview? Should one not allow for a variety of thought and spirituality to co-exist among this marvellous and possibly unique species?*

George leaned back and thought a bit more about this. His answer had to be a definite 'yes', he mused, but only if religion was not linked to indoctrination of the innocent young, as was happening in pathetic and backward Quranic

medreses or Christian kindergartens and schools with religious curricula, and if it did not instil hate and violence through jihadism and war, aggressive post-colonial missionary zeal, and the narrow-minded and pathetic branding of friends and neighbours according to their different belief systems.

But George was nonetheless willing to give his gullible and indoctrinated compatriots the benefit of the doubt. After all, as all forms of religion had a vision of heaven and afterlife, religious belief was, first and foremost, about fear of death. As a psycho-therapist he knew very well how this fear guided most peoples' innermost angsts, and that any promise – as stupid as it may seem to outsiders – of redemption or life after death was eagerly accepted by people who did not want to acknowledge that death was simply the end of everything, the ceasing of the body's chemical, biological and electrical functions and processes, the termination of brain activity that defined a person's personality and 'soul', and the stopping of the heart whose tireless rhythmic action had made all these processes possible. *Dead was dead, and that was it!*, George thought, or, in Nabokov's words, life was just a brief crack of light between two eternities of darkness. No heaven, no angels, no awaiting virgins, no paradise, no redemption, no forgiving of 'sins', indeed no possibility to redeem one's shitty and wasted life! You had one shot at life, and if you messed it up – like almost everybody did at one

point or another – that was it! You better made the most of it while you were alive, and, in George's mind, you did not need the lame excuse of religion, the weak façade of religious indoctrination, and the hiding behind a belief imposed upon you by bearded male chauvinists, to live a full, happy and fulfilling life. Religion – any form of religion – was increasingly a thing of the past, a remnant from an ill-informed and poorly educated pre-modern and pre-enlightened civilisation, a relic in a modern world where the recognition and acknowledgement that each individual life was unique and irreplaceable was increasingly accepted as the ultimate orthodoxy. *You various gods out there, beware!*, George felt like shouting. *Your time is over, your artificial pedestals are crumbling, your fake surroundings disintegrating and vanishing into nothingness.*

George let out a loud sigh. At times like these he felt as if the whole world was weighing heavily on his shoulders and that his thoughts were almost too intense for him to bear. Why was it up to him to think about and help sort out pathetic humanity's weaknesses, inadequacies, prejudices and misconceptions? And now this issue with Marlies and his body's unprofessional behaviour! But then he was a psycho-therapist after all, and his business was to try and understand his fellow citizens, scrutinise their shortcomings, and dig deep into the nooks and crannies of their often-deranged minds. George scanned the people on the wooden decking again. The two young men had left and were

standing with a third even rougher looking bloke at the entrance of the café, talking avidly and gesticulating with their hands. *Maybe their drug deal has turned sour and they are about to pull a knife?*, George thought, imagining a looming scene of carnage and blood-and-guts on the pavement not far from his table. The table where the young mother with her two toddlers had sat was empty, the discarded food attracting wasps and flies. George could not remember seeing the three of them leave as he had been so absorbed in his anti-religious rant. The old couple had finished their fish and chips. They were no longer holding hands over the table and were looking away from each other with distant gazes. The old man was watching a young woman dressed in a provocative pinkish outfit walking past the café. His wife followed her husband's gaze and smiled tiredly and knowingly back at him, suggesting both remnants of love as well as deep regret and sadness, but also forgiving. The woman who had reminded George of Martina was still animatedly chatting to her friends, still smoking what must have been at least her third cigarette.

George looked up from the people around him and scanned his wider surroundings, watching the Devonmouthians go about their day-to-day business. Not for the first time he thought that his daily dealings with patients made him increasingly immune towards his own or his family's psychological problems, especially as he knew that many of his family

members were more in need of therapy than many of his patients. *Could I ever leave the cool theory-laden ballast of my job and engage 'normally' with other people?*, he thought reflecting back on his analysis of his fellow café-goers. Everything he did, everybody he met was psycho-analysed, even while trying to relax and sipping a coffee. He knew that even just scanning the people he was seeing walking past the café now underwent the glib assurance of diagnosis, but he could not stop himself: it was not just the people in the café itself he had so arrogantly assessed over the past hour or so, but it was also the old depressed granny walking hunched over past the café, the panic in the hurried young man not looking at the shop windows, the harrowed woman with a trauma hurrying past, the homeless with a psychosis sitting in front of the entrance to a bank, the sociopathy of the hooded loner, the bulimia of the obese blond girl looking at him from a distance with a vacuous stare, the agoraphobia of the withdrawn and gaunt looking elderly man at the street corner. *Everybody has some form of mental disorder!*, George thought not for the first time. What was 'normal' anyway? Assessing mental illness was more like a fashion that has changed through the ages. People seen as ill and 'weird' in the past, such as witches, would be seen as 'normal' today. Shamans, clairvoyants, or people with 'psychic' powers were often powerful in the past, but were mostly laughed at today. Nowadays it was almost fashionable to have a mental illness! *How*

will a psycho-therapist assess the people walking past here in 200 years? What will the new fashionable fad of mental illness be then?, George wondered.

George looked at his watch with a surprised sigh. It was much later than he thought, and he had better get back to his practice where his next patients were waiting. He had to admit to himself yet again that the boundary between 'patient' and 'non-patient' was very fluid. Who needs treatment and who deserves treatment was a quandary psychology had never fully resolved. George rushed back towards his practice. He could not remember who he was seeing in the afternoon, but he hoped they would be easier and less intense cases than that of Marlies.

*

Over the last few days George had thought a lot about Marlies and had come to no decision as to whether to see here again or to pass her on to one of his colleagues. He had also not written yet to Dr Cranston at the hospital to find out more about Marlies's case or to discuss her case with him. Could he simply abandon her case like that? Would not every male psycho-therapist have the same bodily reaction he had when Marlies had hugged him? Or did she hug him because she liked him? But then she hardly knew him, this had been the first session they had together. And what did it matter anyway if Marlies liked him? After all, she was only a child and George knew

that he should not even contemplate the fact that Marlies may be keen on him. *Dream on, old man!*, he conceded to himself.

George sighed loudly while leafing through his old-fashioned paper diary on his desk to check on the list of patient appointments for the day. He had the impression that Daniela had looked at him differently since he had first seen Marlies and her mother. *Did Daniela suspect that something had happened?*, George wondered. *I should ask her how Paul had dealt with Marlies and why notes had been ripped out of Marlies's file?*, he thought, but he somehow had not found the right opportunity, nor the courage, to ask. This was not the first time in his professional life that he was reluctant to confront a possible problem with a patient head-on.

He pressed the buzzer that signalled to Daniela that she could let in the next patient. Daniela let in a couple who were in their early forties. George motioned them to sit down in front of his desk. The woman, Beth Rigby, was a slim woman who would have stood out as very attractive and fit-looking in the sea of obesity and plumpness that characterised most Devonmouth women. She looked self-assured but also stern and had an air of steely determination about her. Her husband, Reginald, was a stocky-looking laddish character with short-cropped hair and a thick rugby-type neck and a big nose who seemed to fit much better into George's image of what Devonmouthians normally looked like. *How could two so*

seemingly different people decide to get married?, was George's first thought.

He flicked through the notes in front of him. The Rigbys were among the few new patients George had accepted since taking over the practice from Paul Sutherland, and this was their first appointment. They had been referred to George by the family unit of Devonmouth Social Services, where several meetings had apparently taken place and where the couple had discussed 'severe marital problems'. In George's professional experience, such cases were common, and the increasingly stretched social services budgets often allowed for only superficial treatment. When cases became 'stuck' – in other words, when social service budgets and expertise were insufficient to help couples with severe marital problems – they were often passed on to psycho-therapists. George knew that often these cases straddled the thin line between social care and psychology, although the two were most commonly closely interwoven. Marital problems led to increased psychological stress among couples which, in turn, could exacerbate marital problems through a vicious circle of complex feedbacks. Probably a quarter of all cases George was seeing were people whose psychological problems were closely related to marital difficulties.

George welcomed the Rigbys and asked them to explain in their own words what their problems were. Beth and Reginal looked at each other with unease. As George had expected it

was Beth who spoke first. “We are having problems with our marriage.” She hesitated a bit, nervously fiddling with her fingers. “Social services will have informed you that we have had problems off-and-on for years, and we have seen both social services and marital counsellors several times.” George observed Reginald while Beth was talking and could see how uncomfortable he was feeling with this situation. Beads of sweat had begun to appear on Reginald’s forehead and he was rocking back and forth in his chair, clearly distressed. Beth glanced at her husband with a look George interpreted as disgust, disdain and hate. At this early point in their meeting, George already concluded that this marriage was probably doomed. “We met when we were students”, Beth continued, “but it was difficult from the start. “Reginald had always been a heavy drinker …” – Reginald’s rocking motion intensified – “… but his drinking problem became worse after we got married.” Reginal now looked down at his feet. Sweat was pouring over his face. *Poor bloke!*, George thought with a hint of pity. Probably the usual story so typical for this country, which starts with peer-pressure-induced binge drinking in their teens, more intense male-bonding drinking during their studies, and the subsequent inability to leave the laddish, shallow and primitive beer-swigging culture behind. The sad outcome was often broken marriages and destroyed lives.

"At one point I had enough", Beth admitted, "and told him to either stop drinking or get out. To be fair, he stopped drinking and he has never touched alcohol again."

Reginald was still swaying back-and-forth. He had not looked once at either his wife or George. Beth's last statement came as a surprise to George, as more often than not alcohol addiction led to the breakup of marriages. A clear effort had been made in this case to help the marriage survive. Maybe Devonmouth Social Services had even played a positive role in this? George waited for Beth to continue. "For a few years our marriage improved, Reginald got a good job as a lecturer at Devonmouth university, and we had two wonderful boys, Josh and Jack." Tears began welling up in Beth's eyes. "But Reginald was not happy and became increasingly depressed …" Beth broke down in tears and hid her face in her hands.

For the first time Reginald looked up at George, almost imploring George with his gaze for help. Tears also began running down Reginald's cheeks. "My family has a history of depression", Reginald said with a voice that was much deeper and that sounded more self-assured than George had expected. "My father was also an alcoholic. I am not using this as an excuse, but there was clearly some family baggage that made it easier for me to slip into alcoholism." *Good*, George thought, *the key step in addressing alcoholism is the recognition and acknowledgement that one is addicted to alcohol*

in the first place. That is a good sign! "When I stopped drinking", Reginal continued, "I found it liberating at first. I love Beth and I love our kids and I really enjoy my job, but there is always something in the background nagging me. My depression got worse and worse and it was hard not to be able occasionally to drown my sorrows with alcohol. I am trying … I am trying so hard …", and he broke down, his heavy body convulsed with loud sobs. *This is turning out to be a tough session!*, George thought, *but at least both Beth and Reginald are willing to talk openly about their problems. Maybe there is hope for them after all.*

"You are not trying!", Beth shouted suddenly looking angrily at her husband. "Instead of trying to cope with your pathetic problems you are hitting me … and the children … you have become so aggressive!"

OK, that puts a new and unexpected twist on things, thought George. "Why are you hitting your wife and children, Mr Rigby?", George asked.

"I … I don't know", came Reginald's timid response. "Sometimes the anger inside me just boils over and I can't stop myself. I know that I love them but something inside me forces me to hit them. The tiniest of reasons, Josh spilling water from a glass over my work papers, Jack interrupting me when I speak, is enough for me to suddenly lose all control. I hit them … I hit them hard …".

George knew from the notes sent over from Social Services that they wanted him to help in their assessment whether to separate Reginald from his family. Social services were beginning to fear for the children's safety.

"This is a very serious matter", George said to both, "and we need to find a solution to this, otherwise Social Services will force Reginald to leave the house. I will need to see Reginald on his own for several psycho-therapy sessions over the next few weeks. Only then will I be able to send an evaluation to social services as to what would be best for you and your family. If we can find a solution that deals with Reginald's deep-seated frustrations and depression, we may be able to prevent the breakup of your family and marriage."

Both Beth and Reginald looked at George with their tearful faces. They looked at each other and for the first time George could detect a hint of remnant love in their eyes. They agreed that this was the most logical course of action, thanked George for his time and help and left the room.

George felt rather exhausted after this session, but he still had to find the energy to write up his notes about the meeting. However often he had dealt with cases like this before, he could not hide the fact that each case still affected him as a fellow human being who had his own problems do deal with. It was impossible as a psycho-therapist to completely disassociate himself from his patients' stories, histories and

problems. He sincerely hoped that he could help the Rigbys.

George's next patient was Ralph Miller, the patient he had seen the week before and whom he had referred to Devonmouth's Citizen Rehabilitation Group. After satisfying himself that Ralph was attending the group meetings and enjoying them, they had a lengthy discussion about Ralph's current circumstances. George was happy that Ralph's attendance at the rehabilitation group, and his currently more settled and secure lifestyle, had substantially reduced the risk of suicide, but he also knew that Ralph's situation needed regular monitoring.

After Ralph had left, George looked at the paperwork for his next patient. It was the first appointment for Anwar Barhoum who was a Syrian Muslim refugee, currently living in accommodation allocated to refugees in Devonmouth. Since the Syrian civil war and the dramatic increase in refugee numbers in Europe, refugees had become an important part of the mix of patients George was seeing. Of the forty or so patients George had taken over from Paul Sutherland, a handful were refugees from African or Middle Eastern backgrounds, some of whom George was seeing regularly. They often came with severe psychological traumas associated with wars or extreme poverty that had driven them away from their home countries, or linked to the dreadful conditions they had experienced while making the hazardous journey to Europe in the hands of ruthless smugglers and

rapists, on leaking boats that were often death-traps that caused the drowning of hundreds of refugees every year. George ruffled through the notes sent by the Devonmouth Refugee Services. In Anwar Barhoum's case, his psychological trauma appeared to be less related to his background or journey as a refugee, but to the fact that his 12-year old son had recently disappeared, but there was not much information in what looked like hastily scribbled notes by an overworked aid worker.

George pressed the buzzer and Daniela let in the Syrian who timidly took a seat in front of George, nervously crunching a battered cap in his hands. Anwar was a small thin man in his mid-thirties, with balding black hair that already showed hints of grey, a week-old beard covering a tanned face, black piercing eyes, and ill- fitting clothes that had probably been given to him by the refugee aid agencies. He wore shiny white new trainers that seemed out-of-place with his otherwise dishevelled looks. Anwar looked scared and ill-at-ease, like a frightened animal caught in the headlights of a car.

"Welcome Mr Barhoum", George said, stretching out his hand towards the Syrian. "I have been assigned by the Devonmouth Refugee Services to help you, as they have reported that you are feeling rather depressed. Do you speak English and do you understand what I am saying?" George knew that language was often an issue with recent refugees, and in cases in the past he had needed a translator to communicate

with refugee patients, which could make a discussion about deep psychological problems difficult. “Yes, I speak English”, Anwar replied to George’s relief. “I took English at school in Damascus and also had to learn English as part of my training as a pharmacist.”

“Devonmouth Refugee Services have sent me some information, but please tell me in your own words about your problems”, George said encouragingly.

Anwar shuffled uneasily from one side of the chair to the other, reluctant to speak. “Thanks for seeing me, doctor. I need help … I … My son … my son has disappeared!”

George looked expectantly at Anwar, hoping he would continue, but the Syrian had fallen silent again. “How did your son disappear?”, George enquired.

“He … he was here in Devonmouth with me … He suddenly disappeared. My wife and I had fled from Syria in 2015 with our son who was seven at the time. It was … it was a very difficult journey …” Anwar kneaded his hands nervously. “It was difficult to cross from Syria into Turkey. Then it took us a month to make our way to the coast where we paid thousands of dollars to a man who owned a boat that took us to a Greek island. We all nearly drowned … Then we walked through Greece, Macedonia and Serbia. My wife … Afraa … my wife was separated from us in one of the camps … We have not seen her since.” Anwar was overwhelmed by emotion and put his face in his hands. “Somehow my son

Rawad and I made it to Germany. After two years we were among a few Syrians who were officially accepted as refugees by the UK, and we were allocated to Devonmouth Refugee Services who provided us with accommodation and some financial help. My son … my son was put into a primary school. It was difficult at first as he did not speak any English, but he learned very fast and even made some friends with some of his schoolmates. He … he enjoyed school… And then, a few weeks ago, he just disappeared."

"Have the police been informed?", asked George.

"Yes. I told the Refugee Services and they immediately contacted the police. We have been looking for Rawad ever since, but there is no trace of him!"

George could see the despair in the man's face. Not only had he had to cope with the traumatic escape from war-ravaged Syria, but he had also lost his wife and now his son. George leafed through the notes sent to him by the Refugee Services. "Were there any signs that your son was unhappy, or that he had problems at school?", George asked, not finding the information he needed in the notes.

"No … no … he seemed very happy. As I said, he had begun to make friends, and after two years his English was perfect. Although the flat we have been allocated is very small, Rawad enjoyed where we lived. He had been playing outside with a friend just outside our flat, and then he didn't come home. I looked everywhere,

neighbours helped, then the police. I don't understand what could have happened to him. I am completely devastated and I don't know what to do. I have thought about killing myself ..."

Judging from Anwar's dishevelled appearance, George had already surmised that this was a man in deep trouble. He had clearly let himself go over the past few weeks, and the nervous twitching in his face betrayed deep emotional and psychological stress.

"I am very sorry to hear about your son", George said in his most sympathetic voice. "I can assure you that we, myself and the Refugee Services, will do everything in our power to help you. I will see you regularly, which will give you an opportunity to talk about how you feel. It is fully understandable that you are feeling very stressed and depressed by what happened, and I will, in the first instance, discuss with you whether the tranquilisers and anti-depressants prescribed to you by your GP are helping in easing your depression."

George knew that it had been over 30 years since a genuinely new type of antidepressant had come to market despite the fact that globally over 300 million people were suffering from depression. Most antidepressants were based on the 'monoamine hypothesis' which held that most depressions were caused by low levels of a class of monoamine neurotransmitters such as serotonin, norephinedrine and dopamine in the brain. But George also knew from his experience that many patients failed to respond to these

drugs. The severity of Anwar Barhoum's symptoms had led his GP to prescribe a new type of antidepressant based on ketamine, which, originally, had emerged as a recreational drug and which contained the new compound esketamine. *How closely linked recreational drug-taking and antidepressant treatment are!,* George wondered not for the first time. Widely used as an anaesthetic, George had read that esketamine blocked specific chemical receptors, especially glutamate which was often implicated in depression, and which took hold within hours rather than days.

"Your GP will have told you that this new stronger drug should alleviate your symptoms almost immediately, but you will need to let me, and your GP, know how you arc getting on with it. As you know, you take it as a nasal spray, and you will see that it should alleviate your anxiety and it should also help you feel a bit more positive about life." While George was speaking, Anwar had taken out the spray from his pocket and looked at it. George's suspicion that the Syrian had not yet begun to take his medicine was confirmed when George realised that the package containing the nasal spray was still sealed shut.

"In the meantime, I hope that the police will find your son. Maybe he has just run away? After all he is twelve now, so he should be able to fend for himself, at least for a while." But deep inside George knew that it could be difficult to find people who had disappeared after several weeks

had elapsed. Rawad had been gone for over a month now and the chances of finding him diminished with every passing week. It sounded almost as if Rawad had been taken or kidnapped, but he could not remember reading about it in the local news or hearing about it.

Anwar thanked George profusely by shaking his hand vigorously and promising that he would take the medicine. They agreed on another session in a week's time. George leaned back against his still badly adjusted backrest. He had a feeling that Anwar's case would preoccupy him for a while.

Part 2

Darkness

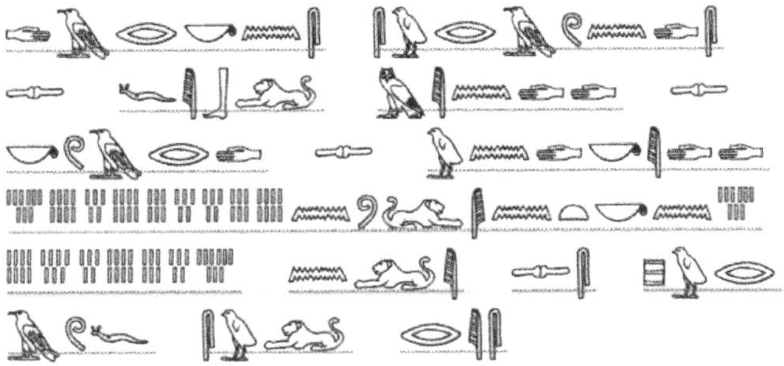

Darkness surrounds the feeble-minded, the coward, the undecided
Only those pure of soul rise towards Ra the redeemer
The saviour and the eternal
Cast aside those behind you, the depraved hordes of simple men
And behold the pharaoh who has risen beyond the abyss of death

(Inscription on tomb of Ramses VIII, BC 1129, Valley of the Kings, Egypt)

Heavy rain splattered the windscreen on George's small Korean-made car as he was winding his way from home to work through the narrow Devonshire lanes, the Dartmoor hills just visible smudging the horizon. The sky was as grey as a dead mackerel. Not for the first time, George admired how neatly cut the hedges were on either side of the lanes, and how these wonderfully biodiverse linear habitats added to the beauty of the farming landscape around his village. Despite the heavy rain, he admired the flowering hawthorn, the golden rape fields swaying in the gale, and the gnarled, wind-bent and dripping-wet sessile oaks standing guard at the side of the road. George opened his window slightly to inhale the smell of the wild garlic that grew in the sessile oak woods which made him think of lamb roast, but the incoming rain made him quickly close the window again.

So far, he enjoyed living in this part of England, and he felt very lucky that he had been able to afford to buy a house in one of the beautiful estuarine villages not far from Devonmouth. All in all, and despite of the difficulties in taking over the practice and patients of a psycho-therapist who had mysteriously disappeared, and the unresolved issue with Marlies which had continued to nag him over the past week, so far he was happy to have taken the decision to leave his London-based practice and move to this part of the UK.

His upbeat mood took a turn when he had to stop his car on the narrow lane behind an old

woman who was walking her dog. In the pouring rain the woman had not heard his car approach. Her dog was huge, a mixture between a pitbull and some straggly beast, its wet black fur dripping water onto the wet pavement with every swaying motion of its ugly canine body. George waited a few seconds before honking his horn which made the old woman jump with surprise. She looked back angrily at George and tried to control her mongrel who was barking heavily and trying to jump at George's car. George could see the disgusting saliva dripping from the mongrel's mouth, its yellow teeth full of putrefied meaty food remnants, and its bloodshot eyes oozing anger, and he was glad that the car door was separating him from the dreadful animal. *It's not my fault if you didn't hear my car approaching, you stupid old and deaf cow!*, George thought angrily while pressing the throttle to quickly whiz past the angry dog.

What did people see in pets, dogs in particular?, he wondered while watching the woman and her beast recede into the rainy gloom in his back mirror. *I can see the human need for pets in the past where they were used as food-waste recyclers, and where dogs were used for protection, and cats to rid farms of rats and mice, but what use are they today? OK, from a psychological viewpoint dogs and cats make sense as they can provide vital comfort to depressed people making them healthier through more exercise with their pets and possibly less anxious, and some studies suggest that they also*

help children learn vital care-related skills, he thought while trying to see the road through the rain-splattered windscreen, *but in many cases pet ownership is also about power, about asserting one's human supremacy over another being that is hopelessly at the mercy of humans' whims, moods and urges of subjugation.* While breaking heavily ahead of a sharp bend he should have anticipated but had not seen in the murky light, George thought about many of the owner-pet situations he had witnessed in both his professional and private life and how, in most cases, the pets, especially dogs, had been used by their owners to assert their superiority and mastery over them. While George had some sympathy for cats and their seemingly more independent minds, it was dogs in particular that annoyed George with their need for hierarchy, their cowardice when alone and not in a pack, and their constant feeble and servile attempts to please their owners. George was particularly annoyed at dogs shitting everywhere, and their owners not cleaning up after them despite of the new-fangled rubbish bins for dog poo and signs everywhere for owners to pick up the crap. *Just imagine how it must feel to pick up your dog's moist and still-warm poo in a thin transparent plastic bag and then to carry it with you to the next poo-bin!,* George thought with disgust. *What dedication! Many humans would not do this even for their own children!* George thought about the fact that many otherwise feeble, unimportant and rather sad men, in particular,

used their dogs to make them feel stronger and superior, and the worst a weak man felt in life, the worse he usually treated his dog. Or about the many women with large dogs they could barely control, like the woman in the lane just a few minutes ago. *Why would a woman want a large dog these days, a dog she can barely control nor master? Was it peer pressure, or maybe just the fact that her stupid male partner had forced her to accept a large dog as a pet? And then think about all the dog and cat food that has to be produced to feed the billions of useless pets on the planet, the carbon footprint associated with this, valuable agricultural land used up to produce food for these despicable and useless beings that are often old, diabetic and increasingly suffer from sensitive digestion! They have it right in parts of Asia*, George thought, *where people still regard the best place for human's best friend as not the sofa but the stewing-pot with some onions and a pinch of seasoning! In China dogs are even rounded up and slaughtered on the ground that keeping pets is 'bourgeois', and how right they are!* George shook his head, wiping the mist on his windscreen with his sleeve. *So much rain! This will be a long journey to work!*

George had caught up with a plumber's van that was struggling with the windy, wet and steep lane. The van's number plate, WF51TYH, showed that it had been built in 2001. George had always wondered about the UK's complicated number plate system which

required some detailed understanding of how it worked for people to see the age of a vehicle. Was this really important and useful information? In other countries such as France or Germany the number plates rather suggested which region or town a car came from. Was their system more informative? Was the UK system only there for people to show that they could afford a slightly newer car than their neighbours?

George continued to follow the van on the windy lanes. He smiled while reading the ad on the van's mud-smeared rear door which said 'Miller's Plumbing: New York, Paris, London, but mainly Devonmouth'. The van swerved in front of him, avoiding the mangled and still bloody carcass of a female pheasant lying prostrate in the middle of the road like a squashed dead insect with its legs sticking in the air. The van almost hit a pair of crows picking on the mangled pheasant remains who had waited until last minute before hobbling off into safety onto the side of the road. George quickly turned the steering wheel to avoid the dead pheasant as he did not want the bird's bloody remains to become encrusted in his tyres. About 20 metres further on a male pheasant, beautiful with intense blue and red head feathers gleaming colourfully even in the rain, was watching the two vehicles rush past. *Possibly the dead pheasant's mate?*, George thought. *Had the bird realised what had happened to his partner? Was there sadness, sorrow and an understanding about death among these animals?*, George had always

wondered when he passed the many pheasant carcasses littering the small lanes around his village. How come these seemingly so stupid birds had survived evolution for so long? They were clearly not suited to survival on busy roads! And yet it was humans who, with their clearing of forests and the creation of the beautiful Devon farming landscape, had created the habitats in the first place for these birds to thrive. But their untimely and brutal slaughter by cars was another thing that put life into perspective, George kept thinking.

Still following the plumber's van, George had turned onto the main road leading to Devonmouth. The road was busy and rush-hour traffic was building up. *I look forward to the next recession when there will be less traffic on the road!*, George thought half-seriously. In places the road was narrow and the van in front of him had to slow down suddenly behind a cyclist. A queue of cars was rapidly building behind them, but lack of visibility prevented the van from overtaking. George looked at the blue LED clock display in his car and realised that it was later than he thought. He had cut it a bit fine with regard to his first patient for the day and hoped they would not be held up much longer. The cyclist was a woman clad in lycra, with rather large hips, probably in her thirties. She was just approaching the steepest stretch of the road and had slowed down to a crawl. It was till pouring with rain. Cars behind George had begun to honk their horns impatiently.

Why does she choose to cycle on this road during morning rush hour and in this dreadful weather?, George thought angrily while looking at the cyclist's swaying bottom. *She knows that she is holding up traffic and that it is incredibly dangerous to cycle on this stretch of road! Why not use the new path that has been built by the local farmer which runs parallel to the road? Sure, there are a few gates to be opened and some sections are rather steep, but the path is certainly much more pleasant than putting herself in danger and slowing traffic, especially in this weather!* The van finally managed to pass the woman, followed by George and a few other cars behind him. Shortly after, they passed a male cyclist, dripping wet and looking rather miserable, who had pulled up into a bus stop looking impatiently at his watch. *Here we go!*, George thought without sympathy. *It's the usual story about a struggling female cyclist who only cycles because her bloke wants her to cycle, instead of doing what really interests her. Why can't the woman stand up to her man and tell him to get stuffed with his stupid cycling on dangerous roads, and that she would rather prefer to do a sport that interested her rather than him, and tell him off for choosing such a stupid time and place to cycle! But maybe it was her who insisted on cycling and he is the one pissed off as he would rather be sitting in his nice and dry BMW?*

George's iPod, on random shuffle mode, had just selected one of George's favourite songs,

and he turned up the music to almost full volume, already forgetting about the struggling cyclists who had held him up. George was very proud of his collection of 20,000 songs on his 120 MB first-generation iPod which had taken him a good ten years to copy, compile and select, based on a combination of digitised old vinyl records, cassette tapes, ripped CDs, and downloads from external hard discs from friends. He found that copying thousands of songs from friends gave him a deeper insight into their real inner self and told him more about them than any in-depth discussion ever could. Indeed, the selection of music and songs people had on their individual devices was one of the most personal and intimate windows into their souls, beliefs and convictions, ranging from those with sad and moody tastes, to head-bangers who had never grown up, to lovers of classical music because it made them feel more 'sophisticated', to those with genuine interest and knowledge of a specific music era like the magical 1970s that, in George's opinion, had shaped rock music like no other decade.

While weaving his way through dense commuter traffic on the outskirts of Devonmouth, George thought cynically about how he had compiled the list of 20,000 songs on his iPod as a clear expression of his need to be in control – a need he had not just with regard to music. He had the same strategy about movies, documentaries and sports events which he assiduously copied using his old-fashioned Sony

DVD recorder, and then copying the DVDs onto a massive external hard disc for use at any time on his laptop while he was travelling and on holiday. Control was everything in his life, control over his career, his well-endowed pension, his own psyche, but all of this possibly hiding a deep sense of insecurity. Even as a child his mother had always said that he was a 'control freak', a kid who created a lot of lists and who constantly was quantifying his life in order to 'keep on top of things'. For a while he had been obsessed, for example, with questions such as why farts, his farts at least, did not last longer than six seconds? Or could he break his own record of holding his breath over two minutes and twelve seconds? Why did one wake up at the precise moment one did, and why not a few minutes or seconds earlier or later? And then there were all these lists he had started as a kid: how many times did a person vomit or masturbate in a lifetime (the vomiting list he discontinued due to insufficient occurrences despite of some heavy drinking spells in his youth; the masturbation list was still going with more frequent entries since his divorce), how many books did one read, how much money did one earn cumulatively over a career (starting with pocket money at age 12), how many miles would he drive in a lifetime in his car and on his bike, and how many altimeters would he climb in his life? Getting bored in traffic jams shortly after he had learned driving, George had even started a list that scored the severity of jams,

where he would start his stopwatch as soon as the car stood still and then measuring how long it took to drive a mile. Anything over four minutes he classified as a jam rated 'F' and going up incrementally to 'A*' for jams lasting more than thirteen minutes and twenty seconds. But even he realised after a while how stupid such a list had become when he had started incorporating stopping at traffic lights as part of a 'jam', suggesting that the methodology he was using was totally flawed.

From a psychological self-analysis, George was still not sure why such quantification made him feel more in control. One aspect was about 'ownership' of information. Once you owned data, on traffic jams, on metres climbed, on movies recorded, or on how often you jerked off, you took control over segments of your life – a form of quantitative compartmentalisation of life stages, a drawing of boundaries around the life-induced abyss. But it was also an important way to reduce reliance on unpredictable other people, on processes over which you had no control, such as what movies were shown when and what songs were offered on the radio. The internet and providers such as Netflix or Spotify had of course added a crucial element of pseudo-control, but George was relatively old-fashioned in that respect and strangely reluctant to engage with the new internet-based freedom and control that should have suited his psyche perfectly. George certainly did not like having to rely on the radio when listening to music in his car, for

example, as he felt that he could not control what kind of music was being played, and he got particularly annoyed at the constant interruptions by radio presenters, especially when they were fading out a song he liked, often just when a fantastic guitar solo was at its magnificent crescendo, in order to babble about something totally irrelevant, boring and uninteresting. Worst of all, the radio forced him to listen to idiotic ads selling crap, shit, and rubbish to a gullible, sedated and brain-washed audience. The 20,000 songs on his iPod gave him complete freedom and control in that respect, and George looked down fondly at the little machine jammed in between the cup holder and the handbrake, thanking its now dead genius inventor, Steve Jobs, for building a device that suited his control-freakish nature perfectly.

George was approaching an intersection which was busy with cars and pedestrians trying to cross. It had stopped raining and the sun had come out through holes in the clouds. George had lowered his window to let in a bit of air and enjoy the sun's strong early summer rays. The iPod had selected a disco tune that George did not enjoy very much. It was a song he must have copied years ago when he block-copied thousands of songs from one of his friends in London. George had a system whereby he wrote down songs on his iPod he did not like (yet another list), and it had taken him years to delete thousands of tunes. He used a classification system from 0 to 10, with 10 being the best songs

and 5 being the threshold at which tunes would be deleted. Inevitably this led to a clustering of songs around 5.0 and 5.1, and the current song, a forgettable mid-80s disco tune performed by a female singer George did not recognise, fell into this category. *But the tune is not quite bad enough to delete*, George thought, as he listened to an instrumental part within the song that was ok-ish.

George was amused at himself thinking about the fact that his mood strongly influenced whether to delete a song or not. In the mornings, when he was often grumpy, songs near the 5.0 threshold were more likely to be earmarked for deletion than in the afternoon or evening when he was usually a bit more cheerful. But once a song was gone it was gone forever, there was no way back. *The current song just about makes 5.0*, George thought, so even in his grumpy morning mood it just about made the threshold. Yet the song was bad enough in his mind that he did not want the people at the intersection to hear the music he was listening to, so he closed his window before passing them. *I am such an idiot!*, George thought, not for the first time. *Why am I so self-conscious that I don't want to admit that I sometimes enjoy listening to a trashy shallow disco song? Who cares what these people standing at the intersection think of me? I will never see them again in my life! And still I close the window!*

George shook his head in anger at himself. *It's not just about control, it's also about your*

image, isn't it?, he chided himself looking at a young schoolboy next to his window wondering whether the boy really cared what music people in passing cars were listening to. *If it was a heavy metal song by Deep Purple or Queen, or a Pink Floyd song, you would gladly open your window and indeed turn up the sound, as this is the image you want to portray of yourself to the outside world, isn't it? So why not admit that part of yourself is also about listening to trashy disco music that is not quite so 'cool' and a bit more boringly mainstream?*

George had also ripped the whole Mozart collection of 180 CDs. *Would I also close the window if the iPod had chosen to play a Mozart tune?*, George thought, tapping the steering wheel impatiently. *Yes, I would!*, came the immediate answer, *as Mozart would be seen as 'uncool' by most Devonmouth citizens. But maybe not by Londoners, so I am sheepishly adjusting my music-listening behaviour to my surroundings! Again, you are not sincere with yourself, it's all about image and appearance!*

But then he also had to acknowledge that he could not jump over his shadow, that this was just the way it was, whether analysed from a psycho-therapist's perspective or just from a perspective acknowledging human fallibility, small-mindedness and peer pressures to conform. Whether he wanted it or not, he was part of a wider community, a fellow local and global citizen, with all the demands, pressures and exigencies such a role entailed of a human

being. He could not be an isolated island. Nobody could. One had to be at least part of an island chain, or, better still, part of a large continent with interconnected bits. But, surely, that then also meant that one had to share societal norms and pressures with other human beings, be they religious rubbish, outdated social mores, or, indeed, conventions about music tastes and fashions? Only those who chose the pathway of complete insanity were allowed to opt out of these human systems and to seclude and shield themselves from external pressures, conformity and the need to 'fit in'. George pressed the throttle and hurried through the traffic towards his practice and his first appointment.

*

After careful consideration, George had decided to see Marlies again. Despite what had happened, his professional ethos forbade him to give up on a patient too easily. After all, he was there to help vulnerable patients like Marlies who had gone through one of the most terrible traumas imaginable, not to farm them off to another colleague who may end up facing exactly the same dilemma. But Daniela had given him a strange look when he asked to schedule another appointment with Marlies. Indeed, he had to constantly remind himself that, as a psychotherapist, he was seeking to get his patients to acknowledge and accept that they were in trouble, and that they were empowered to do

something about it. Patients like Marlies, even at her young age, should be helped to identify what it was about them that needed to change, and what needed to remain the same.

About ten days had passed since George had last seen Marlies. Although his life was very busy with new patients, a new house, and still getting acquainted with his new surroundings, George had often thought about Marlies. For their next appointment he had come better prepared. He was wearing more lose fitting trousers that would, should the 'problem' reoccur, make an erection less apparent. But first and foremost, he was determined not to get his sexual attraction to the young girl in the way of his professional duty to treat her. Although the couch was probably still the best way to allow Marlies to talk freely about her problems, he would sit at a distance, away from any temptation.

Daniela had let Marlies and her mother in. After brief greetings the mother left the room, reminding George with a stern and unfriendly look that she would be in the waiting room. Esther also left no doubt that she continued to see the meetings between her daughter and George as a complete and utter waste of time. Marlies sat in front of George, one leg raised up and resting on the edge of the chair. George scrutinised Marlies's face to gauge whether he should mention the 'incident' from their last meeting. But Marlies's face remained inscrutable. George could not stop himself from looking at Marlies.

She seemed even prettier than the first time he saw her. This time she wore cotton trousers and a pretty blouse that accentuated her slim features and the smallness of her breasts. George again could not believe how young she looked, although the way she glanced at him seemed to suggest a much older person. George tried to focus on Marlies's face rather than her body. In preparation for this meeting, George had decided to use what in professional psychological circles was called 'insight-oriented psychotherapy' which focused on revealing or interpreting unconscious processes. This was meant to encourage the verbalisation of all the patient's thoughts, including free associations, fantasies, and dreams, from which George could identify the nature of the past and present unconscious conflicts which were causing the patient's symptoms and traumas. As the cause for Marlies's deep-seated psychological problems was well known – her father's dreadful rape and abuse – future discussions could focus specifically on Marlies's response to this traumatic experience, her catatonic phase and, most importantly, how it affected her own perceptions about her body and feelings.

"How are you Marlies?", Paul asked trying to break the ice.

"I am feeling ok", Marlies replied immediately and self-assuredly. "I was hoping that you would agree to see me again as I feel that talking to you will, like, help me overcome my problems."

George had to admit to himself that he was very glad about this response. Maybe they could just put the 'incident' behind them and focus on a long-standing professional doctor-patient relationship?

"That's great, I am glad to hear that", George replied. "I would like to start to work with you using an approach called insight-oriented therapy. Can you remember Dr Sutherland mentioning this to you?"

George realised that this betrayed the fact that he did not appear to have the full information about how his predecessor had treated her case, but in order for the therapy to be fully effective he needed to establish what treatment Paul had used with Marlies.

"No, that does not ring a bell", Marlies replied, placing her chin on her raised knees and hugging her lower legs. "He certainly used the couch a lot though, and had, like, really deep discussions with me".

"How did you feel that helped you?"

"Well it … it forced me to talk about what happened … like, what we discussed last time I saw you. Although it's really hard for me to talk about it … it … it seems to help me when I speak about what my father did."

"Ok, that sounds good. How comfortable are you to lie down on the couch? Does it make it easier for you to talk?", George asked fully aware that the couch may have been part of the problem at the last meeting. Her lying down and him sitting next to her inevitably put him in a

position of power and authority compared to the more egalitarian setup of sitting in a chair where they could see each other eye-to-eye.

Marlies looked at the couch. "Yes, most definitely. I like lying on the couch. It makes me feel more relaxed", and without being asked she walked towards the couch and lay down. True to his plan, George placed his chair at a greater distance away from the couch.

"OK. Are feeling comfortable? What I would like to discuss is how the terrible things your father did to you may have affected how you feel about yourself, your body and …", George hesitated a bit, "your attitude to sex". George was fully aware that Marlies was only sixteen and that asking her about her sexual feelings was possibly premature.

Marlies closed her eyes and the painful look on her face suggested that she was trying to recollect what her father had done to her. "I think my initial reaction was to not fully understand what had happened. I was too young to understand that what my father did was, like, having sex. I guess that's why I retrenched into myself by … by not talking for two years … not being able to do anything really."

Marlies opened her eyes, but her thoughts seemed far away.

"After … after it was all finished … and after my father had gone to jail, I did not want to look at my body at all or think about sex. I hated all men and ran away from any boy in my class who approached me. They all thought I was … like

… a total weirdo … you know … like a nut-case!"

She looked at George with large sad eyes.

"I fully understand your reaction", George said. "That is absolutely normal under the circumstances. How are you coping at school now?"

"We moved away and mum transferred me to another school. That made things much easier because … like, nobody at the new school knew about me, and we didn't tell them anything about my past. I was accepted and also started to behave a bit more normally, I guess".

"Have you got a boyfriend?", George asked hesitantly.

Marlies again looked at him with an undecipherable look. She hesitated.

"I think about having sex. I … I want to have sex like my schoolmates … I want to be normal. But …" She looked George deep in the eyes. "I saw what happened to you last time …"

George looked at her aghast and blushed. She had brought it up after all! For a moment he was speechless. "I … I am sorry", he stammered. "That should not have happened …", he admitted sheepishly.

"You don't need to apologise, Dr Williamson", Marlies said, sitting up. "I kind of liked it …", and she reached out her hand and placed it on his penis bulging uncontrollably in his trousers.

George was too stunned to react. He knew that he should move away immediately, that this

was the end of their professional relationship, that he should never see her again, and pass her on to one of his colleagues. How could she be interested in him after what her father had done to her? What complicated psychological processes were at play here that would explain her behaviour? Thoughts were racing through George's head. He knew he had to act quickly. His mind told him to retreat, to flee, to run away, but his body reacted differently. He did not move and let her small hand gently caress his rapidly stiffening penis. Instead of hiding the rising bulge, his cotton trousers accentuated it. His penis stood erect and was clearly visible and accessible. George was still so shocked at both the girl and his reaction that he could not move. He knew that he should get up immediately and end their session, but his body was frozen, immobile, and seemed to have a life of its own, disassociated from his willpower. He could not stop looking at Marlies's boyish features, her small breasts, her child-like buttocks, her pretty face with the cute freckles around her nose. His penis hardened further. Marlies had unzipped his trousers and was now holding his throbbing penis in her hand, moving up and down. George closed his eyes and started breathing heavily. *Don't let her do this!*, he tried to convince himself, but it had been a while since a woman had held his penis like this! While all his senses were still primed for escape, for stopping this ludicrous situation, his body still refused to respond to his will. Marlies was leaning forward

and placed his penis into her mouth. *My God! Probably her father had forced her to do this to him!*, he thought in panic. Marlies was now sucking him hard, moving her mouth up and down his increasingly aroused organ. Although George had been married twice, and had had girlfriends before he got married with plenty of sexual experience, this was one of the most beautiful blow-jobs he had ever experienced. The wonderful feeling of reaching the point of no return quickly began to overwhelm him, shutting out everything else from his mind. His whole body just became one huge, pulsating penis. George came in Marlies's mouth with one of the longest and intense orgasms he had ever experienced, while Marlies swallowed his sperm. He let out a loud groan of pleasure. As his erection abated, Marlies let go and looked up at him with a smile. A smear of sperm was visible on the side of her mouth, which she quickly licked up and swallowed.

"I …I …", George stammered, but he was lost for words. He had let himself be overwhelmed by the situation, his body had dictated the agenda, he had completely lost control. What was he doing? What would Marlies's mother, sitting at earshot in the waiting room, think about this? This was the end of his career and his life as knew it! If this came out, he would be disbarred from practicing ever again!

"You don't need to say anything, Dr Williamson", Marlies said nonchalantly as if nothing had happened. She casually wiped her

mouth to remove the last remnants of sperm. "I told you that I want to have sex. Maybe I need to have sex to make me feel better."

Still shaking from the aftermath of his climax, George had gradually come back to his senses and his professional psycho-therapist mind kicked back in. He surreptitiously tucked his now flaccid penis back into his trousers. Could this be interpreted as part of Marlies's complex psychological coping strategy? To have sex with your doctor, or maybe with anyone, in order to overcome the dreadful wrong that your own father had done to you? Had she internalised her father's behaviour – introjected him, as psycho-therapists would say, through her own sexual projection – embedded him and his behaviour deeply into her unconscious, only to re-enact her father's atrocities? Or was this about her asserting control over a man, rather than the other way around? George knew that he was clutching at straws, that these were just limp excuses for the abuse he had just perpetrated on a young and vulnerable patient. But, after all, it was Marlies who had initiated everything, it had not been him, it was her! *But then she is only sixteen and a mere child! How can you blame her and pretend that it was not you who wanted it as much as she did?*

George was still sitting flabbergasted in his chair. Before he could think about what to say, Marlies had stood up, walked towards him and hugged him tightly. She pressed her lips against his mouth. She kissed him intensely and pressed

her tongue into his mouth, and George could feel the sharp taste of his sperm still lingering in her mouth. George closed his eyes and grasped her tight bottom with both his hands. He could feel the outline of her knickers and felt her small breasts pressing against his chest. He was completely and utterly entranced by her body.

"Don't worry, Dr Williamson", Marlies said with her face very close to his. "This will be our secret. I will not mention this to anyone, I swear!"

George finally found the courage to speak. "I believe you Marlies, but you know that what we did is forbidden and that I could lose my licence to practice if this ever came out", but he immediately regretted threatening her like this rather than admitting what he felt for her. "I like you very much", he quickly added. "and you can see that I am very attracted to you, but this could easily be interpreted as me taking advantage of you. I am your doctor and I also am old enough to be your grandfather!"

Marlies laughed out loud. This was the first time George had seen her laugh and it made her even more attractive. "That does not worry me", she said while walking over to the washbasin in the corner where she rinsed her mouth.

It is almost as if she has done all this before, George began to wonder. Did she do the same with Paul Sutherland and then walk over to the washbasin to clean herself up? George could not believe that this would have been the case, and he was at a complete loss about what to do next.

Should he pretend that nothing happened? Should he see Marlies again? What would happen next time he saw her? Could he stop thinking about her, he wondered, after how she had made him feel just a few minutes ago? He could see himself becoming addicted to her. Of course, he had to see here again!

Marlies did not give him time to reply or reconsider. She wiped off her hands on the towel next to the washbasin and, with a hint of a smile, she left the room. The door closed with a loud bang and George still sat in his chair, wondering whether this had all just been a dream.

*

George closed his eyes and tried to focus. He had messed up his second fairway shot on the previous hole, so he did not want to repeat the same mistake on this difficult Hole 15. Due to a bad back injury years ago, he could not fully rotate his body when performing a golf swing, which meant that he was using his arms more than he should and, as a result, his drive and fairway shots were shorter than those of most other people. But, although he found it difficult, he loved his golf, as it gave him regular exercise and a good opportunity to meet new people from his village. He found golf one of the most fascinating sports, especially as, even as a psychologist, he could not explain why he played one shot well, and why the next one could be

completely miscued although he thought he had used exactly the same stance, swing and mental preparation. *Why were humans so inconsistent?*, he had always asked himself. But most importantly, golf provided an important avenue to forget about work, to distance himself from his patients, and to relax. This is why he had started playing golf years ago when he was practising in London, although he had never played regularly enough to improve substantially.

And yet he could not ban one thought from his mind at all: *Marlies, Marlies, Marlies!* How wonderful his orgasm had felt in her mouth! George placed his three-wood against the yellow Calloway 2 ball that was sitting neatly up on the fairway after a good drive with his new Cobra offset driver. *Concentrate!*, he ordered himself, *don't mess this one up! Try not to think about Marlies for at least a little while! Hole 15 is a tough and long uphill par 4 and you don't want to mess up the second shot!* For the third time he looked towards the distant flag, just visible to the left of the bunker behind the brow of the gentle slope marking the edge of the fairway. He performed his usual routine which involved a practice swing in front of the ball, and then placing the club in front of the ball to get a feel for the exact distance between himself, the club and the ball. One final look at the flag, eyes back on the ball, one swing back … *Keep your head steady!* … and George grounded his club deep into the turf, way short of the ball, grass and earth flying into the air together with a gigantic divot.

As the club had lost almost all its energy by hitting the ground prematurely, it barely touched the ball which rolled just a few metres at a 45-degree angle to the left. "Bugger!", George swore loudly, looking embarrassed at his three playing partners who were all politely looking away after witnessing this debacle. There was an unwritten rule in golf that one commented mainly on good shots, but that bad shots were seen largely as rare aberrations, although, with players of George's ability, they happened all too regularly. Sam Worthington, one of his playing partners and an old friend from the London area who had recently retired to the south-west, was standing to his right and ventured a comment with a slight smirk on his face. : "Happens to the best … !", he said as nonchalantly as possible while beginning the routine of addressing his own ball.

George could not take any solace from Sam's comment. Despite all the concentration and the explicit fact that he had wanted to hit his ball as well as possible, he had completely messed up his shot. How was this possible? Why could he not repeatedly perform the same stroke over and over again? After all, golf was the simplest of sports: hit the ball along a neatly mown surface and get it into a hole at the end. How could this be so complicated? But, of course, George knew that, even after countless years of playing golf, the sport was anything but simple. Slight unevenness of terrain affecting your stance, mud on the ball in summer when the rules implied you

could not place and clean your ball, slight subconscious adjustments of your arms, shoulders, torso, pelvis, legs and feet that could mean that you were a few millimetres out when hitting the ball, movement of your head, or just simply a lack of concentration involving a misjudgement of the distance between you and the ball, or of the direction in which to hit it – all these factors meant that every shot was unique and different, and that a successful previous shot did not guarantee a successful subsequent shot. And then there were all these distracting thoughts about Marlies …!

George enviously watched Martin, his third playing partner and from the village where George had bought his new house, hit an excellent five iron directly towards the flag. "Good shot!", he and Sam shouted simultaneously, and a bit jealous, as Martin's ball bounced a few times and rolled towards the edge of the green. George walked the few steps towards where his wayward shot had landed. His ball had left the fairway and was stranded in thick rough grass, about two metres from the edge of the first cut behind a small tree. *As if I wasn't unlucky enough to have completely mis-hit my shot*, George grumbled, *the bloody ball had to lodge itself close to a tree! Now I don't have a clear line to the flag, which makes the third shot very difficult.* At least the ball was sitting up a bit in the rough grass which should allow reasonable contact between club and ball. "Have you got a line to the green?", Sam shouted

after having played a halfway-decent second shot which had stopped about 40 metres from the green. George stood behind his ball to evaluate the line. "Not really!", he shouted back. "I may need to play it back onto the fairway and lay it up!"

For George, golf was all about statistics, and, true to his quantitative and obsessive self, he kept a meticulous list of all his golf results, colour-coded into different categories. He was working hard to get his handicap to at least 28 which, before new rules had come in, had traditionally been the worst handicap you could have. Now you could have up to 54 handicap which, some ardent golfers thought, was watering down age-old perceptions about what made a 'good' golfer, but the new rules suited George and many of his playing partners who struggled to record results that warranted a 28 handicap or better. After regularly handing in scorecards, George's handicap at the moment was 28.8, rounded up to what he thought was a respectable 29. Based on how handicaps were calculated, every stroke counted, and George's aim was to achieve a round of 99 or better. In his statistics he colour-coded his results, with anything below 100 coloured green, 100-109 red, 110+ coloured yellow, and a dreadful 120+ coloured grey. He had played well so far, with a few glitches and several good holes with even a bogey at the difficult Hole 6, and his score after 14 holes stood at a very good 77 so far. This meant that he could take at most 22 strokes on the last four

holes to reach his target, which was just about possible with three sixes on the par 4 Holes 15, 16 and the very difficult 18th and a four on the easy par 3 17th. Now it looked as if his third shot on Hole 15 would not even get him close to the green, which made a six virtually impossible.

While his three playing partners were waiting patiently, George stood back and looked at the line for his third shot again. Maybe it was possible to play a shot with a lofty eight iron towards the flag that would just miss the tree? George though again about his stats. *Come on!*, he tried to encourage himself. *Just do it! Who dares, wins!* He grabbed the 8-iron from his bag, went through his routine addressing the ball, and hit the ball as hard as he could. In the thick grass the contact was far from clean and the ball went straight for the tree, hit the trunk with a loud smack, and ricocheted off to the left at a ninety-degree angle to end about twenty metres from the tree inside a bush. George closed his eyes in disgust. He could not believe it! Why had he taken the risk? Why not just play an easy rescue shot to the right of the tree that would have safely landed on the fairway, followed by an easy fourth shot towards the green that still made an overall score of six or seven possible? But no, yet again he had been driven by his obsessive statistics and forced to attempt to minimise his score by playing risky shots. Now he was facing the possibility of not being able to play his next shot at all from inside the bush, replacing the ball

and losing a stroke as a result, and still not having an easy fifth shot towards the green.

Sam, who stood closest to George, looked with deepest sympathy towards him. This time he said nothing. They all had gone through what George was facing, they were all mildly ambitious about their scores, and they all wanted to perform well in front of each other. But George had learned to be philosophical about golf as, at their weak level of play, this was the only way to continue to enjoy the sport. As he walked towards the bush were his ball had lodged itself, he thought for the hundredths time that golf was much more than just a sport and that one had to be cynical about all this scoring. In the grander scheme of things, what did it really matter whether one scored 99, 109 or 129? Who cared anyway apart from himself what he scored? Golf was as much about the social aspect, meeting friends, having a drink at the bar afterwards, and enjoying each other's company, as it was about competitive scoring. As long as they enjoyed themselves!

George looked at the beautifully manicured parkland scene around him, with scattered trees in blossom, neatly trimmed lawns, and bluebell-clad hedges and small copses. *Isn't golf equivalent to a 'meditation in green', a spiritual and psychological journey of self-discovery?*, George often thought to distract himself after having played a dreadful shot. *But it can only be men who would be stupid enough to chase a small ball towards a tiny hole!*, he admitted with

a smile, *and most women have way too much common sense to obsess about chasing a small ball into a tiny hole, when there is so much else to do in life!* In the end, wasn't golf just mimicking what bands of men have enjoyed doing for tens of thousands of years? A small male hunting party, out to 'hunt' and 'shoot', occasionally grunting acquiescence of a good shot, but keeping talk to a minimum and concentrating instead on the task at hand in their own narrow-minded masculine world? In other words, and as with many things in so-called 'modern' society, George saw the activity of playing golf as a subconscious continuation of human hunter-gathering activities deeply engrained in the species, but all currently hidden behind the shallow veneer of a sophisticated technology-driven, but ultimately utterly shallow, culture. *Man, the hunter!*, George thought. *All I am doing here is emulating the activities of my hunter-gathering forebears, just with different tools, and instead of shooting the prey I am shooting the ball towards a hole. Golf is, thus, just like any other sport, mimicking age-old traditions of war, fighting, competing, aiming, shooting and scoring, stuff that men enjoy deep inside!* At this thought, George imagined with a smile all his forebears lined up one behind the other on this golf course. Picturing them standing chest-to-shoulder behind each other, this line of people would not stretch too far back to reach the first ancestor who would have lived as hunter-gatherers

somewhere in Europe or the Middle East. Assuming generations of 25 years, this meant 40 individuals per millennium. Following one ancestral line that led back to European Mesolithic hunter-gatherers until about 7000 years ago, this only meant 280 individuals, mothers and fathers, one behind the other for only about 25 metres. George looked at where he was standing near the bush where his ball had disappeared and estimated that this ancestral line only reached to about where Sam was standing. *Hello hunter-gathering ancestor!*, George shouted in his mind towards his imaginary fur-clad ancestor standing next to Sam. *Here we are doing roughly the same thing: you are hunting and shooting a deer in what was a densely forested landscape with your flint-tipped spear, while I am hunting and shooting a small plastic ball with a rubberised core. How little has changed in 7000 years!*

George looked up from his daydreaming towards Sam and realised that his friends were impatiently waiting for him to take the next shot. He had found his ball, deeply lodged and unplayable in the small bush. He took the ball out, walked back from the bush as far as he wanted, roughly in line with the flag, and dropped the ball from knee-high into the rough grass. He took out a 9-iron from his bag, went through his routine, addressed the ball, and played a magnificently struck fifth shot that landed not far from Sam's ball forty metres or so from the green. *Maybe there is hope after all for*

a 99!, George mused with a wry smile on his face. *Now I just need to two- or three-putt from here for a seven or eight, and then try to get not more than 14 or 15 over the last three holes!*

*

George had finally mustered the courage to ask Daniela out for a lunchtime coffee. Since George had started seeing Marlies as a patient, Daniela's attitude towards George had undoubtedly become frostier, and her initial enthusiasm of working with George and filling him in on Paul's patients' histories had clearly waned. George Had not even dared ask Daniela again for help with his many persistent IT-related problems. In addition to this, official-looking letters had begun to arrive from the National Association for Psychology, but George had not dared open them for fear that they could be related to Marlies. George worried whether Marlies's awful mother had reported him to the Association. The two unopened letters that had arrived so far had disappeared into the bottom drawer of his desk.

Daniela had been very reluctant to leave the practice unattended for even an hour. "All the phone calls we are getting!", she kept saying. "We can't afford to lose more patients, and if I am not there to answer the phone we may lose more!" George knew that Daniela was right. In the two months since he had taken over Paul's practice there had been a gradual attrition of

previous patients, like the slow leaking of liquid from a poorly fitted barrel. George was not sure whether it was just coincidence, or whether it was linked to the fact that he had found it more difficult to focus on his patients after he had started this 'affair' with Marlies. He had indeed been rather unconcentrated in his job lately, and on two occasions he had even missed appointments because he had overslept, resulting in rightfully scornful remarks by Daniela. But in the end, she had grudgingly agreed to come for a 'quick cuppa'.

As they were walking towards his favourite café, the one with the wooden decking, George could not help thinking that he knew virtually nothing about Daniela. He knew she was about 50 and that she liked perfume with a hint of roses, lemon and lavender, but was she married or did she have kids? It occurred to George that it would have been polite to talk to Daniela much earlier about these personal matters, as it may have facilitated breaking the ice. But then he had been so busy in the first two months in the job and getting his new house organised. They walked through the moderately busy Devonmouth pedestrian area. It was warm in the strong June sunshine, but a strong wind was blowing. Heavy gusts were blowing plastic debris, discarded wrappers, dead leaves, and dirty napkins around the pavement in little whirlwinds that created an irregular mosaic of tiny ephemeral and ever-shifting waste heaps that scraped along the pavement with a dry

rustling sound that reminded George of water trickling down a dried-out riverbed.

They sat down at a table on the wooden decking, the wind gusts playing with Daniela's black curls and forcing her to flick away a strand of hair that was persistently brushing the side of her face. The wind was so strong that George worried that the froth on his cappuccino would blow onto his freshly cleaned and ironed shirt. He stirred his coffee quickly and took a sip which reduced the height of the froth.

"Daniela, I apologise that we haven't had a chance to talk earlier", George began. "We should have done this much earlier."

Without answering, Daniela looked down at her latte macchiato which George had paid for.

"I have the impression that something is bothering you", George continued. "Is there something we should discuss? Have I done something wrong?"

"I appreciate your candour", Daniela replied, now looking him straight in the eyes. "Yes, it's nice to have a chat, but there is nothing specific I want to talk about".

George looked at her and was not sure whether Daniela was entirely honest. Was she hiding something from him?

"Ever since we started working together, I wanted to ask you about Paul", George said frankly. "Why did he give up the practice so quickly and where has he disappeared to? It would have been so helpful for me to discuss some of his former patients directly with him by

phone, but I have no information about his whereabouts."

"Yes, I warned you from the start that this could be a problem", Daniela admitted. "But Paul … Dr Sutherland … left explicit instructions that he did not want to be contacted …"

"But was his decision to leave the practice very sudden?", George interrupted Daniela. "Was it linked to a problem, maybe with the practice or with some of his patients?"

Daniela hesitated, taking a sip from her coffee. "No, as you know the practice was still in good financial health when you took it over, we still have a reasonable number of patients, although we seem to have lost a few lately, and as far as I know there were no problems with any of Paul's … Dr Sutherland's … patients."

"But why would someone like him with a successful practice then suddenly upend sticks and leave from one day to another without leaving contact details? Something must have happened?"

Again, Daniela did not reply and looked away towards children playing loudly among shrubs lining the pedestrian area.

"It wasn't linked to Marlies and her mother, was it?", George asked outright.

Daniela turned her head with her mouth wide open. George had clearly taken her by surprise. "Why would you think that, George?", she replied after regathering her composure.

"I have the feeling that your attitude towards me has changed since I started treating Marlies, that's why I'm asking", George said, wondering whether Daniela had guessed what was happening between him and Marlies but was too embarrassed to talk about it.

"No … no … not at all", Daniela stammered, but she had clearly lost her self-confidence.

"Did something untoward happen between Marlies and Paul?", George asked bluntly. "Did they have an affair?"

This time Daniela looked George straight in the eye. She was clearly carefully thinking about her answer and weighing up her options.

"Don't worry, Daniela", George tried to reassure her. "I will treat anything you tell me as strictly confidential. I have no interest in slandering Paul who I respect immensely as a colleague. I just want to know what happened."

Daniela looked down onto her half-empty coffee cup. One of her hands was twitching nervously, holding the paper napkin jammed under the plate.

"Yes, I think he had an affair with that young girl", she said with a suddenly rather timid voice. She looked up again. "But I am not entirely sure. She is just a kid after all, and she looks so young! And she is a patient! … How could he …?"

Daniela pulled out the napkin and dabbed her eyes. George grabbed her hand to console her. "It's ok, Daniela", he said gently, "whatever happened is not your fault. So, was that the reason he left so suddenly?"

“Yes … yes, I believe so”, came Daniela’s barely audible answer.

George had a dreadful sinking feeling in his stomach. His worst nightmare had come true. Not only was he completely besotted with a young vulnerable patient, but his predecessor also had an illegal affair with that same girl, and, rather than confronting the situation head-on, Paul had decided to cowardly vanish and to tell nobody about it. George had to stop any interaction with Marlies and pass her on to another colleague, maybe with some subtle warning. At least it did not appear that Daniela suspected that George had had sex with Marlies yet, but George felt bad and ill-at-ease that he could not tell Daniela about what had happened. He was almost ready to admit it to her, but he knew that he could not discuss what he had let Marlies do to him. His sense of self-preservation was simply too strong.

George gently patted Daniela’s hand. “Thank you for telling me. That explains a few things to me about the girl’s behaviour and why several pages seem to be missing from Daniela’s medical file”.

“I did not know about that”, Daniela immediately said in self-defence, and George realised that he had made it sound as if he was blaming her.

“No, no, Daniela, don’t worry”, he reassured her, “I am not blaming you for this. But it looks as if Paul was trying to burn all his bridges before disappearing. It was utterly unprofessional

conduct …", But George realised immediately how hypocritical he sounded and hoped that Daniela was not reading between the lines about what he said. But Daniela seemed preoccupied with her own feelings about the affair. Under normal circumstances, George would have immediately reported Paul Sutherland's misconduct to the National Association for Psychiatry to have him disbarred from work, but now that he was embroiled himself with the same patient, he knew that this was an impossible course of action. For the moment, Paul Sutherland was getting away with his improper and unprofessional conduct.

For a while they said nothing, and then their discussion drifted towards some of the day-to-day issues linked to the practice, but George knew all along that Daniela felt ill-at-ease. On their way back to the practice George was deep in thought while Daniela walked next to him saying nothing. On the one hand, George was relieved that he had more clarity about the reasons for Paul's sudden departure, but, on the other hand, he was deeply worried and unsure about how to make clear to Marlies that he could never see her again. He should really talk to this Dr Cranston at the hospital who also saw Marlies regularly! Maybe talking to him would make things easier for George, but he was not sure whether he was ready yet to see him and talk about Marlies. George also worried that Cranston would be a psychiatrist through and through, which often meant a specialist wary of

psycho-dynamic thinking who favoured more biological, chemical, and practical 'solutions', compared with George's 'deep' sessions involving lengthy talking and discussions that, George believed, allowed much more insight into a patient's mind and deepest fears and anxieties. *'Deep' sessions indeed, you bloody bastard and hypocrite!*, George thought guiltily, remembering his erect penis deep in Marlies's mouth.

*

Although the attrition of patients from George's practice had continued unabated, the following week in the practice had proven to be very busy. George was, yet again, procrastinating about referring Marlies to one of his colleagues, and he had still not had the courage to contact Dr Cranston. *I am so weak, weak, weak!*, he kept thinking, *what would the MeToo movement make of me taking advantage of Marlies like this!*, he thought with a shudder. But something held him back from signing the transfer papers, a niggling feeling of great sadness, an admission that he was sexually besotted with the girl, maybe even the fact that he still wanted to help her overcome her deep-seated psychological problems. In many ways he felt great pity for the vulnerable girl. As far as George could remember, this was the first time he was lost about what to do about a patient. Although Daniela's attitude towards him had slightly improved since their discussion

about Paul Sutherland over a coffee, George could not hide the impression that Daniela suspected that something had happened between him and Marlies. But the unspoken words hung in the air of the little practice like hidden whispers between a squabbling couple at the verge of a marriage breakup.

After a few months in the practice, George had now seen most of the patients passed on to him by Paul Sutherland as well as a trickle of new patients who had self-referred, been passed on by their GPs, or, in more serious cases, been referred to his practice by the psychiatric unit of Devonmouth Hospital. George had just completed a session with a mother, father and son, who were struggling psychologically with their ambition to make their 11-year old boy a world tennis star. The parents had talked with both enthusiasm and frustration about the junior tennis circuit in the UK, mentioning the psychological repercussions associated with a highly competitive, and at times outright nasty, sport circuit in which parents seemed to battle each other even more than their tennis-playing children. After what started as a difficult session, George had been pleased about how the boy had gradually opened up and had taken actively part in the discussion. At the end, they all had agreed on what George thought was a workable solution to reduce their psychological stress. George suggested that they should try out a new sporting timetable for their son, with less parental presence for at least some of his matches, and

then to report back to him in a few months' time about how successfully they had implemented these changes.

Ralph Miller, the suicidal and once successful businessman now living in sheltered accommodation, and one of George's more regular patients, told George that he was struggling to regularly attend the Devonmouth Citizen Rehabilitation Group where George had found him a place. Even regular and intense psycho-therapy sessions with Ralph had failed to produce meaningful results so far. Fergus Rumpley, the patient with the 'bitcoin problem', had also suffered a setback and had become over-obsessed again with finding the lost password on his friend's laptop. Fergus found it particularly hard to see a life ahead of him with the boring day-to-day grind of earning money in a 'normal' job, while millions of dollars were seemingly stashed away on the inaccessible encrypted hard drive of his friend's computer. After a tearful and unsatisfactory session with Fergus on the couch, George had strongly recommended to Fergus to throw away the laptop and start life anew, but Fergus had, understandably, strongly resisted this suggestion and had slipped back into a deep depression that required heavy medication that made it difficult for him to concentrate on his new job at the accounting firm. George had also regularly seen Reginald Rigby, the alcoholic who was gradually and inexorably destroying his and his family's life, but was also making very slow and

unsatisfactory progress with this patient. In their last session, Reginald had admitted that he had again beaten up his wife and children in a drunken rage, and George increasingly feared that the forceful removal of Reginald from his family was only one court order away.

George was seeing his last few patients for the day who were all new referrals. First, he saw a woman in her early 20s whose addiction to the new synthetic drug fentanyl had caused several life-threatening psychotic episodes. She was part of a sad trend in the UK and beyond where nearly half of the people admitted for psychiatric emergencies to hospitals were suffering from the effects of drug-induced psychoses. As with many other difficult cases, George applied the relatively new psycho-therapy of 'incremental cognitive appropriation' which consisted of George telling his patients that a traumatic episode can be like a castle or large house whose exploration can be seen as synonymous with revealing the hidden inner self. George recommended to imagine opening one room after the other, starting with easy, unchallenging and comfortable ones such as a living room, bedroom or kitchen, which should be associated with a sense of peace, quiet and relaxation, and then, as the patient's traumas gradually improved over weeks or months, to move on to more difficult rooms such as the attic, often associated with fear, the cellar, frequently associated with childhood anxieties and horror, and even a dungeon, which may reveal the deepest recesses

of the inner self buried underneath complex psychological layers.

Next, George saw a manic-depressive patient who had lived, and gone to the toilet, for a month behind his couch before finally being discovered by Devonmouth Social Services and sent to a mental asylum for a while. Accompanied by a minder from the asylum, this patient was allowed to see specialists such as George on a regular basis, and George had the impression that he could help this patient just by talking, albeit with many sessions over a long timeframe. His penultimate patient was a new patient, referred to George by a local GP, who had been diagnosed with terminal pancreatic cancer and, as a result, was suffering from severe suicidal depression. George was scribbling a few notes about this patient in the papers lying in front of him in an unordered mess, reflecting on the fact that, in most of these cases, psycho-therapists were more or less unable to help. Even with all his training, experience and intuition, there were no words or therapies that could alleviate the suffering associated with the diagnosis of terminal illness, especially linked to a type of cancer that still had no cure and a one hundred percent fatality rate. The only thing George had been able to do for this patient was to discuss the effects that the very strong anti-depressants prescribed by his doctors had on this patient's body and mind, and to talk about how the patient could best cope with the zombie-like existence of chemical stupor induced by the medication

until the day he finally died. George felt very frustrated and depressed after seeing this patient, recognised his inability to help, and acknowledged the limitations of psycho-therapy for patients like these.

George leaned back in his badly-adjusted chair with a big sigh. *Whoever thinks about how all this affects the mental health of psycho-therapists themselves?*, he wondered not for the first time. *How can we be expected to continue with our routines and personal lives after being bombarded with these terrible cases?*, he thought with tears welling up in his eyes. *Why do we become psycho-therapists in the first place?*, George wondered. But he knew the answer, as he had posed this same question to himself multiple times during his career. *We have an interest in psychology because we are damaged people ourselves! We study it to help heal ourselves! Maybe it's the only way we – as psychologically damaged people – can cope with the world. By understanding what damages people in the first place, we may think that it will help ourselves!* But he had also quickly realised that this had been an illusion, and that, on the contrary, being constantly surrounded by ill and damaged people – mad people – often made him feel worse. Yet he also knew that his current frustration was more deep-seated than the mere inability to help some of his patients. Since the incident with Marlies, his mind had simply not been focused sufficiently on his job, and a deep feeling of dissatisfaction had begun to creep in. Had his

lack of ability to commit fully to his patients not also been reflected in the decline in patient numbers in his practice? *You are not only feeling rotten because of your patients*, he admitted to himself, *but because the unresolved and unprofessional affair with Marlies is sapping all your energy and is severely distracting you from your job! You have to sort this out, otherwise you are at risk of losing this practice!*

His hand drifted towards the bottom drawer where the form for Marlies's transfer to a colleague was waiting to be signed. But George hesitated again. *Weak, weak, weak!*, he screamed inside. There was a knock at the door and Daniela's head peeped in. "Sorry to bother you without you having buzzed me, George", Daniela said apologetically, "but Mr Anwar Barhoum has been waiting patiently for over an hour now and, as I told you this morning, I need to leave now for a funeral".

George looked at his watch and realised that he was, yet again, running very late. "Yes, of course, Daniela, please let him in, and please feel free to go, I'll lock up the practice myself", George replied, surreptitiously wiping a tear from his eye, hoping Daniela had not caught him weeping. Daniela let in Anwar Barhoum who sat down rigidly in front of George's desk.

George steadied himself and leaned back against his still ill-fitting backrest, feeling a slight twitch in his back. "How are you today, Mr Barhoum?", George asked with a slightly forced

sympathetic voice, “and how has the new medication worked?”

“I am coping, doctor Williamson, just coping”, Anwar replied timidly in his fluent English. “I just still miss my son so much”, and he burst out crying, turning his head away from George.

George pushed a box of tissues towards Anwar and gave the distraught man a bit of time to recover. He knew how difficult it was for Muslim men in particular to cry in front of others.

“Has there been any further development about your son’s case since we last spoke?”, George asked cautiously.

“No, none at all”, Anwar replied with a snivelling voice. “I think the police have given up! I feel so alone!”

For a brief moment George was at a loss about what to say. “Have the Devonmouth Refugee Services been of any further help?”, George asked after a while.

“Yes … yes … they have all been very nice!”, Anwar replied while loudly blowing his nose, “and the imam from the local mosque has also been very kind to me. He sees me almost every day and makes sure I’m alright.”

George knew about the Devonmouth mosque, but had to admit that he was not sure where it was located. He had heard that it was not a ‘proper’ mosque with its own building and domed roof, but that it was a corrugated iron shed in the backyard of a decrepit industrial

estate located in one of the more run-down areas of Devonmouth, but he was nonetheless glad to hear that some help was provided for Anwar by the Muslim community itself.

"I find a lot of solace in prayer", Anwar said, confirming George's thoughts, "and praying to Allah, praise be, with his immense gratitude and wisdom, has been an immense help for me".

Anwar had rummaged inside the back pocket of his dishevelled and grimy trousers and had pulled out a tattered wallet. He took out a worn picture. "This is my beautiful son Rawad", he said, holding the picture towards George.

George looked at the picture which showed the picture of a boy from the chest upwards. George thought that it must have been taken in haste as it was slightly blurry and taken with a flash at night. So far George had only thought of Rawad in an abstract way through the tearful recounting of his father's story. But looking at the boy's picture amplified the very personal and sad nature of this case. Rawad was an attractive boy with slim features, thin arms and a long neck, and beautiful unblemished olive-coloured skin typical for many children from the Middle East. He had black piercing eyes that were slightly reddened by the reflection of the camera flash, a cute little nose that was slightly pointing upwards at its tip, thin sensuous lips, and an inviting smile that suggested that the young boy had been happy when this photo was taken. But the photo, taken just before Rawad's disappearance, also showed how gaunt and

skinny the boy was, with a haunted look and dark rings under his eyes, which made George wonder whether the boy had been ill just before he vanished. Nonetheless, seeing the boy in the flesh made George realise even more how hard it was for the father to cope with his loss.

"He is very beautiful", George said, handing the photo back to Anwar and not mentioning how sickly the boy actually looked. "I fully understand how sad you must be feeling. Have the police been in touch with you again?"

"No, nothing since we last spoke", Anwar replied. "I think they have given up the search as it is now over two months since he disappeared", and tears were welling up in his eyes again.

"How has the antidepressant your GP prescribed worked?", George enquired trying to deflect the discussion to more practical issues.

Anwar hesitated before replying. "It has worked well, although I feel very drowsy after taking the nasal spray and I have also felt slightly nauseous and have not been able to sleep very well after taking it, but my depression is better, I have had some happy moments over the last few weeks."

George knew that these were common side-effects. "I am sorry to hear about the problems with the medication, but these are not uncommon. As your GP will have told you, it is important that you continue taking your medicine, so I suggest that you continue with the esketamine for a while, and we can always discuss here whether it works for you or not. If

there are problems please tell your GP, and I can also have a chat with him or her if our discussions reveal that you are struggling with the medication." George was somewhat relieved that Anwar's GP had not yet prescribed more heavy-weight psychotic drugs like Risperidone, which were known to cause even more serious side-effects, including changes in personality, loss of body control such as trembling, and severe lethargy. Anwar nodded in agreement, seemingly pleased at George's suggestion.

As Daniela was gone, George agreed the next meeting date with Anwar, escorted him out of the practice, turned the sign on the door to 'closed', and locked the front door. Thinking back about Rawad's beautiful face on the photo and his father's immense sadness, George leaned back in his chair and stared at Marlies's patient transfer form that still awaited his signature.

*

George woke up. It was dark in his bedroom, the morning light was just beginning to shine through the closed curtains. Crows were crowing hauntingly outside, and the trees in his garden, bent by the incessant westerly gales, emitted creaks that filled his room like an infant's wail. The noise must have woken him and he turned around. A black shape was standing near his bed, making George sit up with a jolt, dead scared. The black shape moved closer towards him, it

seemed to be floating rather than walking. George recognised the features of his second wife Mildred, but her face seemed contorted and her eyes appeared to be pitch black, with no white-of-the-eye, and larger than normal. She floated towards him, her black eyes wide open, and a terrible screeching sound came out of her gaping mouth. Her hand moved forward and was about to touch George … George woke up, bathed in sweat, his duvet lying contorted around his waist. *It was a dream! It was only a dream!*, he thought relieved, but he could not banish the thought of his second wife's contorted face from his mind. *What a terrible nightmare!*

George adjusted his pillows and leaned back, sweaty and sticky, against the giant jigsaw that adorned his bedside wall. He wiped the cold sweat from his brow and took in deep breaths to calm himself. He looked at his alarm clock and saw that it was still early, the faint dawn light shimmering through the gaps on the sides of the curtains. Mildred, his second wife! Why did she appear regularly in his dreams, in his worst nightmares? Why her? George had been married to Mildred for over ten years. It had taken him a while to get over the catastrophic marriage with first wife Martina, but by the time he was in his thirties he had been ready to share his life with a woman again. As soon as he met her at a party held in one of the London suburbs by one of his old friends from university, he fell deeply in love with her. Indeed, George had found himself drawn towards Mildred like a plant in a dark

room towards a wedge of light. For many years they had a very happy relationship, and after three years of dating they decided to get married. Everything seemed to work out at the beginning: their sex life was great, they had many common interests and friends, especially sampling the art and culture scene in London where George was employed as a psycho-therapist in the psychiatric ward at one of the large hospitals, and they shared a common interest in exotic holidays which is where he had visited places like the Taj Mahal in India or the Alhambra in Granada for the first time. But after a few years, things had turned sour. For reasons George had never fully worked out, even with his intricate knowledge of psychology, Mildred got bored of him. She got bored of their flat near the Thames which they had both initially so lovingly restored and furnished, she got bored of discussions with George which had so enthralled her in the first years of their relationship, she got bored of their joint friends most of whom she had introduced to George in the first place, she got bored of their holidays criticising that they always followed the same tedious routine, and, most importantly, she got bored of his obsessive antics, his urge to quantify everything, his preoccupation with controlling and planning every aspect of his own life and their life together, and even of his career ambitions as a psycho-therapist trying to establish his own practice in a highly competitive London environment.

The result of Mildred's frustration was that she started cheating on George. At first, she hid the fact from him that she was meeting one or several other men, often colleagues from work, but after a while she became so reckless that George thought that she wanted him to find out about her lovers. At first, Mildred occasionally came home late, offering increasingly lame excuses about her lateness, but later she stayed away entire nights and came home the next day dishevelled and hung over. She accused George of treating personal relationships like psychological experiments and reprimanded him for being too aloof and controlled. She stopped having sex with him and began talking openly about the other men she was seeing. And she boasted about the fact that she was cheating him with several men simultaneously.

The last year of their marriage, their tenth, was George's worst time in his life. He still loved Mildred and yet he knew that their relationship could not last. He often broke down in tears, got rather depressed, and lost all interest in his job. He knew he was on a dangerous path towards chronic depression and even thought about seeing a psycho-therapist himself. Worst of all, he became afraid of his wife as she had occasionally come home at night, completely drunk, and threatening to harm him. It got so bad that he locked himself into their guest bedroom at night. This was the period when he started having nightmares about Mildred, about being stabbed at night, about being choked by her – a

time when she began to appear in his dreams as an evil half-human creature that bore less-and-less resemblance with the woman he had once loved. His nightmare was a dreadful reminder of that time and he hated himself for letting his subconscious allow the memory of his hated wife to come to the surface again, for his dreams to force him to think about her again.

George sat up in bed. It was still very early, but after all these dark memories there was no way he could get back to sleep. He thought about the fact that he had not dreamt about Mildred for a while, but he was worried that his nightmare about her may herald the start of another spell of sleepless nights. Did the fact that he still felt vulnerable about his second wife partly explain his behaviour towards Marlies? Of course, the affair with Marlies – if he could call it that – also had a simpler explanation, namely that he was just starved of sex. Since Mildred, George had been reluctant to meet other women, and it had been years since he had sex with someone before he met Marlies.

George shook his head. It was no use dwelling on the past. If he was to auto-psychoanalyse, his advice would be to move on, leave the past behind, accept the fact that he had experienced two unlucky marriages, and focus on the present and that he was still healthy with a good life ahead of him. But then he was jeopardising his future by engaging in a sexual affair with one of his patients!

In order to leave these dark thoughts behind, George peeled himself out of bed. How he hated getting up early! He really was not an early morning person, and had always struggled to be in his practice for 9 am. In fact, he always thought that he was dealing with patients much better in the afternoon and that he often was not quite up to speed with the patients he saw in the morning. And it was not a question of caffeine, as with many other working people he knew who got energised after their first caffeine shots. Even drinking a strong coffee in the morning, which his stomach did not cope with very well, did not change the fact that both his body and brain just needed a few hours each day to get going, to work to full potential.

George stumbled towards the living room situated at the front of his bungalow in just his underpants and a t-shirt. He usually put on clothes later, just before he went out for work, and greatly enjoyed this privilege of self-determination which his life as a single person allowed him to live. *Nobody here to tell me what to do and what to wear and when!*, he acknowledged with a smirk. Not that he had too much choice what to wear as, pragmatic and rational as he was, he often bought one and the same outfit in multiples, ten t-shirts, shirts and trousers that were all the same to simplify things and to do away with having to choose what to wear in the morning.

Walking towards the living room, he realised, once again, that his house was a mess.

It was not dirty as he tried to keep it as clean as possible, but junk was lying everywhere, discarded clothes, piles of paper, books, DVDs, more piles of paper and books, and various other things. *How did other people manage to keep their houses so tidy?*, he thought angrily. *How come they seem to have time to go about their busy lives, pursue jobs, bring up children, and still keep their houses so neat and tidy? Did people not have a life, hobbies and interests, which, inevitably, caused a mess and the occasional chaos?* Or was it just the tip of the iceberg he saw, i.e. that the people he knew were relatively successful in juggling the vicissitudes of life and that he never saw the ramshackle, dirty and messy houses of the vast majority of people living around him who coped even less well than he did with keeping their houses tidy? Yet it was not just a 'middle-class thing', as he nonetheless knew some middle-class friends who had similarly messy houses to him.

A look at the beautiful view over the estuary from the large French doors in his living room cheered George up. How happy he was to be able to afford a house in this beautiful coastal village. *Forget about Mildred and Marlies and the mess, just look at this view and enjoy!*, George thought making his way to the kitchen, scratching his bottom through his underpants. Not for the first time his thoughts got distracted by the complexity of preparing breakfast which he did with an almost robotic routine: get plate out of cupboard and put on kitchen table; get knife …

no not that one, the other one with the sharper edge; put water in kettle and place kettle on its electric stand, switch on switch and weigh down switch with small spoon as it otherwise switches off too early; get bread from freezer and put frozen slices into toaster, but check setting on toaster as it tended to occasionally mysteriously self-adjust (he really needed to buy a new toaster!); don't forget to put rest of bread back in freezer!; get margarine and jam from fridge, no not that jam, you had that yesterday, but the other one, ideally two that had different colours (why?); balance jam jars precariously towards kitchen table without letting them drop to the floor; open margarine and jam jars; check toast; find teapot which is, again, hiding behind a pile of dirty dishes; get teabag … damn, need to open a new teabag box, so get tight plastic wrapping off with sharp knife without cutting yourself; place teabag near teapot but don't put into pot yet as you, for some unknown irrational reason, think that a soggy teabag will make the tea taste differently; check both toaster and kettle which tend to reach their climax (was that the right word?) at the same time; kettle wins this time, and while toasts pop a few seconds later, pour boiling water over teabag in teapot; get tea mug from tea mug tree without knocking over pile of dirty dishes (would it not be best to just have two dishwashers: one for the dirty stuff and one with clean dishes, so that you could avoid all this hassle with storing clean dishes and leaving dirty dishes all over the kitchen?); take teabag out of

teapot as you like your tea weak; walk over to toaster and take toasts out; put margarine and jam on toasts; grab tray; put plate with toasts, teapot and mug on tray; get milk out of fridge, no not half-fat one but the 1% fat milk which you use for tea; carefully wedge 2-litre plastic milk bottle in right hand while still holding tray with both hands; and carefully make your way to the living room where you will cautiously balance the tray on the armrest of your leather sofa and eat breakfast while you watch the news on the TV.

George sat down on his sofa with an audible sigh. His bare legs were sticking to the cold leather but he was too lazy to put on trousers yet. He could never get enough from thinking about how even a seemingly ‘simple’ task, such as making breakfast, was, in fact, an intricate combination of highly complex actions and thought processes, and he marvelled at how his brain could manage such complexity so early in the day while he was still half asleep and haunted by his nightmare about Mildred. Wasn’t the human body a miracle? And yet so much could go wrong, especially with the brain and its complex chemistry, biology and psychology, problems which provided him with the means to make a living. Just as he was thinking this, George spilled some blackcurrant jam onto his fresh white t-shirt. *Bugger!*, he thought, *despite of all this complex brain activity that allowed me to prepare this complex breakfast, I can’t even manage a simple arm movement from my plate*

to my mouth without messing things up! He scooped up the bit of jam with his spoon and put it back on his toast, but it had left an ugly dark-red stain on his white shirt which, George imagined, looked like, viewed from above, the blood-and-guts leftovers of a slaughtered animal on a vast snowfield. *How do others cope, those in their tidy houses without spillages?*, he thought again, shaking his head, but probably, he imagined that, as he was just thinking this, hundreds of others in the village had just similarly spilled jam onto their dresses, freshly-ironed shirts or school uniforms.

George flicked on the TV and selected Sky News. As was often the case he had just hit an ad break. Some slim woman in a dark dress was applying some kind of deodorant to her shaven armpits. She was looking lusciously into the camera, caressing her olive-coloured skin in a suggestive fashion, inviting the viewer to imagine applying the same deodorant to their smelly armpits or other fetid areas of their bodies. *Another stupid ad!*, George thought, *again trying to sell shit to idiots who are made to think that they need this kind of rubbish, pampering to the most basic and primeval needs of the audience with blatant sexual undertones and using gender stereotypes in the form of a beautiful slim woman to lure in more viewers. Why do women in this country, and many others too, feel that they have to shave their armpits? What is this idiotic societal convention that implies that hair under your armpits makes you*

ugly? Why does it only apply to women and why should men not shave their armpits too, after all they usually are the smellier of the two sexes? It was yet another fashion, something concocted by the global fashion industry with their stranglehold over what products people should smear on their bodies, what they should wear, and how they should look like!

In the end, George thought, there was no difference between western, so-called 'democratic', societies and autocratic societies such as Mao Zedong's China, when it came to imposing certain types of fashion. In the West it was big business with their economic might and stupid ads that indoctrinated people, especially women, to wear rubbish make-up, deodorant and unpractical dresses, while in Mao Zedong's China it was the Communist Party that had imposed a boring dress-code of ill-fitting boiler suits. But at least the Chinese under Mao did not have to think long about what to put on in the morning as all their clothes were roughly the same. George kind of liked that, as his own wardrobe made up of multiples of the same items testified, especially as it took out the artificially manipulated need for difference in what to wear, extolled by the international clothing and fashion behemoths. How could people in the West, in particular, be so gullible and follow the fashion industry's dictate? George thought about one of the tennis grand slam tournaments he had recently watched where all female tennis players appeared to, yet again, be wearing the same

outfits, indistinguishable from each other and tied together through the same clothing sponsorship deals which forced them to parade the same types of clothes like unthinking robots. Where had individuality gone in all this, and did the tennis-playing pros not realise how totally idiotic their fashion dependency was?

Worst of all, George thought, was the hypocrisy surrounding ads. In the weekly news magazine he enjoyed reading, for example, how often had he been annoyed at the fact that an excellent article on some environmental issues – climate change, biodiversity decline, pollution – was immediately followed by an ad for a super-charged, petrol-guzzling, pretentious, arrogant and totally useless four-wheel-drive SUV? Who needed a four-wheel-drive in today's modern urban world with its good roads? It was all pretentious rubbish, arrogant-looking cars usually driven by short men with inferiority complexes, a fashion-thing yet again. And what about the hypocrisy surrounding child protection and television? A ten-year old was not allowed to see a woman's bare breast – oh no, God forbid! – but was allowed to watch people in movies being murdered, butchered and slaughtered in the most brutal ways with blood and guts splattered all over the place. What kind of society was it that thought that exposing children to naked body parts was worse than exposing them to brutal murder and killings? It made no sense at all!

And yet, why did he care? Again, George wondered, like almost every day, why these topics unhinged him so much. Who cared why fashion was so important in today's society, and why did it matter at all? As a psycho-therapist, George was well aware of the intimate connection between his anger at society and depression, aware that it was probably mentally unhealthy to be obsessed about what other people did, why they did it, and the apocalyptic dystopian future this may lead to. Was all this linked to an inner sense of frustration he felt about himself, his life, his failed marriages, his struggling practice, his inability to cope with the situation with Marlies? *Well*, he thought clenching his fist, *it matters to me, both as an individual and as a member of a society I wish to belong to but find it increasingly hard to fit in, with indoctrinatory processes going on left-right-and-centre, ranging from religion, to fashion, to politics!* In his twisted logic, at least somebody had to be critical about what was going on around them, not to merely accept established doctrines, but to constantly question and second-guess why certain societal processes were occurring. Indeed, it was his privilege to be grumpy about life itself, about the 'crooked timber of humanity', and all the things that made the world around him tick! After all, George was brought up as a critical thinker, and his psychology studies and PhD had particularly highlighted that nothing, absolutely nothing, was sacrosanct and immune to critical thinking. Each

time he saw a patient, he needed to unravel precisely those messy influences, those conventions, indoctrinations and influences, that had pushed his patients towards the brink, be it their religious upbringings, the often misguided sexual norms they had been exposed to as children, and the often narrow-minded, bigoted and one-sided conventions that provided the framework for any person's upbringing. But then, could he, therefore, ever be fully part of society, or had he condemned himself to always be an outsider and never an insider, an observer from 'above', aloof and 'objective', always critical of society, a 'visitor' glancing at societal processes from outside? Although friends and family who knew him well kept calling him an incorrigible cynic, George saw himself more as a realist, as someone who was able, at least most of the time, to judge humanity's depravities from an objective perspective. Was this the reason why he had never fully felt part of the 'nation', whatever that meant in a complex political construct such as the UK? Why he abhorred the notion of nationhood and nationalism? Because a realist could never reconcile himself with a misguided trope such as 'the nation' and 'nationhood'? Was that why he often felt aloof, above the daily shenanigans, obsessions, and goings-on of his fellow citizens with their vane, weak and externally-controlled needs and wants?

As if on cue, the ad break was over and the news was focusing yet again on the ubiquitous

subject of Brexit. George hated Brexit, and his attitude towards the UK had irrevocably changed after the disastrous June 2016 referendum. He had always suspected that the UK was full of narrow-minded and bigoted little Englanders, but before 2016 he never had any proof for it, only hunches and indirect information gleaned through the news, personal interactions and observations. The result of the Brexit referendum changed all this, as for the first time, and for the whole world to see, over 50% of British people – at least of the 75% who voted – confirmed that they put their nationalistic feelings above anything else, the narrow-minded 'somewheres' above the open-minded and globalised 'anywheres' in the words of misguided right-wing politicians. Gone was the feeling that the UK was becoming a more globalised place with more positive cultural inter-mixing and a more European feel that had started to grow under the Blair government. Gone was the assumption that the older and younger generations were beginning to break down age-old conservative and entrenched barriers. And gone was the feeling that the UK was, finally, becoming more European in its outlook and lifestyle. *Had the Brexit voters forgotten what the EU was about?*, George thought, clenching his fists while listening to yet another tirade by an idiotic Brexiter being interviewed about the EU. *The EU was not, as most of the news interviews implied, about economics, but about keeping peace in a continent that had torn itself apart for*

centuries!, he felt like angrily shouting at the news presenter. *It was about opening up borders, not closing them, and giving young people, in particular, a chance to live and work in other countries, to sample different cultures and languages, and to increasingly intermix as Europeans rather than citizens and bland bigoted 'somewheres' of a specific country. Give me 'citizens of nowhere' anytime*, George thought with allusion to one of Theresa May's most stupid comments, *rather than being a citizen of a sad and inward-looking Brexit UK!* The news report George was watching while sipping his tea yet again consisted of a panel of politicians from various parties who were throwing around erroneous statistics to support the various points they were making. The Remainers on the panel used certain figures to argue their case, while the Brexiters used exactly the same figures to argue theirs, and on-and-on, round-and-round, the discussion went yet again, rehashing the same old and tired arguments about whether to leave or stay in the EU that no longer convinced anybody.

George loathed the discussions about nationhood linked to Brexit, and he increasingly thought that one of the greatest evils in modern human history was the birth of nation states, based on artificial, bigoted and indoctrinated constructs of what 'citizenship' and 'belonging' meant. In George's mind, the EU should do away with nation states, and instead scale down the political units of decision-making to smaller

regions, such as the French regions, the German Laender or the Spanish autonomous areas. George saw over-identification with the nation state as one of the biggest current evils of humanity which had resulted in the well-known atrocities of the two world wars in the twentieth century, and which continued in a diminished, but still equally worrying, way through the mindless nationalism expressed at team-sports events for the bigoted masses such as football, rugby or the nationalistic farce of the Olympic Games. Every day the news George watched showed that nationalism was still alive, and even getting worse in a Brexit world, and that societies still identified history through the lens of nation states rather than with cultures, languages, identities or ways of life. In George's view, as new governance entities replacing nation states each of his regions should have one capital city and full decision-making powers with regard to taxation, budgets, police and education, and they should send one elected member to a European assembly that would decide on larger-scale issues such as EU foreign policy, a European-based army or how to fight terrorism. But at the same time George knew that Europeans and his fellow citizens were not ready for this, that his thoughts were too radical and premature, and that maybe societies had to go through painful processes such as Brexit before realising that the nation state was a cul-de-sac political evolution, a remnant of a historical past where indoctrinated national armies were bashing each other's heads

in for ludicrous reasons concocted by demented male leaders.

The worst outcome of Brexit for George was that subconsciously he now divided all British people he met into Brexiters and Remainers, even his patients, and he wondered whether this was beginning to affect his professionalism. As a psycho-therapist, George was fully aware of the danger of shoe-horning people into specific camps, of flimsy assumptions made about people based on fleeting comments about their views on certain things, of the fact that he felt that he had to brand and identify people as belonging either to the Brexit or Remainer camps. But he could not deny the fact that his attitude towards his fellow citizens had changed. While in the past he saw most people as part of a spectrum, where he acknowledged that even the staunchest Tory interlocutor may have something good or interesting to say, now, once he had branded somebody as a Brexiteer, he wanted nothing to do with them. He saw these people as those who were destroying his country, the future of young British people, and who were caught up in such ill-conceived and wrong notions about 'Britishness' that it almost made him nauseous.

Brexit had affected him strongly, both mentally and physically, and forced George to think very carefully about himself as a citizen and a political being. While in the past it was easy to brand himself within a specific political camp or way of thinking, post-Brexit-referendum previously clear boundaries had

become much more blurred. He still saw himself as a left-leaning liberal, influenced by living in one of the most ultra-neo-liberal countries in the world, but he now also criticised that people always had to be assigned to a specific political camp. Indeed, Brexit had shown that long-established political boundaries were much more blurred as it cut right across parties, gender divisions, age groups and communities. One middle class family in a neighbourhood could be staunchly pro-Brexit, while their middle-class neighbours could be staunch Remainers. Members of one family could be split right down the middle, with mum and son staunch Brexiters while dad and daughter were fervent Remainers. While young people tended to be Remainers, this did not preclude the fact that there were also some very enlightened older Remainers, some of whom may have never had anything to do with the EU before.

Listening to yet another idiotic comment made by a Brexit-supporting politician on the news interview panel, George was increasingly convinced that, like people's multiple psychological identities, people could also hold multiple political identities that often did not neatly fit into often meaningless political party boundaries, a fact that had become particularly evident through Brexit. George himself, for example, held left-leaning views on many issues. He was, for example, pro-abortion, pro-LGBT rights, pro-women's equality in everything, pro-legalising all drugs, pro-immigration, pro-re-

nationalisation of utilities and services where they performed truly 'public' tasks such as public transport or water and energy provision. But he also acknowledged that some of his views did not fit easily into what was narrowly defined as 'left-leaning' and rather into the right-wing camp, including his penchant for free-market liberalism and free trade, his advocacy of strict policing (but not against drug addicts who were just victims of the wider system), his feeling-at-ease of living in a white-only neighbourhood (although he claimed, even to himself, to have nothing against black and Asian immigrants), his dislike of holidays in developing countries (although he argued that he just felt too guilty as a seemingly rich Westerner when seeing the poverty surrounding him in these places), and, in particular, his controversial support of the death penalty which was interpreted by his friends and family as extremely right-wing. His views on the death penalty had been the cause of many heated discussions with his two wives and their many left-leaning friends. George always explained that he only wanted the death penalty applied to murderers or those who had committed extreme atrocities and who posed a real threat to society, where guilt was 100% unequivocally clear, and where the accused had unquestionably admitted to the crime. He tried to counter his friends' arguments by suggesting that often guilty convicts committed suicide and wanted to die, and that their incarceration, often for life, cost the taxpayer immense sums of

money while social services were starved of funds for even the most basic needs of innocent citizens.

Most of all, after living for 52 years on Planet Earth, George had come to the conclusion that most of his fellow humans were just plain stupid. He was a big fan of one the quotes attributed to Einstein who knew of only two things that were infinite, namely the universe and human stupidity, although Einstein said that he was not so sure about the former. According to George, there was evidence of human stupidity on a daily basis in the news. Not only were the endless roundabout, repetitive and skewed discussions about Brexit evidence of this, but also other rather irrational processes that often showed both the gullibility of people and how this could be manipulated by influential people who knew all too well how to influence the view of the masses. You did not have to go back in time and invoke the Nazi's masterly manipulation of the gullible German masses through Goebbels' meticulous propaganda machine, as more recent examples abounded. For example, the rising global movement against the 'triple vaccine' measles-mumps-rubella, especially among misguided and often poorly educated women, had led to a rise in deadly measles cases among children in many countries around the world and was openly questioning the utility of vaccination as one of the biggest breakthroughs in medical history. Indeed, the gullibility of the British masses, and the rejection of stupid and ill-informed mothers

of the triple vaccine, had led to the country recently being declassified by the WHO as a 'measles-free' country! Or think about the repeated mass shootings in America and the hypocrisy of members of the all-powerful gun lobby indoctrinating US citizens about the inalienable right to bear arms, creating a vicious cycle of murder and mayhem. Yet one of the saddest examples of the power of indoctrination, George thought, was linked to sects and how they manged to control their often insecure and vulnerable members through various means of coercion, misinformation and outright lies. With the morning news blurting on in the background, George checked information on his laptop about three mass suicide events that he remembered well and that had particularly affected him at the time. These included the 1978 'People's Temple' suicides, where nearly 1000 Americans, including nearly 300 children, committed poison-induced suicide led by Jim Jones in Jonestown, Guyana, after the murder by the temple of a congressman, a reporter and three other visitors. In this case Jones had convinced his members to kill themselves (and to slaughter their innocent children!) as an act of 'revolutionary suicide' protesting the conditions of an inhumane world. Even more bizarre were the Canadian 'Solar Temple' incidents between 1994 and 1997 where members began a series of mass suicides leading to nearly 100 deaths. Members stated that they killed themselves as they believed their deaths, all during equinoxes

and solstices, would be an escape from the 'hypocrisies and oppression of this world' and that, through their deaths, they felt that their souls would move to the star Sirius! But the most idiotic mass sect-related suicide surely was linked to the Californian religious group 'Heaven's Gate' in 1997 where 40 followers died in a mass suicide. These people believed, according to the indoctrinations of their group, that through their suicides they were 'exiting their human vessels' so that their souls could go on a journey aboard a spaceship they believed to be following the newly discovered comet Hale-Bopp! Apparently some male members of the group underwent voluntary castration in preparation for the genderless life they believed awaited them after the suicide!

Just as George's thoughts had drifted towards the idiocy of sects and people's at times contradicting and seemingly irrational views, he saw his neighbour's cat crapping onto his freshly-mown lawn. Carefully pushing his breakfast tray aside so as not to spill tea from his half-full mug, George got up from his sofa with the intention of shooing the cat away, although he knew very well that this was futile as the same cat regularly used his lawn as her toilet. *Bloody pets!*, George thought angrily, using the cat's crapping on his lawn as a vindication to support his deep-seated hatred of pets. George hated dogs, but he also could not stand cats. Echoing one of his favourite parts of one of Jonathan Franzen's novel, George thought that cats

seemed like ‘sociopaths of the pet world’, animals domesticated as a necessary evil for the control of pests such as rats and mice, and subsequently throughout human history fetishized in a way sad, nationalist, bigoted and inward-looking countries fetishized their military, saluting and even venerating the uniforms of vicious killers, just as cat owners stroked their animals’ fur and forgave their slaughter of the local avian fauna and their poisonous and fetid turds left haphazardly on other people’s lawns.

George had just unlocked and opened the French doors when his neighbour, Ingrid von Schnollrotz-Beerenbier, the cat’s owner and the divorcee of a minor Austrian aristocrat, suddenly appeared in front of the doors. Ingrid looked deeply into George’s eyes, but was quickly distracted by the large red jam-mark on his t-shirt and the fact that he stood in front of her in his underpants.

“I am so sorry to disturb you, George!”, Ingrid said looking back at his face and glancing sideways at her cat. “I just saw my cat … doing her business on your lawn, and as I know how you hate that, I was going to chase her off your property … but you know how cats are!”

George looked at Ingrid, still surprised at her sudden appearance and slightly annoyed that she had not rung the doorbell which would have allowed him to put on some trousers. George’s relationship with Ingrid was complex, to say the least. George knew that she was keen on him, as

she had admitted so much herself at his latest barbeque where she had been so drunk at the end that she could barely stand. In front of all the other guests at the time, and in the midday sun, she had started caressing his penis through his pants and had started undressing herself. Only with the help of the other guests had George managed to keep her off him and to guide her back to her house where they had left her semi-comatose and half undressed on her bed. George had not seen her since and did not know whether she remembered anything from that fateful day. While thinking about this latest episode and standing right in front of Ingrid, George got an erection. Although Ingrid was still smilingly staring at his face, she could not avoid seeing the rapidly growing bulge in George's underpants pointing at her like a Jaguar's hood ornament.

"Please excuse me!", George blurted out, cursing his penis yet again for having a mind of its own and getting him into trouble once more. He rushed back to the sofa where he grabbed a blanket and wrapped it around his waist. With his erection's bulge still clearly visible through the blanket, he walked awkwardly back towards Ingrid.

"Thanks for trying to prevent your cat from shitting in my garden", George said in a tone that was a bit harsher than he had intended, but at this stage he was willing to say anything that would distract Ingrid from his boner. The cat had finished her business and walked away without even a glance at the two humans watching her,

leaving a rather large light-brown turd heaped in a tidy spiral on the lawn and clearly visible for anyone to see.

"But as you say, cats are cats, and there is not much we can do about it", George continued although he could not hide a trace of disgust on his face. "I'll clean it up when I am back from work this evening", George suggested.

"Oh, let me clean it up, George", Ingrid replied, "that's the least I can do. Maybe I can make it up to you by inviting you for dinner tonight?", she said without hiding a smile and a quick glance at the still visible bulge under the blanket. *After the disaster with Marlies I now have Ingrid to deal with!*, George thought in desperation. *What do all these women want from me? Why can't they leave me alone?*

George began to close the French doors. "That is very kind of you, Ingrid, but …eemmh… I am rather busy at the moment … work and other things, you know, even in the evening … maybe another time", but George knew that he did not sound convincing at all.

Ingrid looked at him with an undecipherable glance and smiled. "Sure, maybe another time", she said, holding his stare this time rather than looking towards his penis. "In the meantime, I'll try to make sure that this …", and she turned her head towards her cat's turd, "will not happen again".

George thanked her and quickly closed the French doors while Ingrid was still standing there looking slightly miffed. He did not quite

know what to make of this renewed encounter with Ingrid, and whether it would encourage her to be even more persistent in future. Worst of all, his bodily reaction to Ingrid had made George think again about Marlies, their next scheduled meeting, and the sad fact that he still had not signed the papers for her transfer to a colleague. *I am so weak, weak, weak!*, he thought yet again, sighing loudly.

While George was finishing his now-cold cup of tea, Sky News had moved on to yet another ad break, this time about a scantily-clad exotic-looking woman advertising holidays in Thailand, followed by an ad with a famous British actor professing utter nonsense about the excitement, value, innocence and beauty of gambling.

Part 3

Depravity

VIDEO LAPSOS PREME MULTITUDO
EIUS CORAM ME
QUOD ANIMA HUMANA FLAGITIA SUA
TENEBRAE MORTIS AMOR CAEDISQUE
AMPLECTERE FERRUM IMPERII
DEFECTIO TAMEN ILLUD
VULGO PRAVITATEM
IN SUIS HOMINI

I see the fallen hordes before me
The beastly human soul
The darkness of death and slaughter
The iron grip of the empire
The futility of it all
The depravity of the common man
Towards his fellow human being

(Roman philosopher Seneca Verus, AD 92, during a military campaign in southern Gallia)

George was very nervous. A week had passed since he had last seen Marlies and he had, of course, not signed her transfer papers, nor had he contacted Dr Cranston at the hospital. A few more letters from the National Association for Psychology had arrived, and George had placed them unopened into the drawer of his desk. He was very worried. George had seen his first morning patients, and Daniela had informed him that both Marlies and her mum were in the waiting room. After deciding not to sign Marlies's paper – for the moment at least – George had instead read articles in renowned psychology journals trying to shed light on why Marlies, after the sexual abuse she had suffered from her father, had willingly engaged in sexual activity with both him and his predecessor Paul Sutherland. Most of the articles referred to the fact that sexual abuse in childhood was well-known to be a major risk factor in the development of long-term psychological and social adjustment problems that could carry over into adulthood. From his training as a psychotherapist, George was also aware that the most common effects of sexual abuse in children were symptoms of post-traumatic stress disorder and psychological distress, which, after the few consultations they had together, were both apparent in Marlies's case. George was, however, most interested in the few articles that referred to inappropriate sexual behaviour of some victims of childhood sexual abuse. One American study, in particular, referred to post-

abuse sexual behaviour akin to nymphomania, in other words similar to persons expressing their sexuality through a seemingly voracious appetite for sex. Did Marlies's symptoms and behaviour fall into this category? As she had not only had sexual contact with one but both of her psychotherapists, George had to rule out the fact that Marlies was interested in him and Paul Sutherland because she was emotionally and sexually attracted to them as individuals. *That would simply be too much of a coincidence, especially as we are both older men who are probably not very attractive in the eyes of a teenager*, George thought, leaning back in his office chair. *Does this mean that Marlies is just using us, myself and Paul, as the most easily accessible males to vent her psychological distress through sex?*

Despite all this research and reading, George had to come back to his original interpretation of what was going on between him and Marlies, and that her recent eagerness to give him a blowjob could be part of Marlies's complex psychological coping strategy with the dreadful abuse she had been exposed to as a child. Did Marlies use sex with both Paul and himself to overcome the dreadful wrong that her father had done to her, as it was her only way to assert control over a man, rather than the other way around? But George also had to admit to himself that he was just looking for a lame excuse to continue seeing Marlies and to not sign her papers, and to argue that the abuse he had

perpetrated on a young and vulnerable patient during their last meeting could even be interpreted as part of her treatment. *This is totally ludicrous!*, George shouted inwardly at himself. *Don't kid yourself and use this pseudo-scientific explanation to excuse your behaviour towards this girl! Instead, try and help her, rather than sexually abusing her! Really try to make her better, that is your job!*

George clenched his fists, determined to see Marlies only as a doctor trying to help her, not as a sex-starved twice-divorcee taking advantage of her situation. He was also trying to push aside in his mind the issue of the National Association for Psychology, as their letters may not at all be related to Marlies. He wondered why he was so reluctant to open the letters, but it was, of course, a strong feeling of guilt that prevented him from taking any action in this regard. He finally got up and opened his office door. Daniela was typing something into her computer but looked up immediately with an inscrutable face as she saw him. George tried not to look Daniela in the eyes, immediately betraying how guilty he felt. Daniela had certainly begun to wonder about all these letters arriving from the National Association for Psychology. Was she suspecting something?

George looked at Marlies and her mum sitting alone in the waiting room. George could not hide the revulsion he felt for Marlies's mum. Esther looked up from a trashy magazine she was reading and acknowledged George briefly with a

nod. George thought that she looked even uglier than last time, her unkempt hair suggesting that it had not been washed for a while, a cheap flowery-purply atrocity of a dress adorning her flabby, pasty and unhealthy-looking skin, a plasticky black handbag and ugly black high-heeled shoes completing the picture of a woman who had no taste whatsoever, or, even worse, who did not care at all about her appearance. Briefly fixing her gaze, George wondered whether the mum knew about what Marlies and him had done during their last meeting. He was sure that Marlies had not mentioned anything, but George could not hide a feeling of intense fear at the thought that this … monster … would attack him if she knew the truth.

George's eyes shifted to Marlies who was sitting demurely next to her mum. Marlies looked up and smiled with the most heart-warming smile George had seen for a while. *Marlies!*, George thought immediately, and, by looking at her slim and immensely attractive features, all of his earlier resolve to act towards her in a purely professional manner dissolved in a flash. His body wanted her so much! George did everything to hide what was possibly a lecherous and lusty glare. "Hello Marlies", he said with a croaky voice that forced him to awkwardly clear his throat. "Please come into my office", and he held the door open for Marlies.

"I'll see you later, sweetie", Esther said, to George's great relief, while getting up from her

chair. "As we discussed, I'll go to the hairdresser down the road and will meet you there when you are finished. Ok, darling?"

"Yes, ok mum", Marlies replied, looking at George with an undecipherable smirk on her face. Clearly Marlies was annoyed at her mother's overprotective behaviour. While George escorted Marlies into his consultation room, Daniela gave George a final look which betrayed feelings of fear, anger and worry. George looked away quickly and guiltily, closed the door behind him and Marlies, and pulled out the chair in front of his desk for Marlies to sit on.

George looked Marlies in the eyes. "So, how have you been?", he asked her with genuine intent, his voice still croaky and shaky.

Instead of replying Marlies got up and walked over towards him. "You seem so formal, Dr Williamson … George … Have you already forgotten what we did last time?"

This was precisely the turn of events George was desperately trying to avoid. He wanted to stay professional, talk about Marlies's treatment, her medication, her emotional wellbeing, and stay in control of their meeting, assert himself as her doctor, but all of that dissolved quickly into nothing as he saw her approaching with her cute little body. Marlies was wearing a loose-fitting cream-coloured shirt, possibly a man's shirt, cut-off shorts that showed her beautiful and slim legs, and white trainers with yellow stripes on the side of a brand George did not recognise. Before George could say anything, Marlies had turned

his swivel chair around and straddled him awkwardly because of the stiff armrests, squatting on his thighs. She took his head into both her hands and gave him a long wet kiss.

George closed his eyes, breathless and paralysed, except for his penis which reacted immediately to Marlies sticking her tongue lusciously and aggressively into his mouth. George tried to move and say something, but his body completely took over from his brain. His hands moved towards Marlies's shirt and started unbuttoning it. Marlies wore no bra, and quickly George's hands found their way towards Marlies's small and pointy breasts. Marlies's shirt flew to the ground while George bent down and sucked Marlies's small red and erect nipples. He could feel her youth as a kind of fragility in his hands, her tiny boyish body that seemed so small compared to his, and he realised that there was nothing quite like the feel of skin and flesh much younger than your own. "Oh Marlies …", George groaned, while she unzipped his fly and took out his erect penis. In a flash her mouth took him in and moved gently up and down. Marlies was now kneeling in front of George's chair and George's body was totally at her mercy. He let his arms hang down the sides of his chair, his whole body completely overwhelmed by Marlies's regular and exquisite movements with her mouth.

Just as George was nearing the point-of-no-return, Marlies stopped and stood up. George opened his eyes from his dazed near-orgasm and

watched Marlies unzip her shorts and slide them down slowly along her long and skinny legs. He could see the faint outline of her black pubic hair under her small red knickers. He placed his mouth on her pubis and sucked in the aroma of her young body. Very slowly and gently he pulled down her knickers, which gradually revealed her shiny black pubic hair and her vagina. He slid down her knickers, which Marlies quickly disentangled from her feet, gently pulled the outer lips of her vagina aside with his fingers and moved his tongue slowly over her clitoris which he could feel as a swollen pea-sized protrusion in the wetness of her pubis. Marlies let out a loud sigh and George hoped that this was not audible through his office door. While he was licking her, Marlies had moved back towards George's desk and lay down on it, brushing pens and papers aside which landed on the floor with a noise like shards of broken ice on a stone surface. Again, George hoped that none of this could be heard outside, but he was now beyond caring and totally consumed by his body's needs. George increased the cadence of his tongue and felt Marlies's clitoris harden further. She came with a loud moan, her hands clasping George's hair as her orgasm shook her entire body in spasmodic convulsions.

When her orgasm subsided, George stood up and took off his shirt, trousers and shoes, while constantly looking at Marlies's beautiful naked body. She was even more beautiful naked, with her small pointy and red-nippled breasts, her

immaculate white skin, her sparse pubic hair that covered an oval-shaped area around her pubis, which maybe suggested only recent growth, and her marvellously thin and long legs. Marlies spread her legs wide, allowing George to look straight into her wet and inviting vagina. She took his stiff penis into her hand and guided him expertly into her. George was now lying on top of her on his office table, moving very gently inside her. He could feel her wetness and eagerness envelop him, consuming him entirely. He now was only a penis, a giant penis inside her, and nothing else mattered, not Esther and Daniela who may be hearing their loud groans, not the letters from the National Association for Psychiatry, not anything else in the world.

Marlies spread her legs wider so that he could penetrate her deeper. He felt the shaft of his penis touching her clitoris, leading her to utter little rhythmic shrieks while she kissed his neck eagerly in unison with his own thrusting movements. George could feel her press her heels against his rhythmically moving buttocks in order to guide him in even more deeply. Together their bodies agreed on a rhythm that maximised the pleasure for both of them. It was as if Marlies's young body showed all experience of the world, by understanding exactly how much pressure to apply on his buttocks, by gauging perfectly the rhythm that kept him just before climaxing for what seemed like an eternity, and by applying just the right pressure on her clitoris to maximise her own

pleasure. After a brief while with their bodies working in perfect unison, of being one intricately entangled whole, two shapes working in perfect coordination, and accompanied by the increasingly loud squeaking of George's maltreated desk, Marlies came for a second time. She panted loudly, sucking on George's left ear while she came, her eyes closed in total bliss. A few seconds later, George could no longer hold back, he was in free-fall, and the longest and most intense orgasm of his life shook his entire frame. While he came, he put his head into the nook between Marlies's neck and shoulder, forcing himself not to cry out with pleasure, supressing the final loud groans that distorted his sweaty face to a mask that would have probably looked hideous to any bystander. Gradually their bodies slowed down their rhythmic motion, Marlies's pressure on George's buttocks slowly abated, her widely spread legs gradually let go of him, and George slowly and gently withdrew his still stiff but utterly emptied penis. He stood up, panting heavily, and watched a trickle of sperm ooze out of Marlies's vagina that left a large translucent and slimy puddle on his desk. Marlies lay still, eyes closed and breathing heavily, her chest heaving under post-coital recovery. George bent down and kissed her intensely on her mouth, her cute little nose, her freckles, her forehead and her eyes.

"I … I …", but George could not find the right words. He wanted to tell Marlies that he loved her, loved her more than anything and

anyone he had ever loved, but somehow this did not seem the right thing to say at this point in time. He was not quite sure why. Rationality came back and he started analysing the situation, first glancing at his office door that had remained safely closed during their intense intercourse. *What would Daniela think if she knew what was going on in here?*, he thought guiltily. *How can I continue to take advantage of this poor girl, me her doctor?*, he wondered while looking at her beautiful body. He knew there was no going back now, that Marlies and him had crashed through every last boundary between therapist and patient.

Marlies slowly opened her eyes and sat up on his desk, carefully avoiding the puddle of sperm and vaginal fluids that had leaked out of her. She again took his head into both her hands and kissed him long and gently. "You don't have to say anything, Dr … George … I liked it!" George put his clothes back on and sat back in his armchair. He watched Marlies wipe her vagina with one of the tissues from the dispenser on his desk, wipe the large puddle of sperm on his desk, throw the tissue into his wastepaper basket, and put her clothes back on with graceful ease. Without another word or look back towards him Marlies left his office and closed the door behind her.

George sat in his chair, flabbergasted at what had just happened. Was it just a dream? Had this really just happened, or was he just imagining it? He closed his eyes and let his thoughts go

through each of the stages of their lovemaking, savouring intensely every second, never wanting to banish these moments from his memory. It had felt very real indeed. Although he had had sex with several women, including of course his two wives, he knew that this was the most intense intercourse he had ever had. And Marlies seemed to know exactly what his body needed, the rhythm, the pressure of her heels on his bum. She had known exactly what was needed to maximise his and her own pleasure. And they had come together! At these thoughts his penis stiffened again and he had to adjust it awkwardly inside his tight underpants. After decades of sexual intercourse with several partners, he had never managed to come simultaneously with a woman. And here was this sixteen-year old who turned out to be the most experienced of them all! *But what about Paul Sutherland?*, George thought angrily. *Had it been the same with him? Had Marlies timed their movements equally well, had they come together with a similarly orgiastic orgasm. Had Paul told her that he loved her? Had Marlies destroyed Paul in the end with her sexual intensity?*

Just enjoy the moment, and stop thinking about Paul!, George chided himself. *This was not just Marlies using sex as a safety valve, as a control mechanism to make herself feel better. She clearly showed that she wanted you, that she wanted you to come at the same time as her, to give you maximum pleasure. There must be some feeling involved here, no person could do what*

she did without feeling something. And what about him? What did he feel? Was he falling in love with her or was it just lust? Could a 52-year old fall in love with a 16-year old? *Forget it!*, George thought immediately. *Just think of her mum! If she ever found out you would be dead! Dead as a dodo! You could never justify to her, or to your friends, that you are genuinely in love with a 16-year old, and a patient on top of this! It is simply impossible!*

Just as George was about to gather himself and get up from his chair, Daniela came into his office. George tried to hide the worried look on his face and briefly glanced at the waste paper basket near his desk to check that the tissue that Marlies had used to wipe away the evidence of their lovemaking was not evidently visible. Daniela looked at the pens and paper strewn over the floor and looked back at George. "Emmmh… I just had a little accident after Marlies left", George said hesitantly, also checking that the remains of the sperm stain on the desk were not visible. "I … I… was trying to swat a fly and threw all the stuff from my desk while trying to hit the bloody thing … Where is it?", and George pretended to look around him. He was hoping that the intense lovemaking with Marlies had not left any olfactory trace for Daniela to detect, the usual pungent, sweaty, and heavy smell of fucking. George looked back at Daniela, but she did not give away whether she had smelled anything or was suspecting that something had just happened between Marlies and George. *But*

she knows about Paul, so there must be a level of suspicion!, George thought immediately.

George cleared his throat. "I… I think it's going quite well with Marlies", George lied, "she seems to be responding increasingly well to the treatment." *Yes, you bloody liar!*, George thought immediately, *your treatment of Marlies with your horny dick! What a fraud you are, Dr Williamson!*

"That… that is good to hear", Daniela replied, clearly suspicious. "Do you want me to clear this up?", she asked pointing at the mess on the floor, "or shall I get you a fly-swatter?"

"A fly-swatter…? Ah yes, of course … yes … that would be great, many thanks Daniela. I need to find that damn fly again first of all, maybe she has escaped into the waiting room", George said limply, knowing all too well that the fly story appeared a bit far-fetched to Daniela.

"Anyway, I came in to say that Reginal Rigby is hoping to see you. He is waiting outside. I know that you were not expecting any further patients before lunch, and he has not made a formal appointment, but he looks … he looks rather worn down if I may say so. I am a bit worried about him …"

"Ah yes, Reginald Rigby …", George replied trying to refocus on the mundane task of treating patients, after the life-changing orgasmic revelation he just experienced. Reginald Rigby's undoubtedly serious problems just appeared so small and distant at this point in time. "Yes, sure, please let him in", George said with a sigh, while

placing the pens and papers strewn all over the floor onto his desk. “Many thanks Daniela”.

*

George was walking back from his lunchtime break. He had been to his usual coffee place, the one with the wooden decking he liked. Before going for lunch, he had not been able to concentrate at all on Reginald Rigby who had come to see him because he was feeling suicidal after having beaten up his wife again. But after the experience with Marlies, George could simply not find a way to focus on Reginald’s problems – problems that suddenly seemed so remote and distant – and he farmed him off with a limp excuse after briefly discussing Reginald’s recent GP’s prescription of even stronger anti-depressant medication. George knew that the affair with Marlies was beginning to seriously affect his job, his professionalism and the way he treated his patients. He realised with a mixture of astonishment and horror that he simply did no longer care about people like Reginald!

After feeling guilty about how he had dispatched Reginald Rigby, George had taken a little detour to his café as he wanted to avoid under all circumstances to bump into Marlies and her mother near the hairdresser’s just outside his practice. He had incessantly looked around him guiltily, but luckily there was no sign of them. George had eaten his limp and half-cold panini

without much enthusiasm and had sipped his cappuccino with only half-hearted interest. He could not stop thinking about Marlies, her body, her breasts, her wet, wet, wet vagina, and their joint orgasm. He had looked at the people around him in the café and had wondered when they last had sex like he just had? Had anyone ever experienced the same sexual bliss? The middle-aged couple sitting next to him in their cheap raincoats to ward of the chill of a cloudy and damp Devonmouth after a brief rain shower? Had they 'done it' recently and had they enjoyed it like he just had, or was their sex just the usual routine, the endlessly rehashed choreography of two bodies too well-known to each other to still elicit much pleasure. George was imagining the man finding it hard to get aroused at his wife's sagging breasts, her wilting skin, her deepening wrinkles. And could she still find the courage to touch her husband's shrivelling cock, to even take it into her mouth, to forget about his swelling beer-belly and sagging buttocks? Or what about that young couple over there? They could not be much older than 18. Had they already discovered the beauty of understanding each other's bodies, of finding the rhythm that maximised their pleasure? They looked a bit shy and awkward with each other, George thought. *Maybe he is a devout evangelical Christian who has sworn to himself and his girlfriend not to have sex before they got married?*, George imagined with a naughty smile. *Maybe she is*

lusting after him and does not dare tell him that she wants him so badly?

George was not sure what to make of his thoughts. Was he suddenly feeling superior to these people, just because he had had fantastic sex with a 16-year old? Or was he rather envying these people for their ordinariness, the fact that they may very well have long-term and satisfying sex lives which he could never have with Marlies? That they were not relying like him on a complex doctor-patient power relationship that led to the sexual exploitation of a patient in a relationship that could not last and that had absolutely no future? George quickly realised the futility of his irrational assumptions about other people's sex lives, and made his way back to his practice a bit earlier than expected.

Daniela was still on her lunch break and the entrance door to his practice was still locked. A young woman was standing outside the door. George briefly glanced at her, admiring her stylish and yet semi-casual outfit, estimating her to be in her early 30s.

"Dr Williamson?", the woman asked with a smile.

"Yes, that's me", George replied, not knowing whether she was a new patient or not.

The woman held out a slender hand and shook George's hand firmly. "I am Detective Prendergast from the Devonmouth Constabulary", she said while showing George a formal-looking card that confirmed that she was

from the police. "I was wondering whether I could have a word?"

George's jaw dropped and he could feel cold sweat developing on his forehead and neck. He blushed, rubbed his neck awkwardly, swallowed hard, and looked at Prendergast with an anxious glare. *Wow, that was quick!*, he thought. *Either Esther or Daniela must have gone to the police immediately after what happened this morning! This is the end!* George closed his eyes. He was suddenly feeling nauseous and slightly faint, he had to lean against the entrance door not to lose his balance. His whole life seemed to be reeling off in front of his eyes, his psychology studies, the hospitals and psychiatric practices he had worked in, the pride he felt in his job. All this was gone now! Finished! Over! And he fully deserved it. He had done what no professional psycho-therapist should ever do: engage in a sexual relationship with a patient, and with a vulnerable young patient at that! He got exactly what he deserved! This was it! This was the end of his life as he knew it!

"Are you feeling alright, Sir?", Prendergast asked with a worried look on her face.

George opened his eyes. "Yes … no … yes… I am ok. Sorry", and he fumbled to find the keys in his pocket and dropped them on the floor.

They both bent down to pick up the keys and their heads collided. "Oooops, sorry!", said Prendergast apologetically and with a smile while handing George his keys.

“Sorry!”, replied George, rubbing his head. “I … I …”

“I’m okay”, Prendergast interjected and rubbing her head before George could say anything. “No harm done!”

George looked at her again. Despite all his worries about the end of his professional career, he could not prevent himself from thinking that Prendergast was not how he had envisaged a Devonmouth police detective to look. With his old-fashioned prejudices, he would have rather expected an older, tweed-jacketed, pipe-smoking, pot-bellied, white-haired and moustached gentleman with a walking stick exuding an air of infallible arrogance and self-assuredness. He fumbled with the keys, his hands were shaking so much that he was barely able to put the key into the keyhole, but he finally managed to open the entrance door. *I must look so guilty!*, he thought, *but maybe it doesn’t matter as my life as I know it will be finished anyway if this is about Marlies!*

“Please come in”, he said with a shaky voice. “My receptionist is still at lunch, and we lock the practice while we are both out.” With still shaky legs he led Prendergast up the stairs, helped her out of her coat, which he hung up clumsily on one of the hooks in the waiting room, and showed her into his office where he pulled out the chair in front of his desk for her to sit on. George sat down and could not prevent himself from looking at his desk and the faint outline of the sperm stain just in front of him. He placed a

sheet of paper on top of the stain, not looking at Prendergast. He closed his eyes again, trying not to think about Marlies.

"How can I help you?", George asked, still with an uncertain tone in his voice. "My next patient is only due in 30 minutes, so we have a bit of time".

"I am here to talk to you about one of your patients", Prendergast replied.

Here we go!, George thought. It is about Marlies!

"Your Syrian patient Mr Anwar Barhoum", Prendergast continued.

George's body sagged deeply into his chair and he let out a clearly audible puff of breath, not disguising how relieved he was. Prendergast looked at him curiously.

"Mr Barhoum is one of your patients, isn't he?"

George sat up straight again, leaned forward, and adjusted some papers on his desk while recovering his poise, carefully avoiding the one that was hiding the remnant sperm stain. "Yes … yes, he is. He was passed on to me by … by the Devonmouth Refugee Services. He is very depressed because his 12-year old son has disappeared."

Prendergast flicked through a notebook she had pulled out of her pocket. "Yes, that is why I would like to talk to you", she said, smiling at him. "Is that ok with you?", and she tilted her head slightly, still slightly puzzled at George's earlier behaviour.

"Yes… yes, of course", George replied, increasingly recovering from his earlier worries. "Although as you know I can't divulge any information that may breach doctor-patient confidentiality."

"Yes, I am fully aware of that and have actually sought legal advice from one member of our team before coming to see you. I fully appreciate if you can't tell me much about your ongoing psychological treatment of Mr Barhoum, but this is what my legal team told me", and Prendergast looked at her notebook. "As sensitive and deeply personal topics are often discussed during psychotherapy, therapists are expected, and usually legally bound, to respect patient confidentiality. The critical importance of patient confidentiality, and the limited circumstances in which it may need to be broken for the protection of patients or others, is enshrined in what I believe is the 'regulatory psychotherapeutic organizations code of ethical practice'. I have been told that examples of when it is typically accepted to break confidentiality include when the therapist has knowledge that a child is being physically abused, or when there is a direct, clear and imminent threat of serious physical harm to self or to a specific individual".

George nodded and rummaged through the top right-hand drawer to pull out Anwar Barhoum's file. "Yes, that is correct and is a good summary of what I may, or may not, be able to tell you. What would you like to know?"

"The Devonmouth Refugee Services contacted us immediately when Mr Barhoum reported his son missing", Prendergast continued, flicking through her notebook. "As you know, all agencies are legally obliged to inform us if they become aware of anything that may have legal implications. I was just wondering what Mr Barhoum told you about the disappearance of his son?"

"Yes … well … I can tell you what he told me about the case as this does not infringe the doctor-patient confidentiality issues linked to his medical condition", George said more confidently while rummaging through his notes to find the right entry. "Ah … here… Mr Barhoum said that his son, Rawad, suddenly disappeared. He told me about their flight from Syria in 2015 when his son was seven, the difficulty of their journey through Greece, Macedonia, Serbia and eventually Germany, the disappearance of his wife during that time, and the fact that they had not seen her since. He then talked about how they ended up in Devonmouth, where the refugee services provided him and his son with accommodation and some financial help".

George looked up at Prendergast who encouraged him with a nod of her head to continue.

"According to my notes, Mr Barhoum's son was put into a primary school here in Devonmouth. Apparently Rawad found it hard at first as he did not speak any English, but, as kids

of this age do, he learned fast, made some friends, and enjoyed school. And then Rawad disappeared. Mr Barhoum said that it was about four weeks before he saw me, so it must have been early April …"

George looked up at Prendergast for confirmation. She flicked through her notes and confirmed that Rawad was reported missing on 7th April.

"That is now nearly four months ago!", George realised with a shudder, "and still no trace of him?"

"No, nothing!", Prendergast replied, "which is why I am here. We have followed every meagre hint, and had a whole team of five officers working the case for a while, but with no results. Now with all the cuts to the police under the Tory Government I am left on my own to work this case, which is very unfortunate as we really want to find the boy. What exactly did Mr Barhoum tell you about Rawad's disappearance?"

George looked at his notes again. "Mr Barhoum said that there were no signs that Rawad was unhappy, or that he had problems at school. He had begun to make friends, and his English was near-perfect. Mr Barhoum complained about the smallness of their allocated flat, but he said that his son enjoyed where they lived. Apparently, he had been playing outside with a friend just outside their flat when he didn't come home. Mr Barhoum said that he looked everywhere with the help of

neighbours, and then he informed the refugee services who then contacted you. Needless to say that his son's disappearance has completely devastated Mr Barhoum, which is why he has seen me regularly".

"Yes, this tallies with the information we have received", Prendergast replied. "We searched the immediate vicinity of their flat for days, interviewed as many neighbours, as well as Rawad's friends and parents, but to no avail. The boy seems to have simply vanished into thin air. We then tapped into the national police database to see whether any boy looking like Rawad had been found or apprehended anywhere in the country, and, through Interpol, have also liaised with our European counterparts. One possible theory was that Rawad may bc with his mother somewhere in Europe, but as far as we know she has never been found after they were separated in the Balkans in 2015. At least she has not been officially registered by any of the European refugee agencies since."

George knew too well about what could happen to refugee women and girls on their long and dangerous treks through Europe and how many ended up as unregistered prostitutes held in slave-like conditions.

"We are still following any leads we may get on Rawad's mother", Prendergast continued, "but we worry that the trail is getting cold. In all honesty, we also feel that the possible link with Rawad's mother is us just clutching at straws, and that it is unlikely that the boy has ended up

finding her if we, with all the access to data we have, can't find her."

"That seems to make sense", George acknowledged. "What do you think may have happened?"

"Well, we don't know", Prendergast admitted. "Of course, we have various theories, including abduction and kidnapping, but so far no information has come to light that would support this and no demands for ransom or anything similar have been reported."

Prendergast hesitated, while looking at George. "Of course, there is also the possibility that Rawad's father has something to do with his son's disappearance."

George looked back at her.

"This is where you, as his psycho-therapist, may come in, Dr Williamson, and the main reason why I came to see you. As you see we are rather desperate now, and we need to explore every possible avenue."

"Of course, I understand", George replied with a nod.

"How often do you see Mr Barhoum", Prendergast enquired, "and has there been any indication in his behaviour that he may have something to do with the disappearance of his son?"

Of course, George had considered the question whether Anwar Barhoum could have something to do with the disappearance of his son right from the beginning. "I can tell you that I thought about that from the start", George

confided, "but I can also tell you that Mr Barhoum has not betrayed any sign or information that he may be behind Rawad's disappearance. I have seen him about once a week since early May, which means that I have seen him", and George flicked through his paper diary, "exactly 11 times. Based on these meetings, I am not breaching confidentiality here by telling you that Mr Barhoum has been very depressed by the disappearance of his son, but you know that already through the information passed on to you initially by the Devonmouth Refugee Services."

Prendergast nodded in acquiescence.

"His son's disappearance has clearly very negatively affected Mr Barhoum, so at this stage I suspect that he has nothing to do with Rawad's vanishing. He even proudly showed me a picture of his son, and he seems to care very much about him."

"Many thanks for your honesty and candour, Dr Williamson", Prendergast said, getting up from her chair and shaking George's hand. "That will be all for now, but please let us know if any further information comes to light during your next sessions with Mr Barhoum which may help shed light on this sad story. As I said, we are trying everything we can to help. In turn, I will keep you, and of course Mr Barhoum, informed of any developments on our side."

Prendergast held George's hand possibly slightly longer than she had originally intended. "One more thing, Dr Williamson. It may be

better if you do not tell Mr Barhoum about our little discussion today, as it may upset him even more if he knew that you are in contact with us. It is probably best if he just purely sees you as his doctor, which may allow him to open up even more".

"That makes perfect sense, Detective Prendergast, I will not mention our meeting to my patient. In the meantime, please do not hesitate to let me know if you need further information from us".

George led Detective Prendergast through the still empty waiting room out of his practice and returned to his desk. *Nearly four months since Rawad disappeared!*, he thought. *I had not realised that it was so long. Poor boy! The chances of finding him will be very slim by now! Maybe I should press Anwar Barhoum a bit harder at our next meeting? But at this stage I can't imagine that he has anything to do with the disappearance of his son.*

George heard Daniela coming back from lunch and shouted a greeting through his open office door. He took a folder out of one of the drawers, ready for his first patient of the afternoon.

*

George took a large swig from his pint. He looked around nervously to see whether he recognised anyone. He had begun the habit of going to the pub in his village on Friday evenings

after work in order to 'meet some villagers', mainly as a justification to himself for leaving his lonely house. George was not in a good mood, and his dour face probably revealed as much. Things were not going well, and he was beginning to wonder whether moving to the South-west had been such a good idea after all. First of all, there was, of course, this affair, this 'thing', with Marlies that he still was not sure how to describe to himself. Was he in love with her? He continuously admitted to himself that it was 'only' sexual infatuation, northing less, nothing more, and that it would pass. And yet … every waking moment when he was not preoccupied with work he was thinking about her, about her body, the sex …

George took another swig of the stale-tasting lager he had foolishly chosen. And then there was his flagging practice. Daniela had recently informed him that they had now lost about half of the patients he had taken over from Paul Sutherland, and all that only in three months! Yes, of course, he had been very distracted lately and had not really focused sufficiently on some of his patients' seemingly small and unimportant mental ailments, but there had to be other factors at play here! Had word got around that something fishy was going on in his practice, probably not helped by the fact that Paul Sutherland had disappeared seemingly without a trace? Were the hospitals and social services shunning him in some atrocious conspiracy because they thought he was an 'outsider', not

born-and-bred in the South-west like some of his other psycho-therapist colleagues in Devonmouth? Or did they simply think that he was just not a good doctor?

George took another swig from his pint. With a shudder he remembered the dreadful nightmare he had had the last night, when he dreamt that he had finally opened the countless letters that had been sent by the National Association for Psychology. In his dream each one had read: "Dear Dr Williamson. We regret to inform you that it has come to our attention that you have engaged in an unprofessional relationship with one of your under-aged patients. The only course of action the Association can take in these matters is to bar offending doctors from practising and to inform the police. We therefore …", at which point he had woken up, bathed in sweat and panting heavily. *I have to find the courage and open these letters!*, George thought again while taking another consoling swig from his beer.

George rubbed his tired eyes in despair. *And now this sudden attention of the police about one of my patients ... what was her name ... Prendergast!*, George thought with a sigh. *Of course, I should have anticipated that Anwar Barhoum's story and the mysterious disappearance of his son would elicit a thorough police investigation, but how do they think I can help them in their search? After all, it is my role to help Anwar first-and-foremost, who is suffering terrible psychological stress, and not*

for me to become a police informer! But then, if there is something untoward about the boy's disappearance, of course I need to help! George took another sip of beer. But possibly worst of all, he had to begin to admit this to himself, was the fact that he was getting depressed himself. He felt very lonely, alone in his big new house, alone in his job, and with only a few friends scattered mostly all over the UK and Europe, the only exception being his golfing partner and friend Sam Worthington from London who now lived a few villages down the road. But Sam and him had never been that close, and he had only seen Sam for the odd game of golf. Although his two marriages had been disasters, he missed the comfort of married life, the predictability of it, and the support his partners had given him, at least for a while.

"Hello George", a voice said behind him and a heavy calloused hand was placed on his shoulder. "Can I get you another one?"

George tuned around. The man who had approached him was stocky, muscular and very tanned. George remembered having met him before in the pub, but he desperately tried to remember his name. George was very bad at remembering names, a problem he had struggled with all his life, made worse here in this geriatric village full of retirees and older people where, he thought, everybody somehow looked alike. All the elderly men had short-cropped hair and were either called David, William, John, James, Richard, Matthew or Steve – as if their parents

had lacked the imagination of going beyond the narrow boundaries of names already familiar in their neighbourhood – with some of the villagers with names where the first names and surnames were increasingly blurred, such as Richard Matthews or Matthew Richards, James Williamson or William James, or Steve Davidson or David Stevenson. How dull, he thought, with a smile while thinking about his own dull surname. Most women in the village appeared to be short, a bit fat, blond rather than dark (or maybe with dyed hair), traditional in their choice of clothes, and, George had to admit, rather dull and uninteresting. Their main discussion topics seemed to revolve around the local tennis club, which had a lot of members but where hardly anyone actually knew how to play proper tennis, the build-up to the yearly rowing regatta which seemed to need 12 months of preparation to get going, or gossip about yet another marital breakup in a village where most people seemed to be divorced and shagging each other.

"Yes … many thanks", George replied awkwardly, vaguely remembering that the man offering him a beer was a local builder.

"I am Richard", the man replied, realising that George had forgotten his name. "Steve and Patsy introduced us last time you were down here", Richard further clarified.

Yet another couple George could only vaguely remember as he stood aside to let Richard through to the bar.

"And how are things with you?", Richard asked, but George was not sure whether Richard was just making conversation or sincerely interested in finding out how George was.

"Oh, you know … Richard … The usual, really", George replied rather unconvincingly. Was it worth telling this man that the way he treated his patients still ran with what George thought was symphonic precision, but how his practice ran overall resembled more and more pure cacophony? That the genius he once may have had to recognise quickly patients' deepest psychological problems flickered on and off like fireflies on a summer night?

"If I remember correctly, you're a … psychologist … or something like that?", Richard said with a frown on his face which could not betray his unease with anyone who was well educated and 'scientific'. *Here we go again!*, George thought annoyed, *another one who can't understand the difference between being a psychologist and a psycho-therapist and who shows the rather common disdain typical for around here for anyone who is well educated and from 'posh' London! Surely the man must be a Brexiter!*, George wondered, less sure whether he should be seen to accept a drink from this man.

"A psycho-therapist … I am a psycho-therapist", George replied with an almost inaudible voice.

"I didn't get that!", Richard shouted back amidst the din and raucous laughter of beer-

swigging patrons around them, and handing George an already half-spilled pint of one of the ubiquitous boring-tasting lagers. "Never mind … how are you settling into the village?"

George had still not finished his first pint, continuously amazed at how quickly the villagers around him were downing their pints. While it often took him a good twenty minutes to finish one and even longer to finish a second, the others were on their fifth or even eighth pints! He awkwardly held both glasses while being tossed around and bumped into by the increasing number of new patrons entering the overcrowded pub.

"Oh, very well …", George lied, "I love it here in the village. It is so peaceful."

Another man had arm-wrestled his way through the throng to the bar and said hello to George. This person George recognised as Steve, one of the people he had recently played golf with. "Hi Steve", George said timidly.

"Oh, hi there George!", Steve replied, "I had not recognised you from behind. How is your golf?"

George recalled his disastrous play during their last round where, after the debacle on hole 15, he had also messed up holes 16 and 18 to end up with a score close to 110. On hole 18 he had lost two balls and had substantially delayed the others who had felt compelled to help looking for his hopelessly lost balls. Steve, on the other hand, had played to his handicap of 13 and had completed the round with a fantastic score of 83,

a result George could only dream of. After their recent round, George had feared that Steve would no longer want to play with him and, for the last few weeks, George had indeed not heard anything from any of his golfing partners.

"I haven't played since our last round", George admitted. "Been rather busy at work …"

"Ah yes, you're a … paediatrician … is that right?", Steve asked politely while skilfully balancing three pints in his hands and nodding towards a group of people waiting for him.

"A paediatrician … Yes, that's right", George replied limply. He just could not be bothered correcting Steve who was clearly eager to re-join his more interesting group.

"Oh well, see you later", Steve replied hastily and moved away.

In the meantime, Richard had used the brief discussion about golf to slip away, and George could no longer see him in the mass of people who had crowded into the pub.

How can people enjoy this?, George wondered, looking around him. *But the villagers clearly love this!*, he thought looking at the mass of people, who, in George's mind, seemed to be swaying back and forth in unison like an amorphous mass, a swarm of fish or a flock of starlings, a multi-cellular organism, where every part knew the other, except for him. He felt like a complete outcast, an outsider, like a cancerous growth in this teeming mass, as if the villagers were wilfully shunning him. The noise levels had grown so loud that a normal conversation was

now nigh-on impossible, which led people to shout even louder, which in turn increased the noise levels, leading to even louder shouting. George suddenly felt panic setting in. He had started sweating profusely, he was short of breath, he could feel his heart pounding hard against his chest. He had to get out! He felt like being crushed and swallowed up by this amorphous mass of fish, birds, and multi-cellular organism, he felt as if everybody was watching him as he elbowed his way through the throng, he felt the resistance of these stocky muscular bodies, of the Davids, Williams, Johns, Richards and Steves trying to prevent him from leaving, of the blond look-alike women blocking his way, with red ugly lipstick-framed mouths shouting obscenities at him, sucking him into their hollow stinking mouths, preventing him from moving.

Panting, sweating and copiously apologising, George managed to muscle his way through the throng of people to the exit. When he opened the door a gust of fresh and cool air hit his face. He staggered out of the pub, utterly relieved and breathing heavily. 'G and G', one of the most notorious alcoholic couples in the village only referred to by their initials, looked up at him from their glasses with surprise. Female 'G' was swaying back and forth and found it hard to focus on George, while male 'G' had obviously just vomited and was leaning heavily against the pub wall. "Hey, mate … what about an … another round for us?", male 'G' stammered in his alcoholic stupor, holding up his glass towards

George. George looked at them flabbergasted, ignored them and started running back home without once looking back, sucking in avidly the cool and moist evening air, back to his large, empty and quiet house.

*

"I just can't work like this anymore!", Daniela had shouted with tears in her eyes when he had come into the empty waiting room of his practice two hours late, having missed several of his patients. This was not the first time George had been late, and he found it increasingly difficult to find the energy to get out of bed in the morning. He was also not looking after himself properly anymore, had stopped shaving, and a stubbly salt-and-pepper beard was beginning to disfigure his chin. His hair looked increasingly unkempt, in the morning he had forgotten to comb his hair, and his clothes did not smell too fresh.

"Look Dr … George!", Daniela sobbed. "I like you, and I have enjoyed working with you over the past few months, but I simply can't continue working here anymore … Sorry … but that's just how it is."

Daniela looked George deep in the eyes, tears smudging her makeup and creating ugly black runnels that followed the contours of the wrinkles around her eyes. "It's not just the fact that you are letting yourself increasingly go … Just look at yourself! You look more like a tramp

than a doctor! What is the matter with you? We have now lost almost all our former patients. Mr Miller is gone, Mr Rumpley has also gone to another psycho-therapist after you missed the last three appointments with him, and even the Rigbys, who seemed most loyal until the end as I think you really helped them, just rang in this morning to say that they found another doctor".

Daniela let out another loud sob and dabbed her eyes with a crumpled handkerchief. "And then … of course … and then there is this … this … thing with the young girl … Marlies Brown!", Daniela continued with a quivering voice. "Of course, I know what is going on between you and her!", she shouted, holding his gaze with reddened eyes. "You didn't think that your … your shenanigans with her would go unnoticed … the grunts and noises from your office … her unbuttoned shirt and dishevelled hair the last time you saw her … your office stationery strewn all over the floor! It was exactly the same with Paul Sutherland! He also went down that slippery path … and look where it got him! He's gone! He is nowhere! I tried to tell you when we went for a coffee recently … but … but I can't tell you what to do … I am just your receptionist … I …", and she broke down in large sobs, holding her hands in front of her face.

George just stood there, flabbergasted. *And what about Marlies, then?*, he wanted to ask. *Has her mum also withdrawn her from our practice?*, but he did not dare utter the question out loud for fear of confirming Daniela's suspicions. But

what did he care about the Millers, Rumpleys and Rigbys! All he cared about was Marlies. *Marlies! Marlies! Marlies!*

Although George wanted to punch Daniela for not telling him whether Marlies was still with them, he gently led Daniela to her chair and sat her down carefully. He did not know how to respond. *Of course, she is right!*, thought George. She was right that he had led the practice go to the dogs, that he had lost most of his patients, that he had … fucked Marlies, and that he had avoided reading the signs of Daniela's increasing frustration and despair.

"Look, Daniela … I am really sorry about all this", George said sheepishly. "I know the last few weeks have been tough … and that I should have spoken to you earlier about what was going on … Yes, we have lost a lot of patients, but we have also gained a few new ones". George tried to sound encouraging, but he knew it was too late. He had let things slip well beyond the point-of-no-return as far as Daniela was concerned. But he was very worried that she would report his affair with Marlies. "Look", he said holding Daniela's shoulders, "I want to assure you that nothing has been going on with Mar … with Ms Brown. The way she looked when she left my practice last time was … was just part of her treatment …"

Daniela looked up at George with a tear-smeared look that George found difficult to decipher. Was it hatred or just abject disgust?

"Look Daniela … I …", George stammered on, but it was too late. Without another word, Daniela took her bag, grabbed her coat from the coat-hanger and left the practice without looking back.

George sat down in Daniela's receptionist's chair, leaning his head into his hands. He felt so tired and so worn out! How could she do this to him? Just now when things were difficult anyway! *And now it will become even more difficult, as it will take me a while to find a new receptionist*, George realised nervously, still holding his head. *I will have to take all the phone calls and arrange all appointments with patients myself! And what if she informs the National Association for Psychiatry about his affair with Marlies and have me disbarred from work?*, George suddenly thought in panic. *But their unopened letters are probably already about my affair with Marlies, anyway! That's it, this is the end of my career! But Daniela said that she liked me and had enjoyed working with me ... anyway, there is nothing I can do about this now! She is gone and that is it! It does not matter anymore anyway!* George nonetheless flicked through the appointments diary on the desk and while the cancelled appointments Daniela had mentioned were clearly visible as big red crosses (with exclamation marks), he was relieved to see that appointments with Marlies still appeared to be scheduled.

George got up from Daniela's chair and was walking briskly back-and-forth in the waiting

room, tearing at his hair with his hands. *What if Marlies, or her oaf of a mum, cancels her appointments? What will I do then?*, he thought in desperation. Just as tears were welling up in his eyes the door opened and Anwar Barhoum stepped in. For a few seconds, George looked at Anwar, not understanding what was happening, when he suddenly realised that the Syrian was here for his weekly appointment. George turned around briefly, wiped the tears from his eyes as best he could and faced Anwar. "Ah, Mr Barhoum. Please come into my office. My receptionist … is off sick at the moment and I have to manage the practice on my own at the moment". Anwar Barhoum glanced at George with a surprised look on his face, unused to his doctor's unkempt appearance. But he nonetheless followed George into his office.

George sat down in his armchair and tried to gather his thoughts. *Stay professional!*, he kept repeating to himself, *stay professional! You are still a doctor, you still have responsibilities for your patients, whatever may happen in future. Honour the oath you gave when you started as a psycho-therapist, at least until you are disbarred for misconduct!*

George cleared his throat and adjusted some papers on the desk in front of him. But he could not hide the fact that his hands were shaking and that cold sweat was pouring down his forehead. His eyes shifted towards the bottom right drawer of his desk containing all these unopened letters from the National Association for Psychology. A

few more had arrived, all marked with red ink 'Urgent and Confidential'.

George looked back at his patient. "How are you Mr Barhoum?", George asked as innocuously as possible. He immediately thought about the recent discussion he had with Detective Prendergast and tried to adjust the strategy for the session accordingly. *I should have thought about this earlier in preparation for this session*, George immediately thought, *but things have just been so ... busy and confused. Daniela is right. I am no longer fit for this job!* George tried to gather his thoughts again, but found it hard to focus on the Syrian and his mental problems. He had to dig deep into the recesses of his psychiatric brain memory to divert his thoughts away from the fact that he had just lost his excellent receptionist, that his practice was going to the dogs, and from thoughts about Marlies and their affair.

"I have not been too well, doctor", Anwar Barhoum replied timidly, again not looking George in the eye. "I am still struggling with the new medication my GP prescribed … I am still very … very sad and depressed … my son …"

We are turning around in circles in these sessions, George thought. *As per my discussion with Detective Prendergast, I need to focus our sessions away from endless discussions whether the medication works or not and onto Anwar's relationship with his son*. "Mr Barhoum, would you mind if we did our session today with you on the couch over there?", George enquired

hesitantly. This would be the first time that he had used the couch with Anwar.

The Syrian glanced rather worried over to the couch. "I … I … don't know, doctor."

"Well, let's try it …", George said more authoritatively and gently led Anwar towards the couch. George placed his chair behind his patient, his favoured position to allow the patient as much free association in his answers without distraction as possible. George could not avoid a brief thought about his first sexual misdemeanour with Marlies at exactly that same spot. Anwar made himself as comfortable as he could.

"In our therapy we have, so far, focused on targeting your depression and anxiety", George began the discussion, "on your current situation in Devonmouth, on how you have found some solace in the Devonmouth Muslim community, and on discussing the right mix of medicine to treat your mental problems. What I would like to do from now on a bit more is to talk about your relationship with your son Rawad."

Anwar tried to turn his head around to see George, but found it difficult as George was sitting almost behind him. "My relationship … with my son?", the Syrian blurted out, evidently finding it difficult to understand what George expected him to say.

"Yes, your relationship. How did you two get on, your feelings for your son, what both of you did together in the evenings … things like that", George tried to clarify.

"I had … I have … a wonderful relationship with my son", Anwar replied. "I love him and he loves me …". There was a longer pause.

I know how hard it is for Muslim men to talk about their feelings!, George reminded himself. He let a few seconds pass before asking whether Anwar and Rawad did many things together.

"Yes … yes …", Anwar replied, clearly hesitating. "I helped him with his homework whenever I could … but Rawad was … is … such a clever boy that he rarely needed help … just at the beginning when his English was not so good. Having been trained as a pharmacist, I could help him with a bit of biology and some of the simple chemistry they did at primary school."

"How were things at home? Tell me about a typical day", George tried to prompt further revelations.

"At home?", Anwar replied hesitantly. "Things were good. As I have said before we liked the flat that had been given to us. It was nice, as Rawad could play out in the street, it was a quiet cul-de-sac, not too much traffic". Anwar hesitated. "I should not have let him out when he disappeared …", and he started sobbing again.

I need to steer the discussion more towards the feelings he has for his son, George thought with reference to the discussion he had with Prendergast, *find out more whether there was possible tension that made Rawad run away.* "Did you always get on well with your son? Were there times when you fought or disagreed?"

Anwar hesitated again. "Fought? … No, never. After the disappearance of his mother in Serbia, Rawad and I had to get on with each other. Back in Syria, my wife Afraa had been very close to Rawad, the two of them were always together, always playing and fooling around … She was very good with him. After she disappeared it was very hard at first. We had to make our way to Germany with thousands of other Syrians. The only thing I had to concentrate on was not to get separated from Rawad. There was never much time or opportunity to talk much to him or to play … that was simply not possible. Only when we were finally accepted in the UK as refugees and allocated to Devonmouth Refugee Services did Rawad and I find a bit more time to do things together … like a normal family … like a father and son."

George leaned back, pleased that Anwar was beginning to talk without having to be prompted.

"We both missed Afraa very much", Anwar continued. "Just the daily chores were hard. Sorting out the school for Rawad took a while, his initial problems with the language … although he learned so fast! … He was … is such a bright boy! The shopping in the supermarkets, all the strange foods you have here … all these dairy products we are not used to in the Syrian heat … Rawad and I found a little shop in the town centre that sells some Middle Eastern food and ingredients, you know the one near the book shop …", and Anwar tried again to look back at George, but George did not want to disrupt

Anwar's narrative and did not reply. "We enjoyed cooking together", Anwar continued. "Rawad particularly liked to make baclava … you know the typical Middle Eastern sweet pastry that we often have with tea. Rawad was very good at making it in the end." Anwar paused again for a while, staring at the ceiling.

"What was your going-to-bed routine?", George asked after Anwar had not resumed his narration.

"Going to bed?", Anwar asked almost incredulously. "When we came to Devonmouth in 2016 Rawad was nine and he would go to bed at about eight o'clock. Now that he is twelve I let him stay up until nine. Sometime we watched a movie together on television or read the Quran together before he went to bed."

George had hoped for a bit more information. "Did you sometimes read the Quran with him in bed, or other books and stories?"

Anwar hesitated. "In the past it was Afraa who had taken Rawad to bed. She would also read him stories … Syrian stories … and back home in Syria I often heard them laugh together. I … I was never part of this. So, when Afraa was no longer there, Rawad would just go to bed on his own … I would just make sure that he had switched off the light."

After some of the intimacies Anwar had revealed about his relationship with his son, George found it strange that there appeared to be no going-to-bed routine with a young child whose mother had disappeared. Surely a ten or

eleven-year old would have liked being read or talked to just before going to sleep.

"So, after you watched TV or read the Quran together, Rawad would just go to bed on his own?", George prompted.

"Yes", came the very short reply.

There was an uncomfortable pause. George was not sure how to interpret Anwar's answers. He could not avoid thinking back about his own childhood. Although he had never been very close to his father and was much closer to his mother, he nonetheless remembered well how his father enjoyed sitting on his bed and telling him what seemed to be a never-ending story about a man and a witch and their adventures. When George was around ten years old he could not get enough of the story and fondly remembered what were probably the most intimate moments with his otherwise rather removed and cold father.

George snapped out of his reverie. "What about your feelings for your son? Were there any instances when you were annoyed at him? When you were arguing?"

Again, Anwar took a while to respond. Clearly his free association narrative had been disrupted by George switching the questions towards the going-to-bed routine. George had the impression that Anwar was re-rationalising his answers, not talking freely anymore. "As I said, I loved … love my son. We have a very good relationship. He respects me as his father, and he listens to what I say, just like a good Muslim boy

should. We lived our lives very much according to the gospel laid out in the Quran. We are good Muslims."

The discussion was drifting away from the direction George wanted to take. As he had expected, Anwar found it difficult, possibly impossible, to talk about his true feelings towards his son. It would be difficult to break through this barrier, George thought, but he was going to make sure that their future sessions, if his practice survived the next weeks, would focus back on the question on Anwar's relationship with his son.

George stayed in his chair, waiting to see whether more information would be forthcoming from Anwar, but the Syrian stayed quiet, staring at the ceiling. "OK, Mr Barhoum, that will be enough for today", George conceded as they both got up. "We will pick up this discussion again at our next session in a week. In the meantime, please continue taking your medicine as directed by your GP, and I look forward to seeing you again soon. Let me show you out as Daniela is not here."

Anwar looked up hesitantly at George while he was being led through the waiting room. *Was there a glint of anxiety in Anwar's face?*, George wondered.

*

The wet gravel crunched under George's feet as he walked through the old Devonmouth cemetery. It was early in the morning and George had reluctantly peeled himself out of bed. Swathes of early morning mist were draped around the old granite tombstones, casting the cemetery in an eerie light. Busy crows, perched on their yew lookout tree, were croaking angrily as George sat down on an old wooden bench. A funeral congregation was visible through the mist like zombie shadows in a cheap horror movie. George looked over at the cluster of people and recognised Daniela, his former receptionist, who had informed him a few days ago of the funeral of Paul Sutherland, the previous owner of his practice.

George put his head in his hands and sighed loudly. He was not ready to join the mourners and needed a few minutes by himself while the funeral ceremony proceeded. Daniela had informed George that Paul Sutherland had committed suicide. *Why?*, George wondered. Had it been because of Marlies and what he had done to her? Or were there other things happening in Paul's life that George did not know about, possibly suggesting that the membrane between life and death may have been very thin in Paul Sutherland's world? After the news about Paul, George felt even more vulnerable. Would the same happen to him? Was suicide the only way out of the utterly

unprofessional conduct both him and Paul had perpetrated on a vulnerable patient? George glanced back at the congregation. A woman who was perhaps Paul's wife was throwing soil onto Paul's coffin with a small trowel handed to her by the priest. She wore a black translucid veil over a wide-brimmed hat and her barely visible sombre face suggested that she was crying. An elderly woman – *maybe her mum?*, George thought – had put one hand gently on the woman's shoulder in a comforting gesture. The other mourners, including Daniela, all looked gloomily at the coffin.

George did not know why he had come. He had never met Paul Sutherland and had only heard about him through Daniela. The only thing that connected the two men was the practice and their unprofessional love affair with the same patient, a weird and unsavoury bond that somehow tied the two men inextricably together. *Is that why I am here?*, George asked himself scratching his stubbly unshaven chin. *Do I feel a connection to this man who just killed himself?* George did not know.

George watched the funeral for a few minutes from his bench, not daring to approach the crowd. He had the impression that Daniela had seen him and that she had imperceptibly waved her black-gloved hand, but George was not sure. George looked away, leaned back against the old wooden bench and let his thoughts drift away from Paul. *I have always had problems with Western burial rites!*, he thought.

This probably stems from my feelings about Christianity, as the way we treat our dead is inextricably linked to our religious beliefs. He particularly lamented the fact that burials in the Western world, whether through cremation or through the interment of the dead in a coffin, were such a sad affair, with everybody dressed in black, crying and mourning. *Should a burial not be more of a celebration of a person's life?*, he almost felt like shouting to the crowd of mourners, but also well aware that a death from suicide was maybe not something people would have wanted to celebrate. *Sure, with his behaviour towards Marlies, Paul Sutherland's life may not have been a paragon of purity and innocence, and ending your life in suicide was not exactly a sign that you had seen your life as a resounding success yourself!*, George admitted, *but did not every person deserve to be remembered for the good things they had done in life, even someone like Paul? The problem with religious people was of course that they saw death and burial as a transition towards a better life, ideally a life in a heaven-like paradise. Yet, you only live once, you have one shot at life and that's it! If you mess it up, that's it! If you live a successful or unsuccessful life, however measured, that's it! Death ended all these amazing bodily functions in one instant, the incredibly complicated biochemical processes going on in the brain, the intricate interweaving of processes associated with the cardiac and nervous systems, even small processes such as*

the minute growth of hair follicles, nails, skin, all these bodily efforts ceased with death. A living and breathing organism just became a solid lump of bone, liquid and flesh, and that was it! So why not have a burial as a celebration, a feast, a party, as an acknowledgement of the utter end of these bodily functions, why this urge to dress death up as a transitional stage towards immortality in a religiously conjured-up heaven, Nirvana, Shangri-La?, George thought, imagining Daniela and Paul's wife wearing bright-coloured dresses, dancing around the coffin laughing and smiling to the tunes of a jolly samba band tucked in between gayly decorated tombstones. After all, George's unorthodox train of thought continued, the only legacy most people left, except for their rotting bodies or incinerated corpses, were the tons and tons of their shit and urine washed down the sewers and eventually ending up in the oceans. Indeed, when you went swimming in the sea, George imagined with a smile, bathers were surrounded by billions of atoms of piss and shit from millions of dead people.

With a jolt, Paul awoke from his reverie. He looked over at the mourners again who were looking even more sombre at the coffin that was gradually being lowered by some hidden mechanical device into the dark grave. *You are doing it again!*, Paul chastised himself with understandable feelings of guilt that he was not feeling more compassionately about Paul and instead thinking about himself and his own

perspective on life. *You are again looking at your own culture, your fellow human beings, your fellow citizens, as an outsider. You are like an anthropologist sitting on a bench watching the strange burial rituals of a foreign society, like a person completely detached from 'his' own culture, like an anthropologist from a distant country observing the mores of the natives, while people around you are dying, even killing themselves.* And yet, George remembered a friend telling him about a holiday to Polynesia where he had been both impressed and astounded at the fact that the female host of the guesthouse, where they were staying on a remote island, had her mum's skull on the mantlepiece and was talking to her every evening. The host had explained that it was common practice for many Polynesians to first bury their dead and then exhume the bones once the flesh had rotted away to display the bones in one's home. To George this suggested a much more intimate relationship with the dead than Western cremation or burial, indeed it allowed a close, intimate and continuing relationship with the dead through the ability to see and touch the remains of your relatives. *Was this a psychologically healthier way of treating the dead than what is done in our Western society?*, George wondered.

As the priest was uttering barely audible religious nonsense about religion, faith and death over Paul Sutherland's grave, George's thoughts were drifting towards his parents and his father Roger's recent funeral. His mum, Nicola, had

died relatively early of a stroke. She had been a school teacher and George had been very close to her. Her sudden death had devastated him, but, paradoxically, his immense sadness had been the moment in his life when he had felt most alive. He remembered thinking at the time that it maybe took unbearable grief to feel life, to yearn for it and to see things in perspective, the pettiness of it all, the misery of humans, and only when somebody close to you died did it all begin to make sense. Most of the time he was devoid of these feelings, more like a zombie going through the motions of life than someone actually living.

The situation had been completely different when his father died. His father surprisingly survived his mum by 14 years, although everybody in the family had always thought that Roger would die long before Nicola, but it was never spelt out why this should be. Ever since he could remember, George had had a fraught, complicated, and tense relationship with his father. Somehow, they were never on the same wavelength, Roger never understanding how George thought and why he did things his way, and George never understanding Roger's behaviour and way of thinking. As George grew older and began to know more about medical conditions, he began to suspect that Roger was somewhere on the mild side of the autistic spectrum, as someone who had immense problems understanding people's emotions and feelings and acted like a sociophobe for most of

the time. Roger had been a well-known scientist, a university mathematics professor who had made his name with research contributions to the theory of prime numbers. He could talk obsessively and for hours about some of his boring latest calculations, and yet found it very hard to answer George's frequent questions about family, Nicola and their feelings towards each other. The fact that Roger often cheated on his wife, and especially the story his mum told him when he was a teenager that his father had a particularly intense love affair with the wife of the university vice-chancellor where he was working at the time, just when Nicola was pregnant with George, led George to intensely hate his father. After Roger's seventh or eighth extra-marital affair, Nicola had enough and divorced him when George was 11 years old. George stayed with his mum and only rarely saw his father, and Nicola did everything to further stoke George's hatred towards his father by providing snippets of information about Roger's cheating.

George recalled one particularly intensive discussion with his mum when he was about 12. "You know what your father did to me, don't you?", Nicola had asked yet again in one of her more depressed moods.

"Yes, mum, you have told me several times already how he cheated on you, especially when you were pregnant", George would reply.

"I should have never married him, you know?", Nicola continued.

"But you also said that you liked him?", George would enquire, not yet knowing the subtle differences at his age between 'like' and 'love'.

"Yes, of course I loved him when we met", was Nicola's frequent reply. "He was very bright and good looking, and I was utterly impressed with him and how much he knew when we first met as students at university. But very quickly he started cheating on me … I don't know why … I gave him everything he wanted, but he always looked at other women … from the moment we were married he looked at other women. Roger should not have had children … He was completely unsuited to being a father …"

George had heard all this before and never knew how to answer. If they did not have children, he would not be here! How could his mum expect him, at the age of 12, to rationally reply to this quandary? But he also knew that the fact that Nicola quickly realised that Roger was not suited as a father meant that he remained a single child. Soon after he was born, Nicola had decided not to have further kids with Roger and she secretly had her tubes tied. George knew that Nicola never told Roger about this, a further sign of their disjointed and malfunctioning relationship.

A sudden rustling of dead leaves in the wind brought George back from his reverie. While the priest was rambling on about what a great man Paul Sutherland had been – *if only he knew the truth!*, George thought with a cynical look at the

congregation who seemed to avidly soak up the priest's every word – George also had to admit to himself that there had been very nice moments with his father before his parents got divorced. He remembered playing badminton on the street outside their terraced house when he was very little, his father's bedside story about a man and a witch and their adventures – which Anwar Barhoum's sad story had also recently conjured up – or his father hugging him while they were sitting on a sunny meadow somewhere near St Albans in Hertfordshire where he grew up. All of this was about 40 years ago, and yet if felt so recent, as if it only happened yesterday. What had happened to all the time in between? What had he done with his life? But he also remembered what was probably his first childhood memory with his father leaning over the Christmas roast, sweating profusely as he always did after even the tiniest exertion, and a drop of sweat dangling rhythmically at the tip of his nose in unison with the cutting movement of his arms. George had waited for the drop of sweat to fall onto the roast and swore to himself that he would not eat one morsel of the roast if the drop of sweat finally detached itself from his father's nose, which, in the end, it did not. His worst memory of his father was when George was probably eight and his father beat him up relatively unprovoked. Sure, George remembered that it was a damp and cold weekend, he had been bored, he had been nagging, and Nicola had also not been in a good

mood in their small terraced house, but out of the blue his father had attacked him and hit him hard on his bare behind with his buckled belt. It really hurt, and George never forgave his father this rather unprovoked attack. Later it seemed to confirm to George that his father disliked him, saw him as an incumbrance to his ordered scientific life, and confirming Nicola's fears that Roger had never really wanted children in the first place. As a result, when Nicola told him at age 11 that she and Roger were getting divorced, rather than being sad George felt relieved. Now he could have his beloved mum all by himself, without the constant intrusion of a father he did not understand nor particularly like.

George looked over at the priest who was still talking. George leaned back against the bench's hard wooden backrest and looked up at the yew trees surrounding him. The crows seemed to have moved on somewhere else as, apart from the priest's monotone ramble and a few gusts of wind, the cemetery was eerily quiet. Of course, from a psychological vantage point, George's father's emotional problems may have stemmed from his own upbringing. Roger had had a very problematic relationship with his own father, George's grandfather John who died before George was born. John was married to Anna-Claire who suffered from such severe rheumatoid arthritis – at least so the story went in the family – that she could no longer make love to John. As a result, John had a love affair with his secretary who ended up living with John

in his house, with Anna-Claire relegated to the former maid's chamber under the roof! Was it any wonder then that Roger behaved so abominably towards his wife if his own father had set such a dreadful example? On one occasion one of the maids in John's house had damaged a valuable doorknob and was too afraid to tell John. She told Roger about it who was 10 at the time and thought – in hindsight rather irrationally – that he would help the maid by removing the knob altogether by hiding it. When his father found out that the knob was missing, and that the door could no longer be closed, he accused Roger of stealing it, which Roger strenuously denied. However, he did not want to implicate the maid who would immediately lose her job, so Roger got the blame for the missing doorknob. John pursued Roger up into his bedroom threatening to beat him up until he told him where the knob was hidden. Roger became so scared that he jumped out of his bedroom window, fell at least 10 metres, and broke one leg and a vertebrae, which left him with back problems for the rest of his life. After this incident, the relationship between Roger and John was permanently strained and, as far as George understood, they rarely spoke together afterwards until John's death. Again, was it surprising that Roger was a poor father after having never learned proper fathering skills from his own father? *As I find out with my own patients,* George thought, *family problems often come in ever-repeating cycles, self-perpetuating*

problems that are passed on from one generation to another. The same may have been the case with my own family, where simple misunderstandings, unspoken tensions, and erratic and at times nasty behaviour established baselines that future generations would follow, not realising the damage and hurt they caused to people they should have loved and cherished. Maybe it is good that I have no children on my own!

A tear rolled down George's cheek. He did not want to cry over his father, he had done this too many times before! He simply refused to still be influenced by the bastard who had made his life so often such a misery. A son does not choose his father! After his parent's divorce, George had rarely seen his father. He tended to visit him once a year for a few days, especially after his mum's death, but their discussions would always revolve around abstract mathematics and science and almost never touch upon issues linked to the family. George did not get on at all with his father's second wife who was a vicar's daughter. His father had been a staunch anti-religionist, and this is where George undoubtedly got his attitude towards religion from. He had always felt that his father had spun a cocoon of thoughts around him, a web of indoctrination from which there was no escape. But, then, does not every parent do this to some extent, and was some of the indoctrination not something that George today felt very comfortable with, such as his own stance against

religion? Was he expressing his father's anti-religious thoughts, or had he rather developed his own anti-religious conviction over the years? Was it possible to identify where such deep inner thoughts came from and whether parental influence was more important than one's own life experience? But George could not keep himself from criticising his father for his hypocrisy regarding his proclaimed views about life and his actual lifestyle which involved marrying a vicar's daughter. But then again, who was he to judge other people, even his own father? Could his father's actions be excused based on his socio-psychological background, the pressures he had been under both as a child, as an adult, and as a mildly autistic man? Should George be more forgiving? Should he have been more involved with his father's funeral?

Glancing over at Paul Sutherland's congregation which was beginning to break up after the priest had finally concluded his meaningless sermon, George admitted that he had allowed his father's second wife to organise everything regarding his father's funeral, the venue, the list of invitees, the speeches. He had not cared. At the funeral he had stayed back, again more as an observer than a participant, listening to the platitudes uttered in the staged speeches, and had himself declined to give a speech to the eternal consternation of his father's wife. Again, even then he had felt like an anthropologist observing the strange rituals of a society he did not understand, did not feel part

of. At his own father's funeral, he had played the remote, unmovable, distanced son who, in the end, had not cared whether his father was dead or alive! He did not know how he would feel about his father in future, his father's death was still too recent and raw in his mind, but he knew that this was certainly not the last time that thoughts about his father would overwhelm him. Had George become interested in psychiatry at an early age because he was psychologically messed up himself – messed up by people like his father? He knew that a lot of psycho-therapists – whether they chose to admit it or not – were, on some level, drawn to the profession because they wished to 'heal' themselves, but could they really ever achieve this?

George was abruptly jerked out of his thoughts by a woman standing in front of him. George had not seen her approaching and also realised that Daniela was standing behind the woman. George stood up awkwardly, still half embroiled in thoughts about his father, not sure what to say.

"Hello George, how are you?", Daniela said while shaking his hand. "May I introduce you to Paul Sutherland's wife, Linda".

George shook Linda's hand. Linda took off her veil, revealing an old-looking face. Traces of tears were visible in the wrinkles around her eyes that looked like crow's feet.

"Linda, this is George Williamson, the psycho-therapist who took over Paul's practice".

"You don't look like a psycho-therapist or a doctor", Linda said bluntly, looking at George's dishevelled appearance, resting her gaze on the dark rings under his eyes, his unshaven chin, his grubby raincoat and shirt with marmalade stains, and his trousers that had not been washed for weeks. George saw Daniela look away in embarrassment and putting a hand in front of her mouth to hide her disgust. "I picture a psycho-therapist more like someone with a suit and tie … someone who looks like you can trust them", Linda said with a sarcastic smile.

"Well … I …", George stammered, but he did not know how to reply. He knew that he looked like a tramp, that he had let himself go these last few weeks, that he had not slept well, that he had not had a shower for a while and that he was probably smelling. *Well then, Mrs perfect! Do you picture a psycho-therapist like your bloody husband who was screwing a patient who was 15 at the time, and who did not even have the guts to carry on living with his guilt?*, George thought with disgust. But, at the same time, he wondered what his parents would think about his unprofessional and dishevelled appearance and the whole state of affairs he was in.

"I … I … I am very sorry about your husband", George stammered, trying to collect himself, but he was not sure whether his face did not betray how he disliked the woman in front of him. "I never met him, but Daniela … Daniela told me much about him".

Immediately as he said it, he knew that this could be interpreted in different ways, in particular considering Paul's involvement with Marlies. Linda looked at George with a face that was difficult to decipher, and George wondered whether Linda thought about asking him about Marlies. Linda glanced at Daniela. The two clearly knew each other, but it seemed that Linda was unsure how much Daniela had told George about her husband and the young girl. George looked at Daniela trying to get a clue as what to say, but Daniela looked away, clearly embarrassed.

"Thank you Dr Williamson. I appreciate your kind words and would like to thank you for coming to my husband's funeral".

George was not sure whether this was intended as a hidden reproach as he had not joined the congregation when the coffin was lowered into the ground. "I … I was late, so I did not want to disturb the ceremony. I … I thought it best to stay back …", George lied. In truth, he still did not know why he had come to the funeral, and he now realised that had never intended to join the mourners in the first place. Judging from Linda's face, George thought that Linda also did not believe his apology.

"I understand Dr Williamson", Linda said with an uncomfortable smile on her face.

There was a long pause as neither Linda nor Paul knew what else to say. What else could George say to the wife of a man who had just committed suicide after having had an affair with

an under-aged patient? What could one say in such circumstances? He certainly knew that it was futile to mention his thoughts about Western burial practices, this was not the right place or time to start an abstract discussion. Nor could George ask about Paul's death as this would immediately lead the discussion towards the taboo theme of suicide. And George did not want any further discussion about anything that may link him to Marlies. George would have liked to talk to Daniela, ask her how she was, but Daniela was still standing half-hidden behind Linda, and it would have been impolite to address Daniela while Linda was still standing in front of him. Instead, seconds passed, nothing was said, the crows were croaking their sad refrain into the rising mist, wet leaves were rustling and whizzing around the steel feet of the bench in the breeze, and in the distance the hushed voices of the mourners leaving Paul Sutherland's grave could be heard. Shaking George's hand, Linda turned around without saying a word, took Daniela's arm, and walked towards the cemetery car park. George stood there for a long time, feeling embarrassed and confused. This encounter had not helped his frail state-of-mind at all.

*

George had rushed through his final appointment of the day. He had seen a new patient – a rare

occurrence in his rapidly crumbling practice – an academic from the University of Devonmouth situated not far from his office. Donald Richardson had self-referred after a severe bout of depression. George knew that many academics, despite of their usually very self-fulfilling and rewarding jobs, suffered from depression, anxiety attacks and low self-esteem. Donald was no exception. He was a Reader in History at the university, and, from what George could make out after a few minutes, ambitious, diligent, and hard-working. Like many academics George knew, Donald was rather under-dressed, wearing a scruffy shirt and battered jeans, a typical statement of many left-leaning academics who rejected societal conventions of dress codes and other unwritten rules, a subtle, but maybe in the eyes of many a rather silly, rebellion against social mores. Donald was frustrated by his repeated attempts at gaining a professorship. He felt that, whatever he did in a given year with regard to research, publications, grants, teaching and administration, a new baseline seemed to be created each time he put in an application. He was particularly frustrated at what he perceived to be unequal treatment of staff at the university, and he became increasingly obsessed with the assumption that colleagues in the hard sciences, such as physics, engineering or chemistry, were being promoted ahead of him. This had led to a worsening depression and decreasing job satisfaction and enjoyment in life. This was not

helped by the fact that Donald had recently divorced and that his wife had taken the three children with her.

Although George was happy to have a new patient, and although the planned regular sessions with Donald would help alleviate George's increasing financial difficulties at least a little bit, George had been unable to concentrate on Donald throughout their meeting. George kept looking at his watch and had to ask Donald several times to repeat what he had just said. The situation was not helped by the fact that Devonmouth was basking in a climate-change-induced mid-August heatwave with outside temperatures hitting a record 34 degrees Celsius for this time of year. The temperature in George's office may have been even higher, further exacerbated by the lack of air conditioning. George's mind was clearly side-tracked by the excessive heat.

As with many other issues affecting humanity George had no faith in people's ability to tackle the climate change problem. Having read a lot about climate change, he felt reasonably well informed about the dreadful state planet Earth was in and, like many sceptics, he knew that there was no solution to the problem of a human-induced warming of the planet. All the political talk about policy change, the seemingly momentous 'Paris Accord' of 2015, the activism of demonstrators like the young Swede Greta Thunberg, all of this, he thought, was futile. Like his favourite author

Jonathan Franzen, George was convinced that humanity should stop pretending that anything could be done to tackle climate change, that the fight against global warming could not be won in a capitalist world where money and growth were all that mattered. Indeed, the changes required by each individual to tackle the necessary reduction in CO_2 emissions would be so great that they could never be implemented by governments. Humans were much too selfish and were lacking the comprehension about complex global climate processes to dramatically change their lifestyles. Even if some did, their hundreds of neighbours did not, negating any personal self-sacrifice. Like Franzen, George thought that it could be liberating for humanity to admit that nothing could be done about the looming climate catastrophe, and that people could finally stop pretending and rather enjoy the last years touring around in their SUVs. *It is too late, there is no hope, let's just accept humanity's lunacy and enjoy our last years on the planet before it is being irrevocably scorched! Let's take the blue pill instead of the red one, unlike 'Neo', the main protagonist in the dystopian movie 'The matrix' who has the courage to look at the 'real' world beyond the stage-show and pretence, let's continue to stick our head in the sand and further indulge in senseless climate-destroying consumerism,* George thought while struggling to return his attention to his patient.

George was sweating profusely while Donald tried to explain the problems associated

with his depression. George's desk was littered with damp tissues George had used to wipe his forehead, but George somehow did not care. At one point, Donald had stopped talking and had glanced at George with a look that suggested that it was George who needed help and not him, the patient. Somehow George managed to come to the end of the session with an agreement on a timetable of 15 further meetings which Donald seemed happy with. But George still had enough self-reflective skills to realise that this had not been a satisfactory consultation. *I am increasingly losing the ability to focus on my patients!*, he thought bitterly while locking the practice behind him and stepping out into the sweltering heat, *but maybe this no longer matters if one accepts that climate Armageddon is inevitable! However, I am clearly no longer a good psycho-therapist, if I ever was one! What is happening to me?*

But he knew exactly what was happening to him. It was his obsession with Marlies that distracted him from everything in his life. Irrespective of the future of humanity in this sweltering heat, for lowly humans like him it was the here and now that mattered, nothing else. He had to see her! She had now missed the last five meetings and he had not heard a word from her or her mum since their last 'session' a while ago. Opening all windows fully in his small Korean car – George did not like driving with air conditioning despite of the intense heat – George drove through the Devonmouth rush-hour traffic.

Twenty minutes driving took him past the centre and then through leafy and relatively wealthy suburbs. He crossed the famous Brunel-built Devonmouth suspension bridge over the river Devon from which many suicidal people had jumped off into the water of the estuary below, killed on impact after a fall of over eighty metres. As a result, locals referred jokingly to the bridge as 'Jumper's Bridge'. George shuddered despite the heat as he passed the low railing on his left. *Why is the city not raising the height of the railing to at least make it more difficult for people to jump off?*, he thought shaking his head. *But then maybe Devonmouth is happy to get rid of people who voluntarily kill themselves, people whose care would have cost thousands?*, he wondered cynically.

After crossing Jumper's Bridge, the urban landscape changed. Areas with a view of the estuary were still rather posh, with architect-built villas nestled on the slopes exploiting the magnificent views to the maximum, but a few streets further on he entered one of the most deprived and notorious Devonmouth estates, Fernworthy, a part of the city he had never been to before. George knew from Marlies's files that this was where she lived. Slowing down while looking at the google map display on his phone into which he had entered his destination, George was again amazed at how quickly urban landscapes changed in UK cities. Maybe it was the same on the continent, but here you were driving in a reasonably affluent and leafy area

one second, while in the next you were surrounded by squalor, cheap and cramped housing and poverty. It was as if you suddenly passed an imperceptible barrier in a flash of a moment between those who had made it in society with their nicely presented houses and SUVs, and, a short drive away, the riff-raff, the down-and-outs, the losers of globalisation, the un- and poorly educated and, dare he say or think it, the predominantly Brexit-voting cast-asides of modern Britain living in the soulless and anonymous nothingness of the peri-urban realm.

Fernworthy was a typical estate for many British cities, comprised of tightly packed 1950s-built poor-quality terraced houses with small front yards often sealed over and converted into parking spaces for battered and busted Beamers, fractured, fragmented and falling-apart Fords, crappy, collapsed, crumbled and crushed Kias, mangled and mutilated motorbikes, propped-up and patched-up Peugeots, totalled Toyotas, nastily cracked and creaking Nissans, hollowed-out rusty shells of Hyundais, and vitriolic and vulnerable-looking Volvos and VWs. *No new SUVs here, and rubbish everywhere especially piling up in the front yards! How can people not care about how their front gardens looked like?,* George wondered, but immediately chastising himself for thinking like a despised toff. *Maybe the people here really have such hard lives that cleaning up in front of their porches is just not a high priority! Maybe it's just about day-to-day survival, the sheer*

weight of living being hard enough to cope with! Life itself!

Google maps told George that he was not far from the terraced house which was his destination, the house where Marlies lived. He parked between the burnt-out shell of what looked like an old BMW and the rusty hull of a small Hyundai and looked over at the house on 44 Pilchard Street. George was listening to Mozart while he was observing Marlies's house which looked completely innocuous with its tatty front garden with forlorn half-dead bushes and hardy weeds with plastic rubbish and paper entangled in them, its flaking façade, its cheap and poorly fitting UPVC windows which had not been cleaned in years, and its crumbling facias and guttering. Five young lads in hoodies suddenly walked past on the other side and George quickly closed his windows, turned down the Mozart, and bent down behind the wheel as he did not want to be seen or heard, especially not listening to Mozart! *Mozart was probably like a death sentence for the listener in these parts, if these lads have ever even heard music like this!*, he thought with disdain. The five boys, who seemed oblivious to the heat in their hoodies and jeans that were hanging down to their knees, revealing Calvin Klein underwear, stopped near 44 Pilchard Street. One of them took out what George thought were several small plastic bags with white powder in them, while the others rummaged in their filthy jeans pockets for change which they handed over to the guy

with the bags. *Shit!*, George thought, *witnessing lads selling drugs is not what I need right now!*, and he looked around him and in the rear mirror to see whether anyone else was witnessing what he was seeing, but the street was empty. He hunkered down further behind the wheel to make sure the boys did not see him. Their transaction was swift and they dispersed quickly after only a few seconds, one walking closely past George's car but, luckily for George, without peering into it. George sat up and waited for the last lad to have vanished from sight before he reopened the windows. It was swelteringly hot in the car and George felt that he was suffocating. *What I am doing here?*, he thought. *I must be completely crazy!*

And there she was! Through the rear mirror George could see Marlies walking up the street, accompanied by another rather fat girl. George smiled. He had estimated well the time when Marlies would walk home from her school bus which must have dropped her and her friend off a few blocks away. George crouched down again so that Marlies and her friend would not see him, as they passed his car on the other side of the road on their way towards her house. *Please, somebody make sure that Marlies's fat girlfriend does not go in with her!*, George was imploring. The two girls stood for a while in front of Marlies's house, chatting and laughing while looking at their mobiles. *How lovely she looks!*, George thought watching every movement of Marlies's slim body. *And what a monster her fat*

girlfriend is!, he thought angrily. The contrast could not have been starker between the two of them, Marlies, slim and beautiful, the other fat, bulky and ugly with a pig-like freckled face, unkempt and dirty-looking red-blonde hair, and legs that stuck out of her ill-fitting school uniform like tree trunks. To George's relief, the two girls parted, the fat one walking further on up the road while Marlies took keys out of her pocket to open her front door. *And now pray for Marlies's mum not to be at home! This is a crazy plan!*, George thought as he locked his car and ran over towards Marlies's house as fast as he could so that her neighbours would not see him.

He rang the bell and waited. For a while nothing happened and George looked nervously around him to check whether any neighbours were watching him. But he could see nobody behind the lace-curtained windows, nor was there anyone in the street. Marlies opened the door and looked at him with surprise.

"Dr … George! What are you doing here?", Marlies asked, looking him up and down and a bit astonished at his dishevelled appearance.

George was acutely aware of his unkempt appearance and was rather embarrassed. He had not even taken a shower before coming here and he worried that Marlies could smell it! He looked behind her to see whether Esther, the fat oaf of her mum, was visible anywhere, but Marlies seemed to be alone. George knew from her file that Marlies had no brothers or sisters.

“Eemmmhh … I … I … You missed our last scheduled appointments … So I thought I come and see how you are”, George lied.

Marlies grabbed George’s hand and pulled him gently into the porch. George was glad to be away from the street and from possible prying eyes and followed Marlies into the living room. The house was as George had expected it to be: messy, with stuff from both Marlies and her mum lying everywhere, the old worn carpets were grimy, and a glance through the open door at the kitchen revealed piles of dirty dishes and the remains of breakfast still on the kitchen table.

“I am feeling better”, Marlies picked up the conversation again. “I really wanted to come to your practice at the agreed times, but my mum didn’t want me to. I think that she suspects something”, she said with a giggle. “And I couldn’t really turn up by myself without my mum, I need her to drive me.”

George’s practice was near the town centre and not that difficult to get to by bus, but he acknowledged that it may have been difficult for Marlies to come to his practice directly from school, or from home, considering how poor lateral bus connections were in Devonmouth. Under the recent Tory government, subsidies for local buses had been further reduced, and George suspected that the connections to poor estates such as Fernworthy had further deteriorated. But, by the sound of it, Marlies was still keen to see George. Maybe there was hope?

"I fully understand", George replied, looking Marlies deep in the eyes. "In truth, I am not really here as your doctor … but … but because I wanted to see you. I … I miss you", George admitted, wondering whether Marlies had thought much about their recent love-making in his office.

Thinking about it gave George an erection which Marlies spotted immediately. She looked down at his swollen penis, then at his face, and smiled. "I enjoyed what we did last time in your practice … George. I have been thinking about you a lot! But don't worry", she continued as she led him up the stairs, "I have not told anyone about us. I know that this would … like … not be good for you …".

George had followed Marlies, mildly surprised at how eagerly she had taken him upstairs, where Marlies led him into her room. The small terraced house only had two bedrooms, and Marlies's room was right next to her mother's, with a toilet and bathroom at the end of the corridor. While it had been a bit cooler downstairs, the heatwave made it insufferably hot upstairs, and George had to wipe dripping sweat off his eyebrows. Marlies's room was like the rest of the house, messy and full of stuff, with clothes lying both on the bed and on the floor, but it also had some style and elegance to it, with neatly arranged posters of the latest boy bands on one of the walls, a little arrangement of dried flowers sitting on top of the chest of drawers which showed both a subtle sense for colour and

artistic arrangement, and some interesting-looking watercolours of people's faces in nice frames on another wall. On one of them George thought he recognised the ugly pig-faced girlfriend of Marlies he had just seen, and he had to admit that the drawing made the girl look more attractive than she was in real life. Looking at these intimate articles of Marlies's life, George felt rather flattered that Marlies was willing to show him her innermost sanctum, but he also realised that he knew nothing about the girl standing in front of him. He knew her medical history, the terrible abuse by her father, he knew her body, her vagina, and he had been inside her and orgasmed simultaneously with her, but, in effect, he knew nothing about Marlies as a person, as a human bcing, as a girl with artistic interests, hobbies and a life of her own.

Before George could ask Marlies about the drawings, her hands had already gone towards his trousers and had taken out his stiff penis and put it in her mouth. This time George did not even start thinking whether what they were doing was right or wrong. They both had left that threshold a long time ago! He admitted to himself that this was exactly why he had come. He wanted her, he needed her body, he had missed her so much! Finding out about her as a person could wait …

While Marlies was sucking him, George placed one of his hands gently on Marlies's hair and caressed her while he slipped his other hand

on one of her tiny breasts. Marlies let out a tiny moan.

"When will your mother be back?", George asked, not completely oblivious to his surroundings yet.

Marlies took his wet penis out of her mouth. "She is usually not back from work before 6.30pm. But my friend Amy may be dropping in later, so we better be quick!"

George liked Marlies's foresight, and read it even more as a sign that Marlies was as keen to make love again as he was. George helped Marlies take off her t-shirt, and he was struck again at the beauty of her tiny, pointy breasts. They both took off their clothes in a flash and George was stunned again by the beauty of Marlies's body. The rays of the hot afternoon sun were shining through the window in such a way that they cast Marlies's body in a silvery glow, further helped by the fact that the heatwave made them both sweat profusely, oiling her beautiful skin. While Marlies continued sucking him, George gently caressed Marlies's breasts while he could feel the sweat trickle down his chest. Marlies had sucked him vigorously and he was already nearing the point-of-no-return with his penis swelling even more in Marlies mouth. Marlies had sensed this immediately and let his penis go. George, with his eyes closed, felt the feeling of the oncoming orgasm gently fade away. He felt like a giant penis, he was a penis, nothing else mattered. He gently pushed Marlies unto her back, looking at her beautiful body

gleaming with sweat in the heat. She had her legs apart and her wet vagina, rimmed with sparse pubic hair, seemed irresistibly beautiful. But instead of letting him penetrate her from top, Marlies turned around and straddled the edge of the bed on her knees. George looked at her beautiful tight bottom, which again looked more like that of a 12-year old boy than a grown woman, and her vagina looked even more inviting from behind. He placed his penis between the outer lips of Marlies's vagina and started gently stroking her. Marlies let out a sigh of pleasure and thrust her bottom towards him, inviting him to penetrate her. To prolong the pleasure, George continued to caress Marlies's vaginal lips and her clitoris with his penis. He could feel that she was getting even wetter. George could not hold on much longer and penetrated her very gently. First, he only put the tip of his penis into her dripping wet vagina, which again elicited a small cry of pleasure from her. Marlies body was urging him to penetrate her more deeply, to fuck her! George pushed his penis in a bit more, waited again, and then penetrated her completely. He felt his penis being enveloped by marvellous wetness and warmth. Marlies let out a cry of joy and, almost immediately, George could feel her vagina tighten rhythmically around his penis as she orgasmed uncontrollably. As he felt her convulsions of pleasure, George began moving his penis in and out, starting very slowly while Marlies's orgasm gradually ebbed away. Then he

increased the cadence gently, caressing Marlies's sweaty back, bending down a bit more so that he could reach her breasts with his hands. While he pushed in and out of her, he felt the nipples of her small breasts harden. Just like the first time when they made love, Marlies's body now worked in complete unison with his, her bottom and rump were matching his rhythm perfectly, they were just one joint moving body enjoying each other's rising pleasure.

George could see the two of them in a large mirror Marlies had on one of her walls, and that aroused him even more. He saw himself, a 52-year old, slim but oldish man, fucking this beautiful young girl whose small and thin body seemed to be completely enveloped by his large hull. *I look like a silver-back gorilla, with hair on my chest and shoulders, humping a young adolescent female!*, George briefly thought with a smile and not without pride. The mirror also showed Marlies face, which George could not see from behind, and revealed that Marlies had her eyes closed, that she was immensely enjoying being penetrated deeply, with her mouth open and emitting louder and louder shrieks of pleasure. George was now so aroused that he could no longer focus on the mirror and, instead, looked directly down at his penis thrusting in and out of Marlies's vagina. He had never been so turned on in his life, and never had the pre-orgasmic phase lasted so long. Marlies tilted her head back and her shrieks of pleasure grew even louder. George could feel the muscles

'relationship', soured between Paul and Marlies? She was probably only 14 or 15 at the time, clearly still a child, but was there something qualitatively different between Paul's relationship with Marlies and George's relationship with her? Had she loved Paul and similarly enjoyed sex with him? All these questions were racing through George's head while he was watching her nestle innocently and comfortably against his chest. *And what about contraception?*, he thought for the first time. *I have not asked Marlies yet whether she takes the pill or has a coil!*, he thought shamefully. *What if she gets pregnant? But I would not want to use a condom with her, that would take all the pleasure away! But then, should I be so selfish? But she has not raised the topic herself, never asked me to put on a condom*!, he thought while gently caressing her arm. Yet, he stayed quiet. He did not want to disrupt this magic post-coital moment where nothing seemed to matter, not his job, not the unpaid bills that were piling up in his practice, not his depressed state of mind. At this moment in time he seemed absolutely happy. *But what about Marlies?*, he wondered. *Is she happy after all this? After all it was me who came to see her, not the other way round ... but then ... the difficulty with buses ...* He put his hand to her chin and she slowly opened her eyes and smiled. "Marlies, I ...", but he was interrupted by the doorbell ringing.

Marlies was up in a dash. "Shit! That's Amy! Quick put your clothes back on!", and they both

rushed back into their clothes. George was very sad for their moment of peacefulness, and possibly happiness, to have been suddenly interrupted, but he was more worried about being seen by someone in Marlies's house. Marlies was ready to go downstairs and to let Amy in who was ringing the bell more persistently, knowing that Marlies was in the house after having left her only a short while ago.

"Ok, you let her in while I wait in the kitchen", George tried to say with a firm voice that betrayed his nervousness. "She should not see me, especially as your mum is not in the house. You take her to your room and I'll slip out quietly."

Marlies nodded but before she could run down the stairs George grabbed her arm. "Whcn will I see you again?", he said pleadingly looking into her eyes. All these things he had wanted to ask her, to discuss with her, to find out how she was feeling after their love-making, to ask her whether she liked him … loved him? But there was no time. The ringing was now persistent. While Marlies moved towards the front door, George slipped into the kitchen and left the door slightly ajar.

"Jesus, Marlies!", Amy said after being let in. "Have you … like … fallen asleep or what? We agreed that we would meet now!"

"Yes, sorry … I was … like … I was in the loo", Marlies lied relatively convincingly. "Let's go into my room and I'll show you that website we talked about …" George heard the two girls

going up the stairs, Marlies's steps feather-like and nimble, Amy's like exploding mortar shells that made the whole house vibrate.

I just hope that Marlies's bed will not betray what just happened there!, George thought as he heard Marlies bedroom door close. He quickly went towards the front door, opened it gently and peeked out to see whether anyone was looking. Satisfied that nobody seemed to be there he slipped out of the house, but just as he had started walking the short distance to the edge of the garden, he saw a large plump figure appear not far from where he stood. Esther, Marlies's dreadful mum! What was she doing here so early? There was no time for George to slip out onto the street, so he quickly backtracked towards the front door and hid behind one of the bushes near the entrance. The bush, some remnant half-dead thing with brown and withered leaves and old plastic bags tangled in its branches, was not providing much protection and George was hoping that Esther would not look his way. Esther, laden with plastic shopping bags and with her usual grumpy look, approached the front door and rummaged in her cheap handbag for the key. "Where are the bloody …", she grumbled as she was sifting through the mess in her bag. Luckily for George, although Esther was only about a metre away from his hiding place, she had turned the other way so that the sun was shining into her bag to help her find the keys. After what seemed like an eternity, Esther fished out the keys, opened the

doors, and disappeared into the house with a loud “honey! I’m home!” shout.

George breathed a huge sigh of relief. He had uncomfortably crouched behind the bush and after his sexual exertions his whole body felt rather stiff. On top of that he had realised that he was crouching right next to a fresh dog’s turd whose smell suddenly made him retch. He quickly extricated himself from his position and walked to his car without looking back. *When will I see Marlies again?*, he wondered. The future still lay ahead of him as a vast empty plain and George did not have a clue which pathway he would take. Was there any future in pursuing this affair with Marlies? Thinking about Paul Sutherland’s funeral again while he was starting his car, he certainly was still not sure where this whole affair with Marlies would lead him. Should he not attempt to rectify his miserable life, find a partner more his age, focus more on his crumbling practice, make more friends in the village? Maybe even make peace with Ingrid von Schnollrotz-Beerenbier and invite her over for dinner? *I am healthy and have, at least theoretically, a good job. Why am I making such a mess of my life?*, he thought, but all the while feeling rather satisfied after the wonderful sex he and Marlies just had. But looking at the miserable houses in Fernworthy Estate made him feel depressed again, especially when thinking that many of the Fernworthy residents had not had the opportunities he had in life. And yet most

of their lives were probably not such a mess as his own …

*

Waclav Fryzlewicz, a new patient from Poland with an unpronounceable name, had just left what had been a tough psycho-therapy session. George wiped the sweat of his forehead. He was sweating not because of the persistent heatwave, but because he had struggled to cope with this patient's psychological problems and with finding a meaningful therapy. Waclav had self-referred himself because he felt an increasing urge to kill somebody, anybody, at random. George had to pull the deepest registers of his psychological training to cope with the aggressive intensiveness, the targeted murderousness, the vicious killing instinct of this patient, and to provide him with a meaningful treatment that would effectively prevent a random person being murdered by this deeply troubled patient. He had discussed the side-effects of Waclav's medication prescribed by his GP, a new strong aggression-blocker as well as the dependence-inducing sedating drug diazepam, and had insisted that Waclav would see him again very soon to monitor the situation. But he also knew that in this case he may need to inform the police if Waclav's random murderous intentions continued after the next session. But he also knew that the police could do nothing

until Waclav actually committed a crime or began targeting specific victims.

Anwar Barhoum had been his next patient, but after about thirty minutes George was not happy with how the session was developing. A few days before George had had another visit by Detective Prendergast urging him to make progress with the Syrian. Prendergast had admitted that the team investigating Rawad's disappearance had been reduced from initially four people to now just herself, and that she was feeling the pressure from her superiors to either solve or shelve the case. Prendergast had even suggested a hidden device to record the next session with Anwar, but George had looked up the rules and regulations of the National Association for Psychiatry which relatively clearly stated that this would not be possible unless there was clear and imminent danger from this patient to other people which, at the moment, and as George had to admit, was not the case.

George, sitting again behind Anwar who was lying on the couch, adjusted his chair. It felt stiflingly hot in the room, but George did not want to open the window for fear that the traffic noise would disrupt their session. For the last 30 minutes, the discussion had, yet again, revolved around medication and the problems Anwar was having while taking it, and Anwar's continuing stress and psychological problems. Spurred on by Detective Prendergast's insistence, George had repeatedly tried to steer the discussion back towards Anwar's feelings towards his son, the

going-to-bed routine, the possible problems Anwar may have had with Rawad. But the Syrian had, either consciously or unconsciously, skilfully steered the discussion back onto more practical topics such as their shopping habits and eating together, the walk back from school, or visits to the mosque. Anwar made it sound as if he usually got on very well with his son and that they had reached a good parent-son arrangement since Rawad's mother had gone missing.

George was feeling very tired, rubbing his eyes and stretching his aching neck, all the while hoping that Anwar was not seeing his discomfort. He had not slept well and did not feel that this session would lead them any further or provide more information about Rawad's disappearance. He was just about to tell Anwar to get up, but then thought the better of it and just waited silently. *Will Anwar continue talking, even when not prompted?*, George wondered. *Maybe I have just pushed him too hard, attempted to steer the discussion in a certain direction, influenced by Prendergast's suspicions?*

George leaned back and said nothing for a long while. Anwar had been lying comfortably on the couch, talking, at times with his eyes closed, smiling occasionally when a pleasant memory about his son had surfaced. But now, in the growing silence, he had opened his eyes and felt visibly increasingly uncomfortable. He tried to twist his head back to look at George, but George was sitting almost right behind the couch

so that it was impossible for Anwar to turn his head far enough to see George. The Syrian started sweating profusely and beads of sweat ran down his forehead and cheeks. But he did not get up. Something compelled him to stay on the couch. After what seemed like a long while, Anwar cleared his throat and wiped the sweat from his brow with the sleeve of his shirt. Tears began welling up in his eyes. George sat as motionless and quiet as possible, he sensed that the situation had changed, that Anwar had almost forgotten where he was and that George was sitting behind him.

"I … I …", Anwar stammered. "I find it difficult to talk about certain things about my son …", he continued. "It was so difficult after Afraa, my wife, disappeared. Although she had been very close to Rawad … I … I … was also very close to my son … but in a different way. I … I was … I am a good father. I always did what was best for my son. But … but … I was also very lonely, even before my wife disappeared."

George did not dare breathe for fear that it would disrupt Anwar speaking out freely.

"We … we left Syria not only because of the war", Anwar continued, "but also because …". He paused for a long while, but George did not dare prompt him. "… because my brother had accused me … accused me of …", Anwar loudly cleared his throat. *This is it!*, George thought, *for the first time we are shedding light on what really happened!* "Accused me of … I can't say it, it is too disturbing!", Rawad sobbed while

sitting up on the couch and looking at George. "My brother accused me of having sexually molested his son!", Rawad shouted. "My own brother! Accusing me of such a dreadful deed! The Quran explicitly says that children are a gift of God and that four male witnesses would be needed to prove such wrongdoing! The whole family got involved, my brother tried to rally enough witnesses, but he could never prove anything! The whole thing was a disgrace and I never wanted to see my brother again!" Anwar was now panting heavily, still sitting on the couch, his head bowed in deep sorrow.

George had to break his own silence and ask the obvious. "Was it true?"

"Of course not!", Anwar replied immediately. "I loved my nephew! He meant the world to me! I would never touch him inappropriately, inch Allah!"

Rawad looked intensely at George, surprised at his own sudden revelations and his emotional outburst, but he gradually eased his body back onto the couch, panting heavily. George sat in his chair for a while, partly surprised that his strategy of not prompting Anwar seemed to have yielded results. He was stunned by what he had just heard and could not stop thinking that there may have been some truth behind Anwar's brother's accusations. *Had Anwar molested his nephew? Had he molested Rawad, his own son? Did his wife know, and was there more to the story of her disappearance than Anwar had let out?* Of course, he could not be sure, but he felt

ready to pass on these new revelations to Detective Prendergast. A few days ago, George had again looked at the National Association for Psychiatry code of conduct and, although instructions about ethical guidelines and doctor-patient confidentiality were fuzzy, and could be interpreted in different ways, he felt confident that there were now sufficiently suspicious circumstances regarding Anwar Barhoum for George to see the police and maybe even tape-record their next session. Yet he also knew that he could not yet prove anything, and that he needed to press Anwar further to talk about his relationship with his son.

George had to pause his thoughts and leaned back in his chair, breathing deeply. He felt completely overwhelmed by the situation and was not sure whether he could cope in his current confused and stressed state-of-mind. *Am I still fit to practise?*, he wondered not for the first time in the past few weeks. *Am I still of sound enough mind myself to see patients with deep psychological problems? The fact that I am losing more and more patients shows that I am not! My own patients realise that I am worse off than they are!* And yet George had resisted taking the same anti-depressants his patients were taking, knowing full well the terrible side-effects these could have. But he also resisted taking medication for fear that this would confirm to himself that he had psychological problems, that he was becoming mentally ill himself! He put his head in his hands and could

not stop thinking that the tense and complicated situation with Anwar Barhoum was the last thing he needed in his current state-of-mind.

In this fragile mental state, George realised that he was not in a fit enough state to continue the problematic session with Anwar, who was now lying on the couch in silence while George had gathered his thoughts. For the moment, George realised, he had probably extracted all he could from the Syrian. He told Anwar that this was it for today's session. The Syrian got up from the couch, clearly relieved that the awkward session was over. For a long while after Anwar left, George thought about the new information that had come to light, the accusation by Anwar's brother about molestation of Anwar's nephew, the real reason why they left Syria, and the mysterious disappearance of Anwar's wife, leaving Anwar in sole charge of a vulnerable boy in a country they both did not know. George knew that their next session, if he managed to fathom the professional and mental energy, would be the most crucial one.

*

Sitting in his local pub, George glanced over the rim of his lukewarm pint towards the other patrons. The ubiquitously named Davids, Williams, Johns, Richards and Steves were there, even the Richard Matthewses and Matthew

Richardses, swigging their beers and furtively looking away when their eyes met George's. George still had the impression that they were shunning him, probably not helped by his recent frantic escape from the seething masses in the overcrowded pub. G and G were there as usual, male G lying face down and hunched over the table in a puddle of vomit, female G completely drunk and leaning back on her chair with her eyes closed, arms dangling down her sides, and spittle leaking from her cracked lips. The patrons formed a wide circle around G and G, on the one hand reluctantly accepting their inevitable presence, but on the other hand put off by the reeking smell of male G's vomit dripping from the table.

George's former golfing partners were also there, standing in a conspiratorial cluster near the bar, looking over towards him, whispering into each other's ears and laughing while pointing at him. George looked away in disgust, partly because they had never invited him again for a round of golf. Did they despise him? George had also not heard anything from his old friend Sam Worthington whom he had known in London and who now was not living far away. Initially Sam had promised to play golf with George at least once a week, but after a few uninspiring rounds in which George had scored above 110 Sam also seemed to have given up on him. This was a shame as George knew that a round of golf would be good for his mental balance, a meditation in green, the calmness and serenity of

his local manicured golf course, but he could not bring up the courage to play on his own. After all, golf was a social sport, and George could not see the point of trying to hit a small ball into a distant hole on his own.

It was September and the heatwave, that had seemed to last forever, had given way to autumnal cool and wet weather. Heavy rain was pounding the windows of the pub whose old wooden frames were rattling in the wind. Ingrid von Schnollrotz-Beerenbier, the female neighbour who was keen on George, came into the pub, dripping wet and struggling to close the heavy wooden door in the gusty conditions. She took off her dripping hood and immediately spotted George. She looked away and George was not sure whether it was bitterness, disgust, or simply naked hatred that distorted Ingrid's face into a frown that made all her wrinkles even more apparent. *There is another person who wants nothing to do with me anymore!*, George thought sarcastically while taking a small sip from his pint, *there is certainly no point in even trying to make peace with her*, he had to admit to himself. Without a further glance at George, Ingrid disappeared into the crowd.

George looked up at the two people sitting with him at the table. His two cousins from London, Glenda and Robert, the children of his uncle Brad, who was his mother Nicola's brother, were visiting him for one day on their way to see friends in Cornwall. George was not particularly close to them but saw them

occasionally either when he was in London or when they came to the South-west. Apart from their childhood, when they had seen each other regularly when their parents visited each other, they did not have much in common. George looked at Glenda who was sipping a gin-and-tonic. She once had nice shiny black hair, but her hair had now gone completely white which, instead of giving her an air of elderly wisdom, rather made her look worn out and old. George remembered that he once thought that Glenda looked attractive, and at the age of 13 he even had a brief crush on her, but he thought that Glenda had let herself go, with sagging breasts, greasy skin, deep wrinkles that made her look older than her 50 years, and sad watery eyes. George had wondered over the past few years whether she had started drinking. Glenda claimed to be an artist interested in photography, although George had rarely seen any of her work and knew that she had never made money from her photos.

In her artistic inspiration, Glenda had been heavily influenced by her father Brad, also an artist who had worked as a photographer at an advertising agency in London. Brad, who had died shortly after George's mum, had always felt that he was selling his artistic skills out to a capitalist enterprise that was not interested in art *per se*, but only in making money and exploiting artists like himself. As a result, Brad had been increasingly frustrated with his career, had started neglecting his photography, and had

eventually been sacked from his job at the age of 50. After that he never found employment again, and the last decades of his life had been marred by alcoholism and depression.

Glenda, who had tried to follow in her father's footsteps, had found it impossible to make ends meet as a photographer, and had instead taken on a completely uninspiring job working in a supermarket where she had been for the past twenty years. Partly for that reason, but also because Glenda had abandoned school at the age of 16 and never completed A-levels or any other form of further education, George, in his arrogant and self-centred way, did not find her particularly interesting. Their discussion topics always seemed to revolve around rather bland themes that did not suggest much depth of knowledge on Glenda's part, except for the occasionally interesting discussion about photography. George looked over at Glenda again with a mixture of arrogant empathy and pity.

Robert, her older brother who was sitting next to Glenda, was completely different. George was well aware of Robert's sad story, as it had been a frequent discussion topic in his family. When Robert's mother, Mathilda, was pregnant with him, the doctors ordered her to stay in bed for the last three months of her pregnancy for fear that she would lose the child. George remembered his mum often talking bitterly about that time, how Mathilda felt trapped, unable to move, and cursing her unborn

child. Possibly as a result of this, and maybe also because Robert was born severely underweight and fragile, Mathilda developed what today would be diagnosed as severe post-natal-stress-disorder and wanted nothing to do with her son. Robert was placed in the care of Mathilda's mother who looked after him for the first three years of his life, with Robert having virtually no contact to his mother.

As a result, Mathilda and Robert never developed a healthy mother-child relationship, a problem that Robert carried with him for the rest of his life. From a psycho-therapist's perspective this meant that Robert as a baby and toddler never had his mother nearby to soothe his distress and to help him make sense of his early childhood experiences. George knew that there was nothing worse for a child to realise that they are not loved when they needed it most. Mothers were crucial in early childhood to help babies and young children slowly learn how to manage their physical and emotional stages. A child's ability to contain themselves directly depended on their mother's ability to contain them – motherly help that Robert had never received nor experienced. As a result, someone like Robert who had never learned to contain himself was plagued by anxious feelings and nameless dread for the rest of his life.

To compound problems Robert's father also never seemed to fully accept his son and, as a result, Robert developed a deep hatred towards his father. In a moment of rare intimacy between

George and his cousin, George remembered Robert telling him that Brad said to him immediately after Mathilda's death that he 'had had to put up with him for 50 years and that he had enough!' Even George, who had heard many sad family stories in his professional life found such a statement hard to swallow, especially at a time when Robert had felt particularly vulnerable after his mother's death.

Yet, when they were young and met reasonably regularly, George always had the impression that Robert was desperately vying for the love of his parents. He became a 'goody-goody' kid who would never rebel, always do as he was told, and always complying with the stern regime his parents were implementing. George remembered the sad and unspoken story in their family – recounted in hushed voices when his parents thought George was not listening – of Robert wetting his bed until the age of 16. A few times Robert had seen his aunt quickly removing Robert's bedsheets in the morning and placing them in the washing machine, glancing left and right to see whether anyone was watching her and seeing her embarrassment. When George, quite young at the time, caught her once with one of the dripping and yellow-stained sheets, Mathilda's embarrassed look stayed with him for a long while, and he remembered feeling proud that he himself had good control over his bladder, while he always shuddered having to touch Robert for fear of getting piss all over himself.

In addition, and to the dismay of his sister, Robert would tell his parents everything about Glenda's misdemeanours, which increasingly alienated him from his sister. In return, Glenda would involve Robert less and less in her life and started lying, cheating and misleading Robert and her family about what she had been up to. This resulted in the fact that, as teenagers, Robert and Glenda became increasingly estranged and had virtually nothing to do with each other. But the saddest thing George could remember was that Robert was never allowed to do anything. While, as a kid, George was climbing rocks, riding his bicycle like a daredevil, and gathering worms and insects from the nearby woods, Robert did nothing. At the age of 12, Robert still could not ride a bike, had never been to the woods on his own, and had no friends. Instead, he was stuck in their dull suburban home, pouring over what George thought were boring hobbies involving electrical trains sets, electronic kits and, later on, when Robert was older, computer games. Because he was mainly indoors, Robert developed a pasty, pale and unhealthy complexion and became rather fat due to lack of exercise. George was certain that Robert never had a girlfriend in his life and had never made love to, or even touched, a woman. Because of Mathilda's upbringing by narrow-minded and bigoted Catholic nuns and her resulting inbred guilt and misguided 'education' of her son regarding all matters sexual, George also suspected that Robert had never

masturbated, although their lack of closeness had meant that they had never talked about such intimate subjects. But George also knew that Robert had at least twice attempted to commit suicide with sleeping pills, but that both times the dose he had taken was too low to kill him – in psychological terms clear cries for help which, George feared, had remained relatively unanswered by both his parents and his sister. As a psycho-therapist, George knew that he should have offered to help Robert during the darkest hours of his life, but he never managed to stomach the courage, or energy, to help him. Instead he had only felt pity for his cousin, had felt aloof and detached from his sorrows. Even as a child George had always behaved rather arrogantly towards Robert, had felt better than him, more 'normal', and constantly boasted with his achievements, his friends, and girlfriends, partly to show Robert his superiority but also to make George feel better about himself at the expense of his cousin.

George looked over at Robert while taking another sip from his now nearly-empty pint. Robert looked pensively at the orange juice in front of him – due to his frail constitution he could never drink alcohol or fizzy drinks – and did not see George's sardonic smile and slight shaking of the head. And yet George was acknowledging to himself that he had no moral right to feel superior towards Robert and Glenda, that he should accept them as people with immense psychological problems, that he should

be compassionate about their misfortunes and sad lives, and that he should make an effort at seeing them more often. *After all, they are family!*, he thought, but not without a bitter aftertaste.

For a while they said nothing. George could feel that his cousins felt uncomfortable, surrounded by strangers and people who seemed to be constantly peering over towards their table, and he began to regret having taken his cousins to the pub. After a while Glenda looked at George with a slightly worried face and asked him how he had been. George looked up from his pint, somewhat taken aback by his cousin's sudden interest in him. He realised that he had not been asked how he was for a very long time, maybe since Daniela had become increasingly worried about him months ago. *All we talk about is the patients, but nobody seems to care how psycho-therapists themselves feel and are affected by all this!*, George thought with a loud sigh.

"I am well … thanks you for asking Glenda", George retorted, knowing full-well that he did not look well at all. In the past few weeks he had let himself go even more, and had to admit to himself that he had not even paid any attention to the clothes he had put on before his cousins came to visit. He was wearing an unwashed and partly ripped t-shirt which made him look like a tramp. Glancing down towards his belly, George realised that it was the very same shirt with the jam stains he had worn months ago during his

brief encounter with his neighbour Ingrid! George also had not shaved for a while and a straggly beard that looked like a patch of untended gorse and broom covered his chin. He had not washed or combed his hair for a while which was standing up in all directions, with greasy hairs strains falling over his face now-and-then which he nervously brushed away with an automatic flicker of his hand which began to look more like a tic. *Maybe that's one of the reasons why the patrons in the pub are looking at me so strangely?*, he wondered. *Maybe it's just the way I look?*

"You don't look too well, George", Robert said with a surreptitious glance at his sister.

George thought for a while. He had no intention of letting his cousins into his life, of telling them about his growing depression, the problems with his practice, and the dreadfully addictive affair with Marlies. He had never really talked to his cousins about his problems, so why start now? After all he had always felt so superior towards them, never admitting that someone like him could have problems of his own. But then he probably really did not look that well, and it seemed to be evident that things were not going well for him at the moment.

"Well, you know … things have been a bit difficult lately", George admitted hesitantly. "Maybe the move to here was not such a great idea after all, Devonmouth is such a small and provincial place, and I have found it difficult to integrate into the village. You know how these

Devonshire people are …", he grumbled while scanning the Richards, Steves and Davids again who, he felt, continued to stare at him intensely from all corners of the pub. "They don't let you in easily into their community. I have played golf with some of them, but I fear that they think I'm not a good enough player for them. Holding them up and annoying them with my poor shots, you know!"

Glenda and Robert could not know, George thought with disdain, as they had never been near a golf course in their lives and knew nothing about the beautiful sport. But he had begun to talk himself into a rant about his life, and he had to admit that it was somewhat nice to have an audience. "Setting up the new practice has also not been as easy as I thought", George continued, "especially as the previous owner from whom I took it over has just committed suicide".

Robert and Glenda looked at each other, not sure what to make of George's sudden candour. "To be honest, the practice is not going well at all", George continued to confess, "and I now have hardly any patients left, I have lost my receptionist who had been really nice and helpful, and the bills are piling up, not helped by the fact that I still have a substantial mortgage which I needed to allow me to live in this beautiful, but utterly expensive, part of Devon. On top of this, one of my patients may be a murderer, and I am struggling to cope with what may come next. The police have come to see me about this … and I am also in love …" George

stopped abruptly, as he had not intended to talk about the confidential problems of his patients or his love-life with anyone, especially not to his cousins, but the beer must have loosened his tongue. Now that the rhetorical floodgates were opening, there seemed to be no halting him. "I can't tell you who she is, but I love her very much. She is so beautiful and so …" But George had to stop at this point. Although it felt good to talk for the first time to someone, to anyone, about his desperate love affair with Marlies, he again realised that he had nothing to say about Marlies beyond her beautiful youthful body. Apart from the few gleaned impressions during Marlies's visit as a patient in his practice and their last encounter at Marlies's house, which allowed him some glimpses about her love for drawings and boy bands, he realised again that he still knew nothing about her as a person, as a human being, as a girl, a woman, with feelings and thoughts. He was simply using his power position as her doctor to fuck her! That's what it was! It was simply about an old man abusing a young vulnerable girl! How could he be so unprofessional, throw away his life and career for a stupid love-affair that had no chance of lasting! Again, he did not even dare think about how the MeToo movement would see his case! *They would slaughter me, skin me alive!*, George thought despondently.

A loud splintering noise rose George from his dark thoughts. In his anger he had crushed the half-full beer glass with his hand! He had cut

himself deeply and was bleeding all over the table, his blood mingling with the beer as it ran down over the side of the table onto his trousers. His cousins looked at George with a mixture of fear and pity, not knowing what to say or do. Despite of the din in the pub, everybody seemed to have heard what happened, and suddenly the whole pub seemed to be eerily quiet. The publican and the patrons were all looking at George, and even female G appeared to have woken up from her drunken stupor and glanced towards his bleeding hand. You could almost hear a pin drop. George looked up at his cousins and the villagers with a look of utter incomprehension in his face. Everybody was looking at him, the people around him felt like one seething being, like a monster wanting to gobble him up! George could not stand it any longer. He got up, holding his bleeding hand, and fought his way through the thick throng of patrons. He felt resistance, hands on his shoulders and throat, Steves, Richards and Matthews trying to grab him, Ingrid moving towards him like a possessed witch wanting to crush him, and evil stares of hatred seemed to bore into his skin from everywhere as he finally managed to reach the door and heaved himself out of the pub into the pouring rain. His jacket was still on his chair back in the pub, but he did not care as he ran as quickly as he could with his sneakered feet splashing through the deep puddles, away from this alien place of evil, away

from the demons in his own head, away from it all …

Part 4

Nemesis

VIDETE PRAVA MACELLARIUS
CETERAQUE FOEDITATE
REI MILITIBUS
ET FRAUDARE MERETRICIBUS DANTUR
MERCEDES
LEGATI DIVERSARUM
GENTIUM ET PERFIDE
QUOD FALSA IMPERATORUM
POST EAS, NISI TENEBRAE
MISERIAE, MORS, OBLIVIO

Beware of the depraved slaughterers
The debased warriors
The cheating whores
The rogue traders
The false emperors
After them, only darkness
Misery, Death, Oblivion

(Aesculab of Constantinople, AD 1453, at the eve of the conquest of the city by the Ottomans)

George was sitting in his small Korean car which was parked close to the centre of Devonmouth. It had taken him some time to find a parking space, but he had finally found one in one of the cul-de-sac side-streets near the main square. It was raining hard, summer heat had now definitely given way to autumnal storms and the wet season that characterised October to December in the south-west of the UK.

George was clutching the steering wheel, a vacant look on his face betraying that he was unsure about what to do next. He knew that he should be in his practice, but, as he had virtually no patients left, he could allow himself increasing periods of absence from the office. Or was it that he had fewer and fewer patients because he was now absent so often from his practice? George watched the few people braving the bad weather walking past his parked car. A thought he frequently had re-emerged: what if everything he saw and experienced around him was just part of an elaborate show, put on by whoever just for him as the main and unknowing character on a global stage comprised of millions of actors. Was this woman walking past, clutching her umbrella in the gale, an actress who had been paid to walk past his car at precisely this moment? Was the car driving past occupied by paid actors, seemingly searching for a parking space, but, in reality, just there to make him feel like he was living a 'real' life? What was reality anyway? Was Marlies real, or was she just a cast in this global movie?

Was Anwar Barhoum real, or had they now even started to recruit actors in Syria for the George Williamson show? *If yes, they are all damn good actors!*, George thought with a smile that betrayed that such fantasies could be a sign of deep psychological problems often referred to as the 'Truman Show Syndrome', after Peter Weir's enigmatic movie of the same name depicting a person who lives a completely artificial life surrounded by actors and, unbeknown to him, living in a giant movie set. George's parents, especially his mother, had always said that, even as a kid, he seemed 'removed' from the real world, a bit of a dreamer who never seemed to be 'quite there', that he also could never take anything seriously, that he was the eternal aloof cynic. *Cynic or realist?*, he began to regularly ponder even early on in his life.

The loud splashing of the rain on his windscreen brought George back to reality. He rubbed his eyes and looked into the rear mirror, feeling very tired. George did not like what he saw: a ragged, dishevelled and unkempt figure with dark rings under his eyes, week-old stubble on his chin, and a pasty and unhealthy complexion. He barely recognised himself and admitted that he had to better look after himself, otherwise his life would completely fall apart.

He had come to this part of Devonmouth to distract himself from his growing depression, from the dark thoughts surrounding his affair with Marlies and his crumbling practice. This

district was where Rawad, Anwar Barhoum's 12-year old son, had gone to school before his disappearance. To take his mind off things and to help him refocus on one of his key remaining patients, George had organised a meeting with one of Rawad's teachers, Mrs Purcell. He was not sure whether he was stretching the boundaries of what a psycho-therapist could and should do, but he knew that an unsolicited approach to someone like Mrs Purcell by a psycho-therapist treating the father of one of their disappeared pupils was unorthodox, to say the least. But he also thought that obtaining a bit more independent information on Rawad, beyond what Anwar and Detective Prendergast had told him, could not do any harm.

George opened the car door and ran towards the school, holding the hood of his rain jacket firmly against the strong gale and pouring rain. He paused for a brief moment in front of the building to orientate himself. Devonmouth City School was a primary school typical for many run-down inner-city districts in the UK, with several dilapidated buildings betraying a severe shortage of maintenance funds, looking even drabber in the pouring rain. The forecourt was empty as all pupils were in their classrooms. George walked through the creaking front doors, took off his dripping-wet jacket, and made his way towards the teachers' room. Mrs Purcell was expecting him. George thought that she looked like a typical teacher, oldish with grey hair and wrinkles, a skirt that accentuated rather than hid

her wide hips, glasses sitting at the front of her nose and held back by a thin golden chain, and standing in a confident pose that suggested years of experience of dealing with unruly and rowdy kids.

“Dr Williamson, how nice to meet you”, she said while shaking his hand with a firm grip and attempting to hide her astonishment at his unkempt appearance.

“Many thanks for seeing me, Mrs Purcell”, George retorted in as firm a voice as he could muster.

“You said on the phone that you wanted to talk to me about the disappearance of Rawad, one of our pupils?”, Mrs Purcell enquired while leading George to one of the chairs in the rather cramped teachers’ room.

“Yes”, George replied. His voice was still not as firm as he intended it to be, so he cleared his throat again. “Rawad’s father is one of my patients, and over the past few months I have tried to help him overcome a deep depression that began with his son’s disappearance”.

Mrs Purcell seemed to be astonished at George’s intimate revelations about a patient, but said nothing. George knew that he was out of his depth here, but he persevered nonetheless. “I was wondering whether you could tell me a bit about Rawad and what your thoughts are about why he disappeared.”

Mrs Purcell shifted uneasily in her chair. “Well … Mr … Dr Williamson. I have already

told all this to the police … to a Detective Prun … Prin …"

"Prendergast, probably", George interjected.

"Yes, Prendergast. I guess you also know her?"

"Yes, I have met Detective Prendergast", George admitted, "and she has informed me that they still have no clue as to what happened. Do you think that Rawad may have simply run away?"

"Detective Prendergast of course also asked me, and some of my colleagues who knew Rawad, the same question. I can only repeat what I told the police. Rawad was … sorry, is a nice child, a keen learner and quick to grasp new things. His English improved very quickly and he is rather intelligent. But sometimes he can be a bit moody and just before he disappeared, early April I believe, he seemed a bit depressed."

Mrs Purcell looked at George and scrutinised his face to see how what she was saying was sinking in. George looked at her, but said nothing, encouraging her with a nod to continue.

"There were marks on his wrist which we could not explain …", Mrs Purcell continued.

This was news to George, as Prendergast had not mentioned anything referring to this.

"What marks?", George enquired, leaning slightly forward.

"I … I am not sure," Mrs Purcell continued. "First, we thought he had just injured himself while playing in the school yard, but these marks seemed to stay for a while, so myself and my

colleagues began to be worried. We asked Rawad about them, but the boy said nothing. I was just about to report it to both the Devonmouth child and refugee services when Rawad disappeared. I am pretty sure we mentioned this to Detective Prendergast."

"How do you think Rawad got these marks?", George enquired more insistently. This could be the lead he was hoping for.

"Well, I can't be sure. As they seemed to reappear regularly, I thought that maybe somebody was binding his hands tightly, either together or tying them to something. But as Rawad would not talk about it, and as we were not sure whether this was not something the kids did as part of a game they were playing, we were hesitant to pursue it further. In hindsight, of course, we think that we should have reported this to the Child Services straight away …"

"Why do you think Rawad disappeared?", George asked.

"Well. There was a lot of speculation at the time …", Mrs Purcell replied anxiously but also relieved that George had steered the discussion away from the marks on Rawad's wrists. "I told Detective Prendergast that we had no information about what happened. I think it is unlikely that Rawad ran away, he was such a shy boy and not very mature for his age, probably because of his migration background and the fact that he did not know the area that well yet, but it is not entirely implausible either. He would not be the first kid of this age at our school to have

run away. We have very difficult children here, you know", Mrs Purcell said while pointing out of the window at the shabby and decrepit neighbourhood.

"Did you know Rawad's father and, if yes, what relationship do you think he had with his son?", George asked.

"I met Mr Barhoum a few times when he picked up his son after school. I was surprised at how well he spoke English. I think he had a good job back in Syria and had learned English at school …"

"He was a pharmacist back home", George interjected.

"That's right", Mrs Purcell said. "I guess being a pharmacist meant that he had to speak some English in Syria, so language and communication never seemed to be a problem, compared to many other refugees we have here. But beyond this, I don't know much about Mr Barhoum. The few times I saw him with his son they seemed to get on well. As soon as they met, Rawad seemed eager to tell his dad about his day at school. Rawad was always so pleased about how well he had done, especially in maths but also in English …" Mrs Purcell stopped and looked down with a very sad expression on her face. "We miss the boy and really hope that he can still be found. I hope so much that nothing nasty has happened to him …", and she looked up at George with tears in her eyes.

"I am sorry to bring this all up", George said apologetically. He knew that he could not ask

Mrs Purcell anything more about whether she thought Anwar may have harmed his son in any way. He knew that they had reached the end of the interview.

George thanked the teacher for her help and saw himself out of the school. The information about the marks on Rawad's wrists was weighing heavily on his mind and was deepening his suspicions that Anwar had something to do with his son's disappearance. He had to find out more about this at their next session, but he was also afraid about what Anwar may tell him and, worst of all, was not sure whether he had the energy, or the willingness, to confront Anwar directly about what happened to his son. *The lines are getting increasingly blurred between my role as a psycho-therapist and a detective!*, he thought with unease as he made his way back to his car in the pouring rain. *But I am now too involved with Rawad's disappearance and it is my duty to find out what happened.* George realised that, despite of the possible unsavoury undertones of Rawad's disappearance, his case was one of the few things that kept him professionally focused.

*

George sat in his car for a long time, listening to the rain pounding the windscreen and wondering what to do next. He had no further patient appointments for the day so there was no need to go back to the practice. Despite the new vigour with which he intended to find out about what

happened to Rawad, he also had to admit to himself that his depression was getting worse. When he was feeling worst, his mind inevitably kept drifting back to Marlies, as if she was a magnet which held an irreversible attraction over him which his weak mind could not fight. It had been a few weeks again since his fateful visit at Marlies's house and his tight escape both from Marlies's friend and her mother. Why had Marlies not contacted him since? Did she care at all about him? George was running his mind through the last sexual encounter with her in her own bedroom. She seemed to have yet again enjoyed having sex with him, and thinking about the intimate details of how he had taken her from behind gave George an erection. Why was Marlies no longer turning up to scheduled sessions? She had now missed all the last six or seven sessions, and George had now given up all hope that he would ever see Marlies in his practice again.

George was convinced that Marlies's mother Esther was suspecting that he and Marlies were having an 'affair', a suspicion probably exacerbated by what had happened before between Marlies and Paul Sutherland. Paul Sutherland's suicide had probably confirmed to Esther that her daughter was in some way involved, but George could not be entirely sure about this. Although he did not like Esther, George could fully understand her position and would have acted the same had he been Marlies's parent. And yet he hated the mother for

withholding her child from him. How dare she? Marlies was 16 and could make up her own mind with whom she did, or did not, want to be and have sex. But then, did Marlies want to be with him, as she had never made an attempt to contact him herself? On the other hand, it had been her who had initiated their first sexual encounter, George remembered, his penis hardening further at the thought of how Marlies had sucked him for the first time in his office. Yet, she could have rung him, enquired how he was, whether he wanted to meet up! But nothing! It had always been him going to see her, making the first move, persevering with his perverse lust for her. In the end it was entirely one-sided! But he could not blame Marlies. What did she want with a 52-year old depressed psycho-therapist! She had her whole life in front of her, she did not want to be lumbered with some frustrated dirty old man! Although she may have enjoyed the sex, even with Paul Sutherland George had to grudgingly concede, that did not mean that she was emotionally bound to George. She was a budding adult who could make up her own mind about who she wanted to see. But George found this hard to admit. He needed Marlies more than anything at this moment in his life where everything around him was crumbling into dust, where the people he knew, including his patients, seemed to emphasise the depravity of humanity rather than its beautiful sides, where individuals were beset with immense emotional, moral and personal problems that seemed almost

irreconcilable and beyond redemption. George banged his head against the steering wheel of his small Korean car in despair. It was raining harder than ever.

I have to see her again now!, George realised. *I have to clarify my relationship with her once and for all, talk to her as two adult beings rather than just having sex with her, find out more about her as a person, whether she loves me like I love her!* George glanced at his watch and suddenly realised that he could be at Marlies's house just in time for her coming back from school. He did not take long to make up his mind. He started the engine and drove towards Fernworthy Estate through streets soaked with rain, behind cars, lorries and buses splashing through giant puddles, and past pedestrians hurrying through the storm, huddled under their half-broken soggy umbrellas. *Maybe they are all actors in the George Williamson show?*, he briefly thought again with a rare smile on his lips.

He drove past rows of boring same-looking bungalows which resembled biscuits in a tin, another one of Devonmouth's misguided post-war planning crazes aimed at giving its boring and dull residents a shot at a detached house with a tiny garden, surrounded by equally dull and boring neighbours with the same uninspired approach to life. To George the housing estate he was driving through confirmed that Devonmouth was not a vibrant city, a place marred by outmigration, attrition of jobs, the loss of its

brightest young people, with leftover older people who were poorly educated and with few opportunities left in life. At first glance all seemed so peaceful in the estates to a casual passer-by, but glancing through the rain-soaked windscreen towards these dreadfully dull houses, George knew that, hidden behind all these innocuous facades, atrocities were perpetrated all the time. George's vivid imagination conjured up images of fathers abusing their daughters, uncles molesting their nephews, husbands cheating their wives, and wives plotting their husbands' deaths, in an often-lethal merry-go-round of human depravity.

George's iPod seemed to sense his dark mood. As if to taunt him, it was playing one rubbish tune after the other on shuffle mode, each song more unsuited to his mood than the other. As leafy suburban streets were making way to the squalor, poverty and grime of the Fernworthy Estate, the iPod was spitting out songs by Abba whose predictable jolliness got on George's nerves, Philip Glass whose repetitive incantations made him particularly edgy on this sombre day, or R.E.M. whose smooth softness, righteous rigidity and morbid morality made George retch. Why had he kept these songs on his iPod in the first place? But then he sometimes enjoyed listening to these musicians. *How complex the human mind is!*, he thought yet again, wondering himself how little he understood how his own mind worked. *How could someone who did not understand himself*

try and understand the mind of his patients?, he pondered, shaking his head in despair. He pressed the button for 'next song' repeatedly, but had given up after the stupid machine kept churning out worse-and-worse tunes. Some melancholic tunes from Pink Floyd, Coldplay or Porcupine Tree would have suited his mood better, but he could not be bothered searching for specific songs on the iPod while he was driving in these difficult wet conditions. The only thing George could do was to keep his windows closed yet again, so as not be spotted as an outsider, with outlandish music tastes, by the hooded thugs walking the streets of Fernworthy Estate. He grudgingly continued to endure the aural assault coming from his music device. Under no circumstances would he give in and switch off the iPod. That would be tantamount to surrender, summing up his wretched life!

George had arrived in the street where Marlies lived and parked his car in almost the same place as he had last time. The heavy rain made it hard to see anything, he had to repeatedly wipe the mist from the windscreen and side-window with his sleeve to make out anything. He sat there for a few minutes, the iPod churning out further awful songs, but with the volume turned down so as not to arouse suspicion among the few passers-by. With his fogged-up windows George felt like being in a cocoon, shielded in his little car-bubble from the squalor of Fernworthy Estate. Why was he here? He did not fit in here at all, felt like an alien from another

planet, an anthropologist visiting a strange tribe, observing the unfathomable mores of the natives.

And then he saw her. She was not alone! Marlies was approaching her house, arm-in-arm with a hooded chav. Like most kids these days they had no umbrella or raincoat, their hoodies and shirts soaked by the pouring rain. The hooded boy was holding Marlies very tight and when they reached her porch they kissed long and intensely. George could see through the misty windows that the hooded chav had slipped one of his hands under Marlies's shirt and was caressing her breasts, oblivious as to whether somebody was watching them. She clearly enjoyed it as her hand had moved towards the boy's trousers and was caressing his penis gently. George was sure that he could make out the bulge of an enormous erection. Marlies and the boy went into the house and George had no doubt about what they were up to next. A few seconds later the light went on in Marlies's room.

George's world collapsed. He suddenly felt so weak, he could not even hold on to his steering wheel. His whole body slumped over sideways, he did not even have the strength to sit upright. The last thing he seemed to have left in this world was gone! Marlies was clearly involved with this boy, was probably having sex with him this minute. George gripped the steering wheel hard, his face red in anger as he was imagining the hooded chav slipping his penis into Marlies's beautiful vagina, the chav's crusty lips sucking Marlies's wonderful youthful nipples, his mouth

all over her pristine and slender body. Tears welled up in George's eyes and he let out a loud, almost inhumane, cry. He did not care anymore whether anyone heard him, whether the other chavs from the estate would come and beat him up. Maybe that was what he deserved anyway! *Marlies! Marlies! Marlies!*, he thought, his body convulsed by loud sobs as he collapsed sideways unto the passenger seat. It was all over now, he would never see Marlies again!

But what was he expecting? Marlies was a very attractive young girl, surrounded by testosterone-filled hooded youths. It had to happen sometime! It probably had happened all the time, even while George was fucking Marlies, but George had always pushed that thought aside, thinking, hoping, that Marlies was just his. His alone to have, to hold, to caress … to fuck. How could he be so naïve? Of course, she would have seen other men … boys her age. Of course, she was having sex with them. George was only a side-show for her, somebody curious, maybe a bit different, to have sex with. She probably laughed out loud when she thought about him after their sexual exertions, smiled at his clumsy sexual advances, at his so-called life-changing orgasms. It was probably all a bit joke for her!

George sobbed even louder and his tears were beginning to leave a wet patch on the steering wheel. But then it was Marlies who had initiated the first sex they had, he had to remind himself. Sure, she had seen that he was keen on

her when he sported his embarrassing erection during their first encounter. But it was her who made the first move, without which George would have never dared persist with making love to her subsequently. There must have been something there, some feeling, some eagerness to get to know him, at least to know him sexually. But she also never asked about him, she never showed curiosity about him as a person, as a human being with immense problems of his own. In fact, she had never been interested in him, George concluded. But then she was only 16, George had to keep reminding himself. What could he expect of a mere child! He had expected too much of her, he had only seen the woman in her, not the young girl. He had used the yardstick of his 52 years of experience to extrapolate how she would think and behave. He could not compare her to George's two wives, Martina and Mildred, who had been women and not girls when they met, who had been able to take mature decisions when it came to their, eventually doomed, relationships. *But a 16-year old is nonetheless able to make mature decisions!*, George thought. Marlies is somewhere in limbo, between the world of a child and of an adult. *Anyway, she seemed to have made up her mind, whether as a child or as a woman, and she was fucking this boy ... this hooded chav ... this ... this prick!*, George was fuming. He clenched his fists, sat up again in his seat, and started the engine, over-revving it as he shot out of the parking space without looking for traffic in his

rear mirror, and sped through Fernworthy Estate in the raging storm.

George could barely concentrate on the road. Luckily there was little traffic, the deluge was keeping people indoors, despite it being rush-hour. George had reached Jumper's Bridge. He suddenly stopped his car in the middle of the bridge. Luckily there was no car behind him, but George did not care anyway. He got out of the car, walked towards the low railing, and looked down into the gaping abyss. Below him the river Devon was making its way towards the nearby sea, not far from where he was standing. George estimated that it was a drop of at least 80 metres. He imagined his body falling and crashing into the river below. No chance of survival, as the many successful suicides from Jumpers' Bridge hat attested. A car blocked behind his car was honking which awoke George from his dark thoughts. *What am I doing?*, George thought, suddenly aware of where he was standing. *I am not going to commit suicide over a love affair!*, he told himself. *Come on, get a grip! Psycho-analyse yourself! You will get over this! Come on, you still have much to look forward to! You have a nice house in a nice village*, George thought, but was immediately reminded of the dreadful times he had in the pub or with his weird neighbour Ingrid. *Ok, at least you have your practice!*, but his thoughts drifted immediately to the fact that he had lost almost all his patients, that he was effectively bankrupt, that several letters from the National Association for

Psychiatry were waiting unopened in his drawer probably threatening to disbar him from practicing, and that he had a very difficult, and probably depressing, session coming up with Anwar Barhoum. *Ok, you still have your family!*, but he remembered the rather dreadful time he recently had with his cousins and the fraught relationship he had with his parents. *Ok, at least you have beautiful nature around you in one of the most wonderful parts of the British Isles!*, but George thought bitterly how he virtually never went for walks and how he had stopped playing golf as his partners deemed him not a worthy enough player. *Right, that about sums it up!*, George resigned himself. *Nothing to look forward then, but there must still be a purpose in life! At least I am healthy, he thought. Think about all the patients you have seen in your professional life who were severely depressed because of unimaginable pain they were enduring, because of a terminal cancer diagnosis, or because one of their children had just died in a terrible accident. In a few years' time you will laugh about this little affair with Marlies and how it affected you!*, he tried to encourage himself, but tears were welling up in his eyes again. *Where is all your philosophy now and what use is it anyway!*, he thought. *All your thoughts about the world, the universe, politics, life and other people? Who cares in the end what you think about religion, politics, climate change, cats crapping in your garden, your hatred of dogs, your narrow thoughts on Brexit,*

your anti-social attitude to advertising and fashion, your stupid breakfast routine ending up with jam-smeared t-shirts, your irrational fear of someone hearing the songs you like on your iPod, your arrogant and self-centred thoughts about people you know and observe and your misplaced thoughts about their lives, your self-centred opinions about your former wives, your family and your friends? All of this seemed so irrelevant at this point in time, so futile, so … small, compared to the immensity of a life about to be extinguished, to extinguish itself. That was big, compared to the smallness of the rest of his life.

The car behind him was honking again, a queue had started to build up behind his car which was blocking the bridge. George thought that he could hear someone shout "C'mon man! Make up your mind! Either jump or get back into your fucking car!", but he was not sure whether it was his imagination playing tricks. Was he still of this world? Was he still alive? Another dreadful thought occurred to him: had he become so deluded that he had made up the affair with Marlies? Had it actually happened at all? Was it all in his mind, after all? Maybe he was more ill than any of his patients? It was almost as if he stood beside himself, looking down onto him by the bridge railing. Nothing seemed real anymore. He was vaguely aware of himself holding his own hand, nursing himself back to his car, gently seating himself into his seat, placing his hand on his own hand to restart the engine. George felt

like a split personality, someone not entirely within his own body, as he sped off away from the bridge into the leafier suburbs of the city.

*

George did not know how he had fathomed the energy to get out of bed, have breakfast, watch Ingrid's cat leaving a brown turd on his lawn, and drive to his practice. He must have been sitting in his chair motionless and numb for a long time. His eyes kept focusing on the drawer in his desk that contained all the unopened letters from the National Association for Psychology. Why was he so reluctant to open them? How could he be sure that they were about his misconduct with Marlies? Would the police not have long arrested him if the letters were indeed about their affair? He was suddenly jolted back to the present by a knock on his office door.

"Come in!", George muttered, quickly pretending to shuffle through random papers lying on his desk so as to appear busy. George knew that his last few remaining patients were scheduled to see him today, but he had lost all sense of time and had forgotten who had been scheduled first. He was acutely aware of his dishevelled appearance, the fact that he had not shaved for weeks, and that he had not washed himself for a long time. In fact, even in his semi-conscious state he could smell the reeking stench emanating from his armpits and crotch and

hoped that he was sitting far away enough from his patients for them not to smell the stench.

Donald Richardson, the depressed academic, walked into his office and sat himself down in the chair in front of George's desk. George guessed that Donald remained one of his last regular patients because George's practice was just next door to the university where Donald worked. *He comes more for convenience than because I offer a good service!*, George admitted to himself. Donald gazed at George with a strange look on his face, not for the first time unsure what to make of the unkempt appearance in front of him. He had looked uneasy at their last meeting, George remembered, but George had then still tried to look reasonably respectable and professional. All that pretension was now gone. Donald sat on the edge of his seat, ready for a quick escape.

George had to concentrate hard to remember the details of Donald's case. He felt very tired, in fact utterly exhausted. He asked Donald a few innocuous questions about how his medication helped with the depression, about Donald's frustration with his promotion prospects, and about his frustration of not seeing his three children often enough after his divorce, but he also realised that Donald recognised immediately that George was not able to fully concentrate on his case. George found it hard to focus when Donald was dribbling on about his problems, and he felt increasingly like shouting at Donald to get his act together, that other

people were facing much more serious problems in life than thinking about career advancement and more regular access to children. But George still had enough self-restraint and professionalism left to at least appear to be interested in what Donald was saying. It was, nonetheless, a dreadful, unfocused, and very short session. George could see the relief in Donald's eyes when George terminated their session, but he also sensed immense despair in his patient who clearly needed intense psychological help, and quickly! George knew he could no longer offer such help to his hapless patients. Donald left the room without saying goodbye or looking back at George, and George was sure that this was the last time he would see this patient. *I can't do this anymore!*, George sighed. *I have to sort out my own problems before being able to refocus on my patients! I have to sort out my own life first!*, he thought, leaning forward and resting his head on his arms, sobbing loudly. Not for the first time he realised that he probably had been drawn to the field of psychiatry in the first place because he needed psychiatric help himself!

He did not have much time to recover his poise. Gone were the days when he made copious and professional notes about his patients after every session, he just could not care anymore! After knocking timidly, Waclav Fryzlewicz entered George's office and sat down. He too looked at George's dishevelled appearance and felt clearly uneasy, probably

realising that George had just cried. George cleared his throat and tried to focus on his patient.

"Tell me how you have been since our last meeting", George said with a voice whose clarity surprised himself.

Waclav was very nervous, his whole body was trembling and he could not sit still on his chair. "Not well, doctor, not well …", he admitted after a while. "I … I … am about to kill my neighbour!", Waclav said with a broken voice.

George still had sufficient professional acuity left to recognise that this was a very serious situation and that the hospital's psychiatric services had to be informed immediately so that Waclav could be placed into a closed ward until his condition improved. After their first session, George had still left options open, waiting to see how the patient's murderous thoughts were developing, but this admission had clearly moved the situation up another notch. Waclav's neighbour, whoever that person was, was clearly in mortal danger.

"Please try and tell me more", George urged.

"I … I … just have to kill him!", Waclav continued. "I wake up every night, and there is a shadow … a ghost … a spectre … standing next to my bed. I am frightened to death. The shadow comes closer and I can feel its ghastly breath. The shadow says that he will kill me if I don't kill my neighbour. I … I … can see his gleaming

and ice-cold blue eyes. He will kill me if I don't kill first!"

George's hazy mind had cleared after hearing Waclav's confession. Deep inside his brain, memories of his psychological training were re-awakened, signalling that Waclav was suffering from severe cognitive disassociation, a condition that often led to patients to implement their intentions of murdering others. Cognitive disassociation – a condition where patients hear voices that tell them to do horrendous things – was often associated with mass murderers. He remembered from his studies that mass murderers such as Ted Bundy or David Berkowitz, the 'Son-of-Sam-murderer', may have been led to their mass murdering sprees by voices inside their heads.

George was very worried and looked at Waclav with a mixture of disdain and professional understanding. "In my view you are suffering from a serious psychological condition called cognitive disassociation", George said. "I was not sure of the diagnosis after what you told me at our earlier meetings, but what you said just now seems to increasingly point into this direction. I need to inform you that in cases like this, we as psycho-therapists are forced to inform the psychiatric services at the hospital, as you may cause severe harm to other people, as you have admitted yourself. I do not have the power myself to hold you here, but please be aware that I will contact the hospital immediately and that they will seek a referral under Section 136 of the

Mental Health Act to take you to a closed psychological ward where you will be kept until your condition improves. I will, therefore, close our session and ask you to wait in the waiting room for the health services to take you to hospital. Do you understand what I just explained to you?"

Waclav's face betrayed a sense of disbelief but also understanding. "Yes, doctor. I understand. I will wait for the … the health services to take me to the hospital. Yes, I understand. That is … that is the right decision. I am very scared …"

"Yes, I fully understand that you are scared", George replied while walking around his table towards Waclav. George gently placed his hands on Waclav's shoulders and could feel how his patient was trembling with fear, fear about what has going to happen to him, but also fear about what he may do to his neighbour. At least there seemed to be sufficient self-awareness left in Waclav about his condition that he could recognise how precarious his situation was. George gently led Waclav out of his office and placed him gently on one of the chairs in the waiting room. George was certain that Waclav would not try to escape and wait for the health services to pick him up, and that Waclav's neighbour would be safe for now. George walked back to his office, rang the health services who ensured him that they would immediately dispatch an ambulance to pick up Waclav. The health officer also confirmed that

they would immediately send an officer out to Waclav's neighbour to inform him of the possible threat.

George put the phone receiver back. He was shaken by what had just happened and was amazed at his professionality in the situation. Waclav's murderous admission had jolted George back from his own depressive brink and forced him to refocus on the job. He felt almost proud that he had handled what was one of any psycho-therapist's worst nightmares with calm and professional panache. Maybe he was ready after all to deal with what could be an even more problematic upcoming session with Anwar Barhoum. George nonetheless dreaded the forthcoming encounter, especially after the information he had obtained from Rawad's teacher. George opened his office door to check whether Waclav was still there. Waclav was sitting stooped over in his chair, his head in his hands, clearly ready for what may well be a long incarceration in a closed psychiatric ward.

Anwar Barhoum had already arrived and was sitting opposite Waclav, scrutinising Waclav with a look of curiosity and possibly fear. As the session with Waclav had been very brief it was still early and George had a few minutes to get himself into better shape. The successful handling of Waclav's case had given George a new impetus to sort himself out. He remembered that he had an old battery-powered razor somewhere among the mess in his drawers and managed to find it after a bit of rummaging

through old papers but still avoiding the drawer that contained the letters from the National Association for Psychology. Although he had not used it for a while, the batteries in the razor still seemed to work. Avoiding to look at both Anwar and Waclav sitting in their chairs, George walked to the small sink and mirror in the patient toilet and shaved off his ragged stubble. George watched his face reappear as the stubble disappeared down the sink. It was the first time he looked closely at his face for a long while, but what he saw worried him. His face looked haggard, he had deep dark rings under his blood-shot eyes, betraying weeks of sleepless nights, his wrinkles seemed to have deepened especially around the corner of his eyes. He thought that he looked ashen, shrunken, and incredibly old, almost a different person from that of only a few months ago when he had opened this practice with so much enthusiasm and vigour. While he was dabbing his chin with a bit of water, he wondered what had happened to him in the past few months. How could he sink so low? How could he let his practice go to the dogs like this? He had lost almost all his patients now, and just today he had probably lost another two, Donald because of his lack of engagement with this patient, and Waclav because he would probably be locked up for a while in a closed psychiatric ward. In fact, he now only had Anwar Barhoum left, and he was not sure whether Anwar would continue to be his patient either. This was it then! His experiment of professionally relocating from

London to Devonmouth had failed! In less than eight months he had managed to destroy his practice, had annihilated his patient base, lost his receptionist, and was basically bankrupt. His love life was in shatters, his friends and family had deserted him, and he did not feel at home at all in his village. Even if his own mental health improved, he would need to urgently sort out his finances, probably sell his house, start anew somewhere else. George's body hunched over the washbasin and he was just about to cry again when he heard the door to the waiting room open. The ambulance staff had arrived to pick up Waclav.

*

After the commotion of the ambulance staff escorting Waclav out of George's practice had subsided, George led Anwar Barhoum into his office. George mustered the slightly stooped man walking in front of him to his chair and thought he could smell a faint whiff of mixed Syrian spices. This reminded him of his second wife Mildred, who had occasionally cooked meals based on Syrian recipes infused with cardamom, marjoram, coriander, cinnamon and cloves. Anwar sat down heavily on his chair, evidently feeling uncomfortable. Without looking at Anwar, George rummaged through the notes he had prepared, to remind him about Anwar's uneasy revelations about being accused of molesting his nephew and the relationship to his

son. George felt very uneasy about what was going to come.

"Good to see you again Mr Barhoum", George lied after clearing his voice. He did not want to betray the fact that he felt relieved that Anwar had turned up for this session at all, as their tense last meeting may well have meant that Anwar would be unwilling to continue with the sessions. But George had also had the feeling that Anwar benefited from their sessions, that there was something Anwar wished to tell him, but had not been fully able to do until now. George was relieved that it was also much cooler now in George's office than during the sweltering late summer heat during Anwar's recent sessions. George's strategy was to gently work his way towards the most difficult part of the discussion he had planned with Anwar. First of all, he led Anwar to the couch, and George was pleased to see that Anwar willingly followed him and lay down on the worn couch with a loud sigh. George placed his chair again behind Anwar as this again enabled the least restrained free association talk by his patient. Anwar closed his eyes, ready for the first questions.

As usual, and to ease the evident tension, George began the discussion with innocuous questions about Anwar's medication and the problems Anwar was having while taking it, Anwar's continuing stress, and his psychological problems. Anwar seemed to relax gradually and talked openly about his problems, referring specifically to his difficulty of going to sleep and

repeated dreams he was having about his son. But rather than focusing on Anwar's day-to-day interactions with his son, which had not revealed much during their last session, George now intended to address Anwar's relationship with his son head-on. *Stop beating about the bush!*, George thought, *this is probably your last chance to find out what really happened!*

"I paid a visit to Rawad's school a few days ago", George said with a voice he knew was betraying his increasing nervousness.

Anwar who had been lying relatively relaxed on the couch suddenly opened his eyes. Like a predator ready to pounce he was waiting for what was coming next. George was carefully observing his patient, trying to read any sign, any bodily movement that could betray Anwar's state-of-mind.

"Rawad's teacher told me about the marks on Rawad's wrists …", George said with a slightly sterner voice.

Anwar's body tightened. He clasped his hands into fists, his knuckles white with tension, but was still lying motionless on the couch.

"The teacher could not explain how Rawad had gotten these marks, but he disappeared before she could ask him directly", George continued. "She was getting increasingly worried about Rawad."

Anwar clasped his hands more tightly into fists, he pressed his hands together so tightly that George could see the nails begin to dig into the flesh. Anwar's whole body was now as tight as a

steel rod, but he remained on the couch. His eyes were now wide open and tears began welling down his cheeks. George said nothing and sat motionless behind his patient. He hardly dared to breathe.

Anwar cleared his throat. "I… I …", he stammered, but he was convulsed with sobs and had to catch a deep breath.

"I … I killed my son!"

Although George had suspected all along that this was what happened, the sudden confession still caught him by surprise. He was not sure how to proceed from here, whether to say anything or just wait. This was the first time in his professional career that he had to deal with such a dreadful case, and even his usually acute professional instinct, or what was left of it, seemed to have abandoned him. Not knowing what else to do, George just sat still and motionless behind Anwar whose whole body was now convulsed with loud sobs.

"I … Rawad was such a good boy!", Anwar continued without being prompted. "He was so brave after his mother disappeared! He almost looked after me, rather than me after him! He was such a help when we first arrived in this strange and alien country".

It was almost as if the floodgates had been opened, and Anwar did not need any prompting to continue. He seemed almost oblivious to the fact that George was still in the room with him, sitting right behind him, anxiously listening, holding his breath.

"We were both so lonely!", Anwar admitted. "We huddled up in bed together every night, we would talk about our day and the problems we had. Rawad was much more than just a son to me, he was my best friend … my … my …" Anwar cried out loudly and put his head into his hands. "What have I done! What have I done!"

George saw that Anwar was about to get up, he was half leaning on the couch, but something made him slump back again onto the couch. "I will tell you everything now, doctor! Nothing matters anymore anyway!"

Anwar seemed to regain his composure. He wiped the tears of his cheek and a resolute look appeared on his face. It was almost as if he had crossed an invisible threshold that had kept him from telling the truth so far.

"I … I … my son became my lover …", Anwar admitted.

This is it!, George thought. In many ways he did not want to hear what was coming next. He despised himself for being in this position, for being what he was at this moment in time, a psycho-therapist having to hear the dreadful confession of one of his depraved paedophilic patients about how he had molested and killed his own son. And yet he seemed to be transfixed to his chair, unable to move, rigid like a statue. He had to finally hear what had happened to Rawad.

"As … as we were lying in bed together …", Anwar continued, "I made love to him .. you know … from behind. I had no wife … I was

lonely … Rawad did not understand at first, he tried to be nice, not to resist. He was so lovely … But I had to hurt him to get my pleasure … and after a few weeks Rawad increasingly resisted. In the end, I had to tie up his hands against the bedpost … I had to … He was beginning to struggle, he was hitting me, telling me to stop … He was getting stronger. But I needed him … I needed his body … I had no wife …!"

George could not stop himself imagining the dreadful scene, a 12-year old boy trying to fight off his brutal father who was raping him repeatedly. He did not want to hear the rest of the story, but the last remnants of his professionalism kept him glued to his chair, unable to move.

"For several weeks I tied him up when we made love", Anwar continued, rage building in his voice. "He understood my needs less and less, he was crying and shouting and I feared that the neighbours would hear us. He threatened to leave me, to tell the teachers what I was doing to him. But … but I needed him, I wanted to feel close to him … I had done the same to my nephew back home! My brother had been right! I had always been attracted to my beautiful nephew …!"

Here we go!, George thought. *Let it all out, you sick shit! Your pretence that nothing happened, that your son just vanished into thin air. All lies! Lies from the start! You are a depraved paedophile and probably always have been!* George felt like getting up and hitting

Anwar for what he had done to both boys, but an invisible force still kept him glued to his seat. He knew there was more to come.

"It became so bad that I feared losing Rawad. I knew that he was about to tell people about what I was doing to him. So, I had to get rid of him … I had to kill him. On our last night … Rawad was struggling so much, I hardly managed to tie his hands to the bed … to … to come inside him … He kicked me hard with his legs, it really hurt. I strangled him there and then … my beautiful boy!"

For over a minute, Anwar was convulsed in sobs and could not carry on.

"Rawad was not very heavy yet. I packed his body into a black bin liner and stuffed him into our old suitcase. I did not want to look too suspicious, so instead of waiting for the dark, I took the suitcase out the next day in broad daylight and walked the long way towards the big bridge … I think they call it 'Jumpers' Bridge' because so many people from Devonmouth commit suicide there … I waited a while in the middle of the bridge, and when there were no people or cars around I tossed the suitcase over the side. It landed with a big splash on the water below … I remember there was a lot of water in the river then … There had been a rainstorm … The suitcase disappeared quickly, it was probably carried by the current to the sea … What have I done! What have I done to my beautiful son!?"

Anwar was shaken again by convulsive sobs. George was stunned and did not know what to do. He had Anwar's confession, but it left him completely numb, unable to fully process what had just happened. He had, of course, not taped this conversation, in his unhinged state he had simply forgotten to do it! Would Anwar be willing to confess all this in front of Prendergast, or would he recover his poise and deny everything?

After what seemed like an eternity, George finally recovered sufficiently to ask the key question: "would you be willing to repeat all this to Detective Prendergast at the police?"

But looking at Anwar, sobbing loudly, George was sure that any leftover will to fight had gone out of the Syrian. He now was an utterly broken man, a mere shadow of himself, an empty shell devoid of any feeling and compassion, a cold-hearted murderer! Anwar got up from the couch, still struggling to keep his loud sobbing under control. George thought that Anwar was about to agree to admit the murder of his son to the police and to wait until they came to pick him up. But Anwar suddenly pushed George hard aside so that he fell over backwards and hit his head hard on the wood-lined floor. In a dash, Anwar was out of the practice.

George staggered back up. He could feel blood trickle down from his head and he felt dizzy. He made it to his chair and sat down with a loud thud, relieved not to be standing. He tried to control his panting breathing, refocus his

mind, recover his strength after being brutally knocked over. He still could not fully focus, clearly his head had hit the floor hard and he probably was concussed. In his daze, George watched a buzzing fly who, in its bestial stupidity, kept banging its head against his office window, thud, thud, thud, not realising that the glass would never allow it to escape. *This fly is trapped like myself!*, George thought, *there is just no way out of this mess!* The fly had suddenly toppled over and was lying on its back, its buzzing motion making it spin around its central axis, its six crooked legs bent upwards in its last death throws. *That's exactly how I feel!*, George admitted to himself, *like Kafka's giant dying insect lying on its back, unable to move, life gradually being sucked out of me!* He felt so weak! What a day this had been! How could humanity be so … so … depraved! A 12-year old boy who still had his whole life in front of him! Why did he have to be confronted with all this, at this point in time when he himself felt at his most vulnerable?

*

George was sitting very nervously outside Prendergast's office. After the session with Anwar Barhoum, and as soon as George had regathered his wits from banging his head hard on the floor, he had rung Prendergast and told her the whole dreadful story about Anwar and his son. On the phone Prendergast had said that, like

George, she had suspected this outcome all along, and she thanked George for making Anwar confess. She had also confirmed that she was sending out officers immediately to arrest Anwar. But a whole day had passed, and George had not heard anything back from Prendergast when she rang him saying he should come to her office. She would not say more on the phone.

Prendergast's door opened. She greeted George and led him into her office. Briefly George again thought that he found her attractive, but these thoughts were quickly dispelled by the seriousness of the situation. George suspected that something had happened, otherwise Prendergast would have given him information on the phone about Anwar's arrest.

"Hello Dr Williamson", Prendergast said while shaking George's hand. "Please take a seat". But George could immediately sense Prendergast's state of unease as she scrutinised his dishevelled appearance. No shaving and taking his first shower in weeks could hide the ravages that the stressful last weeks had left on George's face. He knew he looked like he had aged several years, and he was deeply ashamed of how he had let his body and mind go over the past few months, especially in front of an attractive woman. George almost felt like apologising, but Prendergast did not give him the opportunity to utter a meaningless explanation about his current condition.

"Dr Williamson", she continued, "the reason I did not get back to you about Mr Barhoum's

case is that something has happened in the meantime that forced me to withhold information until we were absolutely sure about what was going on." She paused for a few seconds and wanted to reassure herself that George was ready for what was to come. Prendergast still was not entirely sure as to whether George was in the right state-of-mind to receive further bad news. She cleared her throat uneasily, betraying her own nervousness. "We now have confirmation that Anwar Barhoum killed himself", she said while watching George's facial expression carefully.

Although George was not surprised at this news, Anwar's suicide nonetheless came as a shock. He closed his eyes, allowing his mind time to compute what was happening. He could not hide tears welling up in his eyes, although he felt absolutely no compassion for the child-molesting Syrian murderer. But he felt sad and disappointed in himself, that he had not been able to prevent Anwar from fleeing his practice after his confession, that he had not been able to deliver the Syrian to the authorities as would have been his professional duty.

"He jumped of Jumpers' Bridge, probably from the same spot where you mentioned he had dumped the body of his son", Prendergast continued. "We have just found Anwar's body this morning, several hundred metres downriver from the bridge. That's why I could not inform you earlier, as it took several hours for the coroner to release the body and for the body to

be identified by one of the staff from the Devonmouth Social Services who had worked with Anwar. There has been no sign of Rawad's body and I suspect that we will never find it as Anwar dumped his body months ago". These revelations did not surprise George at all, who was slowly recovering his composure. It made perfect sense for Anwar to jump off the same spot where he had thrown his son's body into the river.

Prendergast was still intensely scrutinising George for any signs that what she was saying may further unbalance him. "But that is not all", she continued, half-heartedly satisfied that George was ready and able to face more revelations. "We just heard yesterday from the Serbian authorities that they think that they have finally been able to identify a body they found a while ago as that of Afraa Barhoum, Anwar Barhoum's 'disappeared' wife and Rawad's mother. As you may remember, Anwar Barhoum had told us that they fled from Syria into Turkey and that they then went through Greece and Macedonia to a refugee camp in Serbia. There Mr Barhoum claimed that his wife Afraa was separated from them in one of the camps and that they had not seen her since. Assuming the remains that have been found are Afraa's, the Serbian authorities have informed me that there is evidence of foul play in Afraa's death. Although the body was badly decomposed, they claim that there is evidence that her throat was cut."

Prendergast paused again to see how George was taking in the information. "I am not surprised at this revelation", George said with a croaky voice. "After all this man has done, molesting his nephew back home, and raping and killing his own son, I would not put it passed him to also have killed his wife".

"Indeed", replied Prendergast, " and after the confession you got out of Anwar Barhoum, I would not be surprised if the molestation of Anwar's own son had not started earlier, maybe even while the three were fleeing from Syria. If it is true that Anwar molested his nephew, then there is clearly a long-standing paedophilic trait in Anwar Barhoum. One could speculate that Afraa may have found out about Anwar abusing their son, and that this is why he killed her? Unfortunately, the answer to this we will probably never know now that Anwar is dead."

George was appalled at the depravity of the man who had been his patient. Again, he was angry at himself that he had not been able to obtain crucial information from Anwar earlier, that he had used an incremental psycho-therapeutic approach that had taken very long to yield any useful information. And now it was too late! Anwar was dead and they would never find the truth!

George was about to get up and thank Prendergast for all the information and revelations, but she motioned him to stay seated.

"There is one more thing, Dr Williamson, and I know that this will come as a further shock

to you, but I may as well tell you about it, now that you are here, as you will undoubtedly hear about it soon in the local news."

Prendergast saw George's very worried look on his face. *What more can there be?*, George wondered. *Haven't we already scraped the barrel of human depravity? Could this be about Marlies? Is the truth finally out?*

"We found a second body not far from where Anwar Barhoum was found." Again, Prendergast let this news soak in before continuing, but George's face did not betray any worsening of his already frail state-of-mind. "I have just heard confirmation that it is the body of another of your patients ..."

George's heart sank. *This could not be! Not two of my patients in one day!*

"It was Donald Richardson's body", Prendergast revealed. "He must have jumped from the very same spot on Jumpers' Bridge ..."

This news did surprise and shock George. Yes, he knew that his session two days ago with Donald Richardson had been one of the worst in his professional life in terms of not at all being able to help a patient, to concentrate on his needs, and to recognise the precarious state-of-mind the patient had been in. But George still did not think that Donald had been in imminent danger of committing suicide. Yes, Donald had expressed suicidal thoughts, but as George had assumed during their last meeting, Donald's problems seemed so small, so trifling, compared to George's own problems. And yet, here it was!

Donald had obviously not found any other way to resolve his problems than to commit suicide, an urge to die obviously stronger than his remnant attachment to his job, his estranged wife, or his children. How said all this was!

"Thanks … thanks … for the information", George stammered, but he found it hard to compose himself. Although Anwar's death had come as a shock, the last remnants of his rational mind could still argue that Anwar maybe deserved to die after all he had done. But Donald Richardson was a different story. George's job had been to help people like Donald, and he had utterly failed to prevent a death that should have been, with the proper psychological care, avoidable. George felt that he had betrayed Donald, himself, and his profession. It showed George that he had lost all sense of perspective, that he was now so subsumed in his own problems that he could no longer objectively address the problems of others. In this instant, George realised that his career as a psycho-therapist was over!

George looked up at Prendergast, who looked back at him with a very worried look on her face. She was clearly regretting informing George about the death of Donald Richardson, but she also knew that Devonmouth Social Services, or the local news, would have informed him soon anyway. She came over to George and put her hands on his shoulders. George's body was shaking and convulsed with loud sobs.

"I am sorry … I am so sorry", George sniffled, leaning his head against Prendergast's arm. "I should go now …"

George tried to get up from his chair, but his body felt like weighing a ton. All the strength had been sapped out of his body, all energy was gone, his will to live was dissipating into thin air. While he had been depressed for months, now he was looking straight into the dark abyss, the beckoning chasm, the alluring pull of death itself. There was nothing left in his life, he thought as he limped out of Prendergast's office, supported by the detective's strong arms draped around his hunched body.

*

A short while after leaving Prendergast's office, George parked his car at the tourist viewpoint overlooking the gorge over the river Devon spanned by the famous Brunel-built Jumpers' Bridge. *How beautiful the view is!*, he thought as he glanced towards the posher villas nestled among the greenery on the steep slopes overlooking the estuary, but he was immediately surprised at how he could think such mundane thoughts and take in the view in a moment like this. *Even now part of your messed-up brain is still rational, still evaluating and calculating. It is almost as if part of yourself is still enjoying life, still with a strong will to live! What a weird psychological creature you are, George*

Williamson!, he felt like shouting out, but he was in no mood to psycho-analyse himself at this point in time. After the revelations in Prendergast's office, the abyss was too close, darkness too overwhelming, nemesis too palpable.

He left his car and walked along the walkway that had only recently been built along the side of the bridge. George wondered again at the low height of the railing and that the authorities were not doing more to prevent people from jumping. This was where Anwar Barhoum had disposed of the body of his son and where Anwar himself had jumped off! This was where Donald Richardson had committed suicide on the same day!

George walked slowly, but his thoughts and senses remained sharp. It was as if he was seeing the world around him with more intensity, that for the first time in a long while he was really alive again, inhaling the not-so-fresh Devonmouth air deeply, his ears picking up every cranking, jolting and spluttering sound from the vehicles rushing past him on the bridge, his mind swirling with thoughts about Marlies, Anwar, Rawad, Donald, his two former wives, Paul Sutherland, Detective Prendergast, and thoughts about his childhood, playing in the sand, throwing a ball to his dad, a cuddle from his mum, a strange-looking insect resting on his tiny hand. Was the affair with Marlies real? Was Anwar really dead? Was any of this real? He closed his eyes to sense this moment even more deeply. It felt real. But was he ready? Despite the

traffic noise, deep inside his head it felt very quiet. “Is it the deep breath before the plunge?”, he heard himself muttering.

George had reached the middle of the bridge and looked over the low railing, down 80 metres into the gently flowing river Devon which was very wide at this point not far from where it flowed into the sea. He was standing at the mid-point of the bridge, probably precisely the place where Rawad had chucked the suitcase with his son’s body into the river. He wondered how strange it was how all the misery in George’s life seemed to be congregating on this bridge, on this very point, as if this was the navel of the Earth, the centrepiece of his miserable life, the focal point where all depraved pathways seemed to come together. The bridge acted like a magnet, attracting all the evil in this world and then helping to get rid of it with one fell swoop. And how his life could not be disentangled from the terrible fate of the little Syrian boy!

How deep the chasm looked below him! Falling from this height, the surface of the water would feel like concrete, it would be certain death. Even the most trained diver would not survive a jump from this height. But then survival was not the aim of people who decided to throw themselves off Jumpers’ Bridge. That was the hole point!

George looked left and right to see whether other people were walking along the bridge. An elderly woman could be seen some distance away carrying a large plastic bag in her left hand.

For a brief moment he thought it could be Marlies, or Ingrid von Schnollrotz-Beerenbier, or his mum, or one of his wives, but these irrational hopes quickly dissipated as the woman came nearer, shouting unintelligible warnings. Although the woman was still far away, George thought she looked rather poor, hunched over, probably weighed down by a life of hardship.

George knew that he had to hurry. He climbed the low railing and placed his feet on the small ledge above the abyss, his arms behind him still holding on to the railing. The elderly woman let out a shriek of anxiety and attempted to run towards him on her short stocky legs, her arms raised above her head and the plastic bag swivelling back and forth with each movement of her body. George looked down. He was very scared. He thought he could feel the spin of the Earth through space, his mind set aloft, high above him, looking down onto the UK, Devonmouth, and his tiny figure perched above the abyss. How unimportant all his problems seemed in the grander scheme of things! Who cared whether he lived or died? Who cared whether the affair with Marlies had happened or not? He was just a speckle of dust on a tiny planet weaving its way through space at 1800 km per hour. How irrelevant his death would be!

But rationality took over yet again, even in this moment of imminent self-chosen doom. George suddenly realised that he should have thought more often about the art of dying well. He should have analysed death and how to die in

much more detail, so that he was better prepared for what he was attempting now and bring his suicide to a successful conclusion. But when would he have been able to direct his thoughts towards how to best commit suicide? Surely not while he still had hope, hope about a relationship with Marlies, hope about running a successful practice, hope about life itself? Probably one could never fully confront the reality of committing suicide unless one was about to do it there and then? In this sense thinking about suicide was like Heisenberg's uncertainty principle: you could not observe an activity such as the wish to die objectively without affecting that wish itself. Had all this gone through the mind of his patients Anwar Barhoum and Donald Richardson before they decided to kill themselves? Had Anwar been able to rationalise his own demise before he actually decided to commit suicide, or was he so subsumed in the utterly despicable act of fucking and murdering his son that death was the only way out?

The ledge George was standing on was not very wide, only the heel of his shoes was supported by it, the rest of his feet was already dangling above the void. He had to concentrate hard not to slip, his hands felt very sweaty on the cold metal railing. George was so scared that he started shaking uncontrollably. Why did he need to hold on so tight and be worried about slipping as he intended to jump anyway? Why not just let go instead of hanging on so tightly? With his fatalist view of the world, George had never been

afraid of death, so why was he not relaxed now, ready to jump? Suddenly a thought he had read about years ago, and somehow remembered, from the atheistic and amoralist Greek philosopher Lucretius came to his mind: 'What has this bugbear death to frighten man, if souls can die as well as bodies can? From sense of grief and pain we shall be free, we shall not feel because we shall not be'. This sounded good in theory, George thought, but in practice this was very difficult to implement, especially when you were standing above the abyss with sweaty hands holding on to a frail railing. Although he could rationalise his own death, George was afraid … very afraid.

George could no longer control his bowels and bladder. He felt a trickle of urine running down his legs and moist diarrhoea began weighing down the back of his trousers, slowly spreading a reeking stench. *That's it!*, he thought, looking desperately with tears in his eyes at the old woman running towards him with her dangling plastic bag. She was not far now, he could see the deeply etched wrinkles in her ragged face probably ravaged by the vicissitudes of a life of hardship in the bowels of wretched Fernworthy Estate. *There is no way back now! … Or is there?* Was this, after all, the first day, hour, minute, second, of the rest of his miserable and wretched life?

Printed in Great Britain
by Amazon

77539740R00181